100% PURE FLORIDA FICTION

*Edited by Susan Hubbard and Robley Wilson*

# 100% PURE FLORIDA FICTION | *An Anthology*

University Press of Florida

GAINESVILLE · TALLAHASSEE · TAMPA · BOCA RATON
PENSACOLA · ORLANDO · MIAMI · JACKSONVILLE

05  04  03  02  01  00  c  6  5  4  3  2  1
05  04  03  02  01  00  p  6  5  4  3  2  1

Cover painting by Mary Ann Carroll

LIBRARY OF CONGRESS CATALOGING-IN-PUBLICATION DATA
100% pure Florida fiction: an anthology /
edited by Susan Hubbard and Robley Wilson.
p. cm.
ISBN 0-8130-1752-1 (c: alk. paper). — ISBN 0-8130-1753-X
(p: alk. paper)
1. Florida—Social life and customs—Fiction. 2. Short stories,
American—Florida. I. Hubbard, Susan. II. Wilson, Robley.
PS558.F6A15 2000
813'.010832759—dc21    99-39571

The University Press of Florida is the scholarly publishing
agency for the State University System of Florida, comprising
Florida A&M University, Florida Atlantic University, Florida
International University, Florida State University, University
of Central Florida, University of Florida, University of North
Florida, University of South Florida, and University of West
Florida.

University Press of Florida
15 Northwest 15th Street
Gainesville, FL 32611
http://www.upf.com

For Kate and Clare,
and Florida readers everywhere

# CONTENTS

# PREFACE

What we learned first as we put together this new collection of Florida fiction is that the variety and vibrancy of the state are remarkable and uncontainable. Florida can be anything and everything a reader wants it to be—a refuge from the cold of the North and from the politics of the South; a theme-parked tourist trap; a haven for surfers and snow-birds; a training ground for athletes; a heady mix of disparate cultures; a meteorologist's casebook of heat wave, hurricane, tornado, and lightning strike; a sociologist's dystopia of ethnic, economic, and religious enclaves. Yet as our work proceeded, we began to sense a peculiar presence in almost all the fiction we read: a common nostalgia and sense of loss that persists even in paradise. Each of these stories has an uneasy heart.

Like W. H. Auden's idea of the "finished" poem, this anthology is in one sense an "abandoned" project; it couldn't possibly embrace *everything* that is Florida. Not that we didn't assign a few boundaries. We restricted ourselves to stories whose Florida setting seemed to us crucial—stories perhaps possible somewhere else, but not probable—and we confined our search to work published or written since 1985. We screened more than 600 stories by as many authors. Our University of Central Florida graduate assistant, Ashley Woods, scoured short story indexes and swamped interlibrary loan with requests for books. We advertised in writers' journals. We searched the internet. We asked around, making nuisances of ourselves to colleagues and friends.

These final selections are varied in setting—from Alligator Alley to the Panhandle, from Key West to Jacksonville, from Canaveral Seashores to Redington Beach. Of the twenty-one stories, arranged alphabetically by author, eleven have male narrators and ten female (we didn't plan that evenness; it just happened), and they are diverse in ethnicity, gender, and class. Their subject matter ranges from love to death and back again and includes such topical concerns as homophobia and child abuse and such timeless ones as loyalty and responsibility. It's certainly likely that we've missed some excellent Florida stories, but we think the group assembled here is both representative and impressive. The stories showcase some authors who are already well known, and they introduce others just beginning their writing careers.

\*　　\*　　\*

Looking down on Florida from the sky, as astronauts (and those of us who watch the NASA cable channel) do, you're struck not so much by the land as by the water—the Atlantic, the Caribbean, the Gulf—waters that define this familiar peninsula. Coming closer, you notice lakes—not only prominent Okeechobee, but thousands of others—that punctuate the green land. Closer yet, you see countless turquoise swimming pools scattered through suburban neighborhoods. More than any other element, water appears to define Florida, and it isn't surprising that in many of the stories offered here, water is a major character.

Sometimes water appears in the form of rain, which often stands as a metaphor for truth, or for awakening to truth. "Larroquette," the Frederick Barthelme story which opens this collection, concludes with a frustrated mother being sprayed with a hose in a dusty Panhandle town. She tells her son, who's wielding the hose, "Go on. Rain some more. Rain harder." In John Henry Fleming's "Wind and Rain,"

rain creates the moment of violence upon which the story turns. In Wendell Mayo's "Jagged Tooth, Great Tooth," the water of the Gulf "walked onto the beach, then ran out in smooth, overlapping sheets." At its most extreme, rain rides a hurricane, as in Jeffrey Greene's "The Blind Gambler" (a story, by the way, that features another staple of Florida fact and fiction: the con artist).

Water imagery takes myriad forms. Steve Cushman's "Me and Dr. Bob" introduces us to two losers whose finest moment comes when they offer a glass of water to a jogger, and whose only real life occurs in kayaks paddled off Canaveral National Seashores. "The Ferdinand Magellan," by William Snyder, Jr., is a surrealistic tale of what happens when a ship appears in a small lake near DeLand. Alison Lurie's "The Pool People" and Aracelis Gonzalez Asendorf's "The Gossamer Girl" both use swimming pools as sites of retribution (each, incidentally, offering the reader its own kind of ghost).

★   ★   ★

Like water, heat and humidity saturate the stories collected here. In Tom Chiarella's Redington Beach story, "Foley's Confessions," the summer is "long and Florida heavy"; its protagonist remarks, "The saltiness of the place began to overwhelm me." Similarly, in Abraham Verghese's "Tension," the coach of a professional tennis player "almost chokes as the Florida air clogs his nose and throat, like a hot, wet rag." In Philip Cioffari's "Dangerously the Summer Burns," we visit Key West during the hottest summer in the island's history, when the weather itself turns outlaw.

Nature is lush and abundant here, in rural and urban settings alike. While the traditional southern story may feature plantations (often as a symbol of decay) or characters who embody the grotesque, the Florida story is richly embellished with exotic flora or fauna. In Elisavietta Ritchie's "Shopping Expedition," the "scarlet hibiscus and purple bougainvillea entwine with pale clematis, innocent honeysuckle and Virginia creeper mingle with poisonous pink oleander." In "The Gossamer Girl" we encounter a "picuala plant . . . a vine [that] blooms most of the year with sprigs of flowers that blossom white, turn pink, and become crimson once they mature."

Sometimes the flora and fauna are faintly sinister, as in Karen Loeb's "Fauna in Florida." A woman opens her door to retrieve the morning paper and "almost lost her wedding ring and charm bracelet which she never took off . . . because there was what looked like to her a real-life gray-green four-footed slimy-mouthed alligator waiting for a meal. His two front feet were on the plastic wrapper of the paper." Alligators, like homeless people, are considered commonplace nuisances in contemporary Florida—intrusions in a culture that increasingly encloses itself to create an illusion of safety from such threats, each enclosure only enhancing the problem.

Besides gators, this anthology is populated by snakes, sharks, love-bugs, and—"They're not roaches," says the mother in Patrick J. Murphy's "The Flower's Noiseless Hunger, the Tree's Clandestine Tide"—palmetto bugs. Peter Meinke's story "The Cranes" finds in whooping cranes a symbol of fidelity and eternity; Jill McCorkle's "Migration of the Love Bugs" uses the sex-obsessed bugs as metaphors for displacement and mortality. And in "The Flower's Noiseless Hunger . . ." a preteen boy escapes to the scrubland that borders the Everglades and wishes "away the developments and the cars and the people. A hundred years ago it was the same. A land of water and birds and fish. Albert imagined how it might have been."

*    *    *

The theme of many a Florida story is nostalgia: longing for a past that never was, regret for what might have been, discovery not of the Fountain of Youth but of a paradise lost. Perhaps one reason for nostalgia is the relatively recent development—or *over*development—of the state. Unlike the New England story, haunted by rich colonial history and bound by tradition in its land use, architecture, and customs, or the classic southern story whose roots lie in a miasma of past glory and whose present celebrates eccentricity, the Florida story tends to be more brash yet more uncertain. Retirees, snowbirds, natives—all are at odds with the alligators and the heat. Strip malls, not post offices, libraries, or courthouses, are the landmarks of our communities; abundant fast-food outlets, trailer parks, and pawnshops reinforce an overall sense of transience. Gated residential "communities" are bordered by the ghettos of the poor.

In such a setting, in the story "In the House of Simple Sentences," Louis Phillips's narrator meets an old man named Zeus, and his employer tells him "the reason God came to Florida is not because he needs a vacation, but because he wants to be close to Chattahoochee"—a reference to the well-known state mental hospital.

Contemporary Florida is a place where Nature and society conspire to make the everyday world surreal. Joy Williams's "The Blue Men" follows the family of a man condemned to die in a Florida prison. Enid Shomer's "Taking Names" details a child-abuse jury trial. Shomer's story shows the symbiotic relationship between violence and Nature, linking cruelty to the child with the devastation of a citrus crop; Williams's story ends with its three oddball characters united after— of all things—a car crash; the car's driver tells the police, "I thought it was just a dream, so I kept on going."

*　　*　　*

Mortality and death are frequent in the Florida of this book. Outsiders come here to die, to bury their dead, to learn the disguises death wears. When Elisavietta Ritchie's narrator shops for a coffin in Miami, she discovers that ethnic prejudice crosses over from the living. In Wendell Mayo's "Jagged Tooth, Great Tooth," a retired couple searches the Venice beach for sharks' teeth and for a resolution to their grief—"as smooth and as unfathomable" as the sea—for their dead son. In Alison Lurie's tony Key West, death lurks in the shimmering waters of a private swimming pool. Even at a tourist attraction, death takes no holiday: read Steve Watkins's bitterly funny "Critterworld," which begins when a hundred-year-old elephant drops dead in a decaying small-town theme park.

Yet death need not always be dark and silent. As Peter Meinke's story suggests, it may speak to us of love and loyalty. He captures both in the closing image of two cranes plunging upward, "their great wings beating the air and their long graceful necks pointed like arrows toward the sun."

*   *   *

A last word about the stories' authors—men and women, younger and older, famous and not. Many of them are Florida natives; some have stayed, others moved away, and a surprising number left the state and later returned to enjoy the sun of their successes. All of them, even if they only visited Florida for business or pleasure, give us sharp insights into the state's variety of people, place, and climate. Resort or trailer park, tourist or retiree or native, these settings and characters offer a literary Florida to ponder and to savor.

The editors remain dazzled by these stories. We offer them as entertainment, resource, and enchantment; we hope you will share them with friends, students, relatives—up North and down South.

# ACKNOWLEDGMENTS

"Larroquette," copyright 1999 by Frederick Barthelme. Printed by permission of the author.

"Foley's Confessions," by Tom Chiarella. From *Foley's Luck* (Alfred A. Knopf, Inc.), copyright 1992 by Tom Chiarella.

"Dangerously the Summer Burns," copyright 1999 by Philip Cioffari. First published in *Gulf Stream*. Reprinted by permission of the author.

"Me and Dr. Bob," copyright 1998 by Steve Cushman. First published in *The North American Review*. Reprinted by permission of the author.

"Wind and Rain," copyright 1999 by John Henry Fleming. First published in *The Georgetown Review*. Reprinted by permission of the author.

"The Gossamer Girl," copyright 1999 by Aracelis Gonzalez Asendorf. Printed by permission of the author.

"The Blind Gambler," copyright 1999 by Jeffrey Greene. First published in *The North American Review*. Reprinted by permission of the author.

"Alligator Joe & Pancho Villa," copyright 1999 by William R. Kanouse. Printed by permission of the author.

"Fauna in Florida," copyright 1993 by Karen Loeb. Reprinted with the author's permission from *Jump Rope Queen* (New Rivers Press).

"The Pool People," from *Women and Ghosts* (Doubleday), copyright 1994 by Alison Lurie. Reprinted by permission of Melanie Jackson Agency, L.L.C.

"Jagged Tooth, Great Tooth," copyright 1993 by Wendell Mayo. First published in *Ascent*. Reprinted by permission of the author.

"Migration of the Love Bugs," from *Crash Diet* by Jill McCorkle, copyright 1992 by the author. Reprinted by permission of Algonquin Books of Chapel Hill, a division of Workman Publishing.

"The Cranes," copyright 1999 by Peter Meinke. Printed by permission of the author.

"The Flower's Noiseless Hunger, the Tree's Clandestine Tide," copyright 1999 by Patrick J. Murphy. First published in *Buffalo Spree* magazine. Reprinted by permission of the author.

"In the House of Simple Sentences," copyright 1993 by Louis Phillips. Reprinted with the author's permission from *A Dream of Countries Where No One Dare Die* (Southern Methodist University Press).

"Shopping Expedition," copyright 1992, 1996 by Elisavietta Ritchie. First published in *Flying Time: Stories & Half-Stories* (Signal Books) and *If I Had My Life to Live Over I Would Pick More Daisies* (Papier Mâché Press).

"Taking Names," copyright 1993 by Enid Shomer. Reprinted with the author's permission from *Imaginary Men* (University of Iowa Press).

"The Ferdinand Magellan," copyright 1993 by William Snyder, Jr. First published in *Midland Review*. Reprinted by permission of the author.

"Tension," copyright 1998 by Abraham Verghese. Reprinted with the author's permission from *The Tennis Partner* (HarperCollins).

"Critterworld," copyright 1992 by Steve Watkins. First published in the *Mississippi Review*. Reprinted by permission of the author.

"The Blue Men," copyright 1990 by Joy Williams. Reprinted with the author's permission from *Escapes* (Atlantic Monthly Press).

Many thanks to Ashley Woods for her research assistance and to the University of Central Florida for its support.

100% PURE FLORIDA FICTION

*Frederick Barthelme* | LARROQUETTE

Sheila leaned against her chain-link fence,
fingering the decorative scroll bolted onto
the top of the gate. She was looking across
the street at the Terlinks' garage. The Terlinks were having a Sunday afternoon barbecue. Sheila watched carefully. She hadn't
waved. She didn't know the Terlinks—
Johnson Terlink and his wife, Emma, their
two children, Rita and Herman—had never
spoken to them except in passing at the
mailbox: Hello, how are you? Nothing
more. But somebody else was with them.
A fancy rental car nosed into the end of
the drive, so she knew they had company.
Sheila kicked at Bosco, the dog who kept
winding around her legs, in and out, pant-
ing, occasionally making little yipping
noises.

I

She liked the neighborhood. It was the best she could afford. The houses were wood siding things, falling apart, once painted white with colorful trim. The yards were thick grass, tricycles, colorful volley balls, soccer balls, plastic do-dads and what-nots. A kite twirled on the telephone wire behind the Terlinks' house. The kite had been there since Sheila moved in eighteen months before, after her divorce. Eighteen months, Sheila thought looking at the kite. I should have introduced myself before this.

Sheila worked nights at the hospital, rolling patients over, wedging pillows under them, cleaning bedpans, changing drips and catheter bags. She had six hours before work.

The tall guy on the Terlinks' driveway laughed loud. He looked familiar, she thought. He looked like John Larroquette.

She went inside to get her son, Tod, who was eighteen, in his room watching MTV. Tod had a job at Don't Nobody Eat Pizza? He strapped a Don't Nobody Eat Pizza? sign on the top of the car and delivered all night long.

"Come out here and look at this, will you?" Sheila said. "I think we've got John Larroquette across the way."

"What's he doing there?" Tod said.

"Don't know. I'm not sure it's him. There's a guy who looks like him, somebody. Got a fancy rent car."

"So walk across the street," Tod said.

"I don't want to meet him," Sheila said. "I just want to know if it is him."

"I don't care if it is," Tod said.

"I know," Sheila said. "But I do. So come out, look across, see if you can I.D. him, O.K.? I don't ask too goddamn much."

"You ask everything," Tod said. He rolled off the bed. She followed him and Bosco followed her. They were a little parade.

Tod leaned on the fence, squinted hard, said, "I don't know. I give up," and headed back inside.

"Tod," she said.

"I don't know. I can't see. What makes you think it's him anyway? And why do you care? You never looked at John Larroquette, did you? Wasn't he on *Cheers*?"

"Oh, like you don't know," Sheila said. "*Night Court*. But now he's got his own show. He reminds me of your father."

"Everybody reminds you of my father," Tod said. "Batman reminds you of my father." Tod wore plaid green Bermudas and a soiled t-shirt. He walked around a bush at the corner of the house. "You need a life, Mother. That's what."

"Look who's talking. Come back here." She pointed to the ground in front of her. Tod looked, his hair a tangle of eight-inch spikes. He stood on the back steps.

Bosco tore a limb off the bush and ran around with the limb in his mouth, daring Sheila to chase him. She feinted at the dog and he dodged away.

"What's wrong with me?" Tod said. He held his t-shirt at the hem, staring down at himself.

"You're eighteen and living at home with your mother," Sheila said.

"So I'll move," he said. He opened the screen door.

"You're just like your father," Sheila said.

Tod shut his eyes and leaned his head back and rubbed his left hand through his hair several times, holding his head. "I'm not just like my father in any way," he said. "I've never been like my father. I don't know why a person would say that. I don't know why you would say that. You know I'm not like my father."

Sheila sat down on the ground, gathering her skirt between her legs.

"Don't sit on the ground, Mother," Tod said. "Come inside. I'll fix you something to eat—a toasted cheese sandwich. Would you like that?"

"Nope," Sheila said. "I want to know if that's John Larroquette."

"It's not," he said.

"I saw him on Leno. He's from Louisiana. He said he visits his cousin in Florida, his only cousin. They have barbecues. In the garage. That's what he told Jay."

"I'm guessing he visits Miami or something. Coral Gables. Not likely his cousin lives in Quantum." Tod came down the steps, into the yard, and reached out to help his mother up, but just at that minute Bosco hopped into her lap.

"I could talk to Mrs. Terlink about her dogs," Sheila said.

"What dogs?" Tod said.

"She raises Chihuahuas," Sheila said. "That's what Ellen told me. Ellen next door?" She thumbed to her left where Ellen lived. "Said she raises Chihuahuas. She's got maybe twenty-five Chihuahuas over there."

Tod shook his head. "O.K. Here's what I'll do. I'll go out like I'm getting the mail. If it's him, I'll come get you."

"Why would you be getting the mail on Sunday?" Sheila said.

"I wasn't home Saturday?" he said.

"You're always home," she said. "Everybody knows that."

"Oh. Right," Tod said. He finger-combed his hair over his head, one side to the other.

"Why don't you wash it?" Sheila said.

Inside, she sat on an old green stool by the stove. Tod made her a sandwich out of Rainbow bread and wrapper cheese. She took some wrapper cheese to feed Bosco, made him stand up on his hind legs and go around in circles, then dropped cheese strips from shoulder height to see if he could catch them. Most of the time the cheese went right by him.

She walked out through the dining room into the living room and stood at the front window, pulling back the curtain, peering across the street. "I think that's him," she said. "I'm almost certain that's him."

"It's not," Tod said. "Come eat your sandwich."

"Let's go out in the car. We can get really close."

"I thought you wanted a sandwich. I'm making a sandwich. Are you going to eat?"

In the living room, Sheila picked up three copies of *Family Circle* magazine that Ellen had lent her. She gathered up some of Bosco's toys—a pink ball with a pebbled surface, a plastic bone the size of her forearm, a book he liked to chew on. She tossed all three into a basket in the corner of the living room where Bosco's toys were kept. For some reason Bosco wouldn't go near the basket. When he wanted a toy he would stand about a foot away from the basket and whimper, looking back over his shoulder at her. It would have been easy enough for him to tip the basket over, or reach in and bite whatever toy he wanted. But he would never do that. He just whimpered. Sometimes if a toy went under a chair, or the bench in the entry hall, Bosco would stand there and look, whimpering. He was afraid the furniture was going to jump him.

"Ready," Tod called. She went in the kitchen and ate her cheese sandwich. Tod ate a peanut butter sandwich and stood at the window by the sink looking at Ellen's house. "There are snakes over there," he said. "Ellen came over last week and told me the yard guy found a snake in the back, chased it under a tree stump, so she had the animal control people come out. But they said they wouldn't touch it. That it was her responsibility. If the snake was out in the open, they'd take it. Otherwise, no dice."

"That's a big help," his mother said.

"She was warning me about Bosco, to keep him out of the yard," he said.

"He can take care of himself," Sheila said.

"Said it was a copperhead," Tod said. "I went and looked, but I couldn't see anything. She wanted me to put gasoline in this tree stump and burn it. I didn't want to do that."

"She's fond of you," Sheila said.

"Oh, please," Tod said.

"Ever since the police came," Sheila said.

"Yeah, big turn-on," Tod said.

Two months before, the police had come to the house to talk to Tod about a case they were working on. Some pizza delivery guy was raping women. They called the guy the pizza rapist. They didn't think Tod was him, but they thought he might know the guy. Two uniformed policemen and two plainclothes policemen. They came in and sat in the living room with Tod and Sheila, and in the middle of things, Ellen had arrived.

"Can I help?" she had said.

"No, we're just talking to the police," Sheila told her.

"Oh?" Ellen said.

"They're here to talk to Tod," Sheila said.

"Is he in trouble?" Ellen asked.

"Nothing like that," Sheila told her. "They need his help in some case. It's like somebody he may know or something he may have seen. They want a witness."

"Oh," Ellen said.

She stood on the front porch craning her neck, trying to get a look into the living room at the cops and at Tod. Sheila tried to stay in her line of sight.

"Can you come back later?" Sheila asked her.

"Sure," Ellen said. "Later. If you're sure you're all right."

"We're fine," Sheila said to her.

Ellen was twenty-two and an assistant to the pharmacist at the Eckerd drugstore. She had a junior-college degree and was thinking about finishing a four-year degree at Florida Platinum College. She wore chrome-rimmed glasses and Sheila did not think she was unattractive. She wouldn't be a bad match for Tod, was what Sheila thought. But Tod wasn't interested. He had his face fixed for one of the MTV girls, or any girl like an MTV girl. Somebody about sixteen. He had dated a lot of younger girls when he was in high school, but when he dropped out he stopped dating altogether. He hadn't had a date in a year.

⋆　⋆　⋆

Sheila opened the front door. "I'm watering the beds out front." She had a straw hat and sunglasses, struggled adjusting them.

Tod rolled his head. "Leave the damn beds alone, will you?"

"Just let me water," she said.

"Water the grass," he said. "But don't be staring across the street."

"I'll be careful. I've got these glasses on. They can't tell where I'm staring anyway," she said.

"That will really confuse them. They're not going to have a clue."

"Well, drive me somewhere, then," she said.

"O.K. Fine. Where?"

"I don't care. I just want to go in the car so we can go by the driveway and see if that's him. I'd like to meet him. I'd like to take him dancing."

"Mother—"

"I've earned it," she said. "You're young. Nobody wants to go dancing with you."

"Thanks, Ma," Tod said.

"You know he has a wife. She's very English. That's what he said. He said his wife was 'very English.' Too English. She was upset because they were at this barbecue with his cousin," Sheila said. "Just like these people across the way. He was in the garage just like they are. He said it was cooler in the garage, that's why they were in there. Then his English wife came up and whispered he was a redneck. That's what he said on Leno. He seemed like a real nice guy."

"I'm sure he is. Very well to do," Tod said.

"What does that have to do with? Aren't you putting your contacts in?"

"No, I can see with the glasses," he said.

"We might run into Ellen. We might go to the drugstore."

"We're not going to the drugstore. Do you need to go to the drugstore?"

"I need garbage bags," she said. They went out to the car, an Oldsmobile, green, from the eighties. Tod drove. "Now go slow," Sheila said as he backed out.

"I'm going as slow as I can. If I go slower, I'll be going too slow."

"You're going backwards," she said. "How can you go too slow?"

"Mother," he said. He crawled the Olds past the Terlinks' house, past the driveway, and she stared up there and waved at the Terlinks. They all waved back from the deep shadow of the garage.

Two or three houses down the street there was a brown horse standing in somebody's front yard, tied to a tree. It had a bridle, but that was all. Nobody was paying any attention to it. It was just standing there.

"What's with this?" Sheila said, pointing out her window.

"Horse," Tod said. "Somebody got a horse."

"Well, they should wash it. Look at that. It's going to be hot, its feet are caked. They ought to get somebody over here to wash it."

Out by the shopping center on Palmetto Road there were two police cars with their blue lights flashing.

"Check the heat," Sheila said.

"That really dates you," Tod said. "Heat."

"Oh, god, I'm so sorry," Sheila said. "Forgive me, really. Can you ever?"

When they got close enough, they saw that somebody had driven a panel van into a ditch. Somebody else had gone in right after and landed on top of the van. That person was still sitting in his car, sort of slumped over to the side. The driver of the panel van was on a board alongside the van, deep in a ditch, surrounded by cops and ambulance people.

"It doesn't look good," Sheila said.

"I've seen that head get-up on ER," Tod said. "See the way they've got the Styrofoam thing around his head there?"

"That's not Styrofoam," Sheila said.

"You want some yogurt?" he said. "I'm stopping at the yogurt joint."

"That really dates you—joint," she said. "Look at this guy in the Caddy. He's just perched up there. Why don't they get him out? He looks sad."

"You'd be sad, too. I mean, come on," Tod said.

"What if those cars explode?" she said.

Tod changed lanes to get on the side of the street where the yogurt shop was in the strip shopping center. He pulled up to the drive-in window and asked Sheila what she wanted. She said a waffle cone with fat-free chocolate. He got a cup of vanilla and an oatmeal cookie. When the yogurt came, they paid and then drove the car out to the edge of the parking lot and stopped, rolling the windows down. From where they were sitting, they could see the wreck down to their left, the police and the ambulance, the road in front of them, and two shopping centers across the street.

"I don't remind you of my father, do I?" Tod said after a minute.

"Some ways. What's wrong, you don't like your father?"

"I don't want to be like him. He didn't do well."

"He did fine," she said. "Just ran out of steam."

Tod left the car running and the air conditioning on even though they had the windows down. "I feel like doing laundry. Dishes, too. I'm doing dishes when we get home."

"Fine. Do dishes all night long," she said. "Your father never did a dish in his life."

"I like my hands in the water," he said. "The way water sounds running. I could do dishes for hours—water's warm and soapy, you know, you've got a good sponge and you get some soap in that and rub it on the plates and the plates get a little slippery and everything gets a little slippery so there's some danger to it."

"Yeah," Sheila said. "That's how I feel about it exactly."

"Don't ruin it," Tod said. "Sometimes when you're gone and I'm there I wash dishes and clothes at the same time so I have the washer running and sometimes the washer and the dryer and then I'm washing dishes, too. God, that's great. I really like that. That does it for me."

"You remind me of your father," she said, shaking her head. She looked out her window at a yellow dog that had its nose stuffed in a Burger King sack. The dog lifted the sack up, throwing its head back so that it could get deeper into the bag. It was walking around on the striped concrete with this bag on its face.

"I hope that guy in the van doesn't die," Tod said.

"Me too," Sheila said. "What do you want for dinner?"

"We had sandwiches," Tod said. "I can't think about dinner yet."

"You want to barbecue?" Sheila said. "We could do that in the driveway, just like the Terlinks. Maybe we could go over there, or they could come over."

"We could have a party," Tod said. "Maybe I'll take up with the Terlink girl. We'll become lovers—tonight, after you leave for work."

"They have a daughter?" Sheila said.

"Oh, yeah," he said. "She's a babe. She's a babe and a half. She's a twister. Sometimes I sneak over there and look into her window, crawl around and peep in, see her in her underwear walking around the house. She always wears lace underwear—pink and black and pale blue. She's a real beauty. Sex hound."

"Oh, stop," Sheila said.

"She's probably poking Larroquette," Tod said. "He's grinning that stupid grin of his, revitalizing his . . ."

"Never mind," Sheila said. "Quit."

They were quiet in the car finishing the yogurt. The only thing she could hear was the smacking of their lips. When he was done, Tod squashed the bag the cookie had come in into the cup, broke the plastic spoon and put it in the cup too, then opened his door and set the cup on the concrete of the parking lot.

"Why do you want to do that?" Sheila said. "Here. Give that to me."

"I'm leaving it here," he said. "It's a gift. I don't have dirty diapers or chicken bones, so this is the best I can do."

"Oh, Jesus," she said. "Tod, open the door and pick that up."

"I'm not," he said. He backed the car in a half circle.

She reached over and struggled with the steering wheel, trying to force him to drive back and pick up the cup, but he turned the wheel the other direction and drove diagonally across the lot.

"I need to get a magazine," he said.

"I need to get home," she said. "We need to solve this problem once and for all."

"Dinner?" he said.

"No," she said. "I've got chicken at home. I stewed some chicken. You can have that. I'm having a salad. I've got to get this cheese off my legs." She grabbed her thighs and wagged them.

Tod drove more cautiously than he needed to. She was struck by it. He drove like his father. There wasn't a bit of difference. If she had shut her eyes, or if she had worn blinders to prevent her from seeing who was in the driver's seat, she could have imagined being with Dan. The ancient Oldsmobile was his car, part of the settlement, the conclusion of their marriage. The car and the house—that was her part of the bargain. She had always liked the car, and the house was comfortable. Sometimes, when she looked at *Better Homes and Gardens,* she wished it were fancier, but most of the time she didn't worry. She kept it clean. It had a nice old house smell about it, and sometimes in the summer, when the ceiling fans were going and the attic fan was on and a breeze was being pulled through the house through the open windows, she could close her eyes and imagine she was at her grandparents' house when she was a kid in the fifties, remember the way things smelled, the way the air moved. Her grandparents had a house in Bay

St. Louis, Mississippi, overlooking the Sound, and it had a certain sweet mustiness she always remembered. That was how her house in Quantum smelled.

She hadn't wanted Dan to leave. She'd spent seventeen years with him, but now she didn't know why she had stayed that long. He'd had different jobs—night watchman, car salesman, men's wear sales in a department store. He'd hold on to one for six months or a year, then go crazy after some young girl. Start drinking, start staying out all night, shoving her around when he was home. He wasn't much to miss, and he had always ignored Tod. Still, it broke her heart when he left. It did occur to her from time to time that she would like to have another man around, a boyfriend, but Tod was O.K. for the day-to-day, the routine stuff—watching TV movies and renting things from the video store. He was even fun, because he liked things that were strange to her. She worried she was hanging onto him too much, clinging to him, poisoning him. She worried that keeping him at home, making it easy for him to stay, was wrong. But she'd never really lived alone since college, and even then she had girlfriends, and she didn't think she wanted to start being alone at forty. She'd brought men to the house before, people she knew at the hospital or at the church. There was always tension between the men and Tod. After a while she stopped bringing them. They were just going to sit on the sofa and smoke cigarettes and drink her beer and watch her television and scratch themselves. Tod could do all that.

*     *     *

When they got home, the Terlinks were gone. The fancy rental car was gone and the garage doors were closed. All the windows were covered with mini-blinds. There were a few lights on behind them. It was dark when Sheila rolled the barbecue pit out of the garage onto the driveway. She took off its lid, removed the grill, went back into the garage and got some charcoal briquettes and poured them into the bottom of the grill, sprayed them with Gulf lighter fluid then walked around looking at her flower beds while she waited for the lighter fluid to seep into the briquettes. Tod went inside and came out to tell her there were steaks in the freezer and ask her if she wanted him to defrost them in the microwave. She said she did.

"Are there vegetables?" she said. "Spinach?" He said he'd look. She opened the aluminum folding chair she'd found in the garage and sat on the driveway with a hose spraying water onto the flower bed between her property and Ellen's. She had a five-dollar nozzle on the end of the hose. Tod came out of the kitchen door with two packs of frozen vegetables.

"Corn or lima beans?" he said.

"Both," she said. She released the trigger closing the nozzle and dropped the hose on the driveway while she lit the charcoal. Then she put the grill on top and scrubbed it with a wire brush. She sat down again and started spraying. There was a little breeze and the water from the spray was shifted slightly out of its path, sometimes the mist flew back on her. It felt nice and cool. It felt refreshing. She swung the nozzle and sprayed the Oldsmobile and then started on the bed on the house side of the driveway. She kept an eye on the Terlinks' garage. She wondered what had made her want it to be John Larroquette. She thought it was odd you could want something so bad and never get it. You could spend your whole life wanting something and never even come close.

When she married her husband, Dan, she had been in love with a Black man she had met in nursing school. He was beautiful and powerful and very smart. He knew that she loved him or at least that she had a crush on him. Sometimes he took advantage of it, touching her in ways that he shouldn't have—feeling her waist, letting his hand rest just beneath her breast, testing the strap of her brassiere, casually brushing against her buttocks. It happened too often to be accidental, but that was as far as it went. Later he became the weatherman for a TV station.

On her wedding night, after she and Dan had made love, she had watched this Black man who she was in love with do the weather forecast on the ten o'clock news. She thought he was so handsome.

\*    \*    \*

Tod came out with the steaks on a cookie sheet. He'd put a lot of Worcestershire sauce on them. "How long?" he said, holding the cookie sheet up on five fingers, as if he were a waiter.

"Coals ready any minute," Sheila said. "They're getting gray."

"I've got the vegetables," Tod said. "I did them in the microwave. You want to eat by the TV?"

"Sure," Sheila said. "What's on?"

"Everything," he said. "Probably movies."

"I never watched his show anyway," Sheila said.

"What?"

"Larroquette," she said. "He seemed nice when I saw him on TV. I liked him. He talked like somebody you could like. You know what I mean? He pinched his fingers together and said he was a redneck just about that far under the skin. It didn't seem to bother him. He laughed when he said it. That's such a wonderful thing for a man to do."

Tod looked at her for a few seconds, then brought the cookie sheet down and handed it to her. He pulled a cooking fork out of his back pocket and handed that to her as well. Then he took the hose out of her hand and spritzed it up in the air so that it drizzled on them just a little bit—just lightly.

"Sure," she said. "Go on. Rain some more. Rain harder."

Tom Chiarella | FOLEY'S CONFESSIONS

One summer, long and Florida heavy, I
decided to become a bad person. I went
to St. Petersburg, took an apartment and
found a job in a movie theater that faced
the beach. That was neither the start of it
nor the end of it. It's only what I choose
to open with. This story closes with an
angry theater owner holding a gun to my
head.

I made the decision the night after I was
blackballed by a fraternity at the University of Florida. I'm not suggesting cause
and effect here either, only that another
life occurred to me that evening, one that
I had never considered for myself. I could
split myself, become someone new, someone dangerous—the skulking kid with
the boxed Pall Malls, the one who hung
smoke rings and whirled into the night.

14

I knew the decision was juvenile, that I would be minor-league bad. But my path had been chosen. I went ahead: brooding, drinking, skulking.

I grew comfortable with all of this. When the time came to go home for the summer—north, to my mother's questions, to my father's business—I decided that I needed distance and went off by myself, south, to St. Pete. I took a one-room unfurnished apartment above a drugstore and got a job at a theater—the Beach Cinema—only a block away. There was sand everywhere in the apartment; I could see the Gulf from my fire escape. The world took on an air of finality.

\* \* \*

I had brought with me a duffel bag of clothes, which I lived out of for the summer. In it was a box containing my initiation sweatshirt, with Greek letters stitched across the front. We had been allowed to order these things, but not to wear them—not until we became brothers. Soon after arriving in St. Pete I opened the box, pulling the tissue paper back, like the sheets of a marriage bed, to take a look at the sweatshirt. I could have resold it back at school, but that morning I took out a double-edged razorblade, and began to cut away the letters. There was no plan; I just wanted them gone. I took off two of the letters and left the B—a beta—which I thought was puzzling enough to be left by itself. It stood for nothing. I had simply castrated the shirt. I wore it day after day.

\* \* \*

The section of St. Pete where I lived and worked was known as Redington Beach. There was not much to it in those days—just Gulf Boulevard, a strip of shops built on the edge of a swamp, a dock on the inlet, a post office and the Beach Cinema. People—from places like Minnesota and Wisconsin—were building tiny bungalows all along the empty grid of streets. Someday these numbered streets would be jammed full of houses, but now they were vacant lots, cleared and ready. On the south side, the point where the township blurred into Madeira Beach, someone had posted a sign that read REDINGTON BEACH—PREPARED FOR PROGRESS. At the other end there was another sign: REDINGTON BEACH—CITY OF THE FUTURE. I found disagreement on the motto, but everything there pointed forward.

For an architecture student like myself it should have been heaven. There were jobs galore—as surveyors, carpenters, laborers, electricians—but I liked the submerged quality of life at the movie house. Even as I intently watched the buildings go up, I feigned lack of interest and told phony stories of how I once stole cars.

I fancied myself living incognito. No one there knew my past; no one was much connected to my present. I took a post office box. My parents had no idea where exactly I lived. I had no phone. It drove my mother to tears.

★   ★   ★

I worked for a man named Rudolph Korn, who owned the theater and several lots nearby. I assumed he had plenty of money since his taste ran toward the rare. He drove a Mercedes, a truly foreign car in those days, and collected an assortment of exotic fish, which he kept in recessed, wall-length tanks at the theater. After he hired me, he gave me the tour of the theater. Stopping at the tanks, he ran a finger along the bottom of one and said, "These are meant for effect. To make people feel tropical. Movies should be like a vacation, right?" Rudolph had thick arms and a stomach that looped out over his belt like some giant gland. He wore a sad, untrimmed mustache and liked to let the beard around it grow for three days at a time before shaving. He favored doubleknits, in various shades of white (which he liked to call "buff"). When I first met him, I thought he was sick, but I later realized that he was pasty by nature. I think he was forty-three.

He hired me, and I was grateful. He had several University of Florida students working for him, most living at home for summer vacation. Among them was a nineteen-year-old girl, named Grace McBride, to whom he was rumored to be engaged. Grace worked at the ticket window. I started as an usher, but moved up quickly to the concessions stand—the Snack Bar, as Rudolph called it. He claimed he had invented the term.

Rudolph kept me away from the concession stand until I agreed to try to look happy. When I did work there, I was without shame. I stole and stole and stole. Opening boxes of candy, I ate a few pieces, then resold the box even as I chewed on my third nougat. I devised systems to circumvent Rudolph's inventory—restacking used popcorn boxes in among the new, substituting counterfeit drinking cups for the real thing. I pocketed an extra ten dollars a night. There were other rituals, just as mean-spirited as my stealing. After clocking out, I liked to watch the end of the late show while taking short pulls of Jim Beam. The theater was mostly empty. I sat in the back, with my feet up, laughing out loud in all the wrong places. Occasionally someone would stand up, or walk back, and ask me politely to shut up. Rudolph never got wind of it.

As I've said, all of this was a pose. I knew that even then. But I began to feel that I was almost dangerous. The detachment from my former lives—the one in Gainesville and the one before it in upstate New York—was what I liked. I rarely called my parents that summer and wrote no letters. With no one to talk to, I walked constantly—not often on the beach, more often along the streets of the undeveloped township, listening for the sound of people's radios, for the old Minnesota men on their new electric organs.

★   ★   ★

I was heartsick for Grace after the first week. This threw my planned isolation out of whack, since all I really wanted was to be with her, happy or sad, clothed or naked—and this required extensive talking and a general curiosity, both of which violated the discipline I'd set up for myself.

The first time I met Grace was on the sidewalk outside the theater, just before it opened one afternoon, as we waited for Rudolph to unlock the doors. She had just been to the beach and I could see beads of sweat forming on her skin.

I said nothing to her, staring straight out at the water as if it held some message for me. Then Grace introduced herself. "What's the B stand for?" she asked, nodding at my sweatshirt, at my chest.

As I looked down, I thought about the possibilities. I wanted to say something dark, something scary, but I could only come up with "bird" and "bench" as these were the only B words in my line of vision. I lied.

"It stands for Barnes," I said. "That's my name." She nodded. "It's what people call me. Just Barnes."

She called me Barnes that whole first night, apparently thinking that it was my first name. Even when I told her the truth—that my name was Dan Foley—I did so with a lie at the ready. I was changing my name, I would tell her; I was in the middle of a painful split with my family. I braced myself when I told her, somehow expecting that she would care, that she would even be angry when I told her the truth, but when I said "Foley," she only smiled.

"Pretty name," she said, trying it out for herself. "Foley," she said. "Foley." She called me only that from then on. Even after she found out that other people called me Dan, she rarely called me anything else. I loved it.

\*       \*       \*

When Grace sat at the ticket counter I watched her back. I loved her straight spine, her slender shoulders. When she was next to me, doling out popcorn, I caught little whiffs of soap. Once I asked about her relationship with Rudolph—were they engaged?—but she laughed and said nothing. I was left to figure.

I began to watch Rudolph's hands, picturing his soft palms, his many-ringed fingers, cupped around one of Grace's breasts. In this vision, the two of them met at one of the beach motels—The Galleon, The Tides, The Ship's Mate—while I prowled the streets, looking to bust in and end it all.

Once Grace claimed she was worried about Rudolph. He had openly wished for cancer. I pshawed and dug into the mound of popcorn.

"He said, 'Cancer. I want it.'" She looked earnest, concerned. "Those were his exact words." I was hitting off a box of Whoppers stashed under the cash drawer. I popped one in my mouth and took an order. "Rudolph is morbid, Grace. Don't let it get to you." For the moment, I wanted yet another persona; I tried out the sensible, stalwart Foley. "I'll talk to him if you want."

"You don't have to sit there with him every night like I do. He's so dark, Foley. It rubs off."

I took another Whopper in my mouth, crunched down on it and sucked until it dissolved. "Try getting him angry," I said, casting a glance at the office door. "Get the life force flowing." That was the best advice I could come up with.

She was not consoled. I spent the rest of the night wondering where the two of them went together and what it was they did. He took her to dinner, I guessed, to the expensive Cuban restaurants in Tampa or to swarthy Eastern European spots, where everyone's arms were as thick as his. In those places he talked low and suicidal to her.

\*　　\*　　\*

I now think it's funny that I never tried to figure out Rudolph's death wish. I couldn't appreciate the subtleties of motivation and I didn't try. Nothing seemed explainable. More importantly, Grace kissed me quite suddenly on the beach that night. I began to learn that she liked to take giant leaps, with or without me. We said nothing to Rudolph.

We began to go to dinner together, but more often we walked the beach, despite my passion for roaming the streets. "There are palmetto bugs running all over the pavement at night," she said. That's what she called roaches. All Floridians did as far as I could tell.

Sometimes we ended up in a clinch, on the beach if the tide was low, or in her apartment. I loved the feel of her dresses against my chest. The buttons, the pins, the edges of her pockets. I tried my best to be a gentleman—yet another version of myself, my new night persona— and did not rush her. Once I got my hand up under her skirt, where I brushed the inside of her thigh. She took a deep breath and said "Thank you" as if I had just told her I liked her new hairdo. I pulled my hand back immediately, figuring she was betting on my honor.

She kept seeing Rudolph, though, and it ate at me that Grace wouldn't tell me what they did together. I asked if she loved him. Again she laughed. "It's nothing like that," she said. "He's harmless."

\*　　\*　　\*

Once, a long time after all of this, I recounted this story to Grace and she remembered saying, "He's harmless. It's you I love." But I cannot say I have any memory of her saying this, nor can I figure out why she loved me so quickly, so surely. "At first you seemed scary," she told me once. "Then I realized you weren't anything to be scared of. I liked it that way."

★   ★   ★

One night Rudolph and Grace left me to close the theater by myself. We had a particularly long movie showing, one that took place in France and involved knives. Grace knew it drove me crazy that she still went out with Rudolph, especially since I had begun touching her breasts, but she reassured me. "Only a week or two more," she said. "Then we'll be done."

When they left that night Grace shot a knowing smile over her shoulder at me, Rudolph waved merrily and I was suddenly alone.

Leaning out the door, I watched them turn off the boulevard a few blocks down. They were moving toward Rudolph's house.

I checked the ticket count. In the theater behind me, there were thirteen people, watching the last thirty-five minutes of the show. I could duck out, follow Grace and Rudolph for a block or two, and still get back before the credits. At the very least I'd know if they ended up at his house.

So I locked the cash drawer and the office, leaned out the glass doors, looked around as if someone might see me—as if someone might care—and took to tracking them. But there was no adventure in the chase. They ended up at Rudolph's house, as I'd suspected. I watched them through the blinds, which were only half drawn. Grace walked in, took off her clothes and sat in a large hammock. Rudolph backed away, opened a closet, wheeled out an easel and began to paint.

★   ★   ★

The saltiness of the place began to overwhelm me as I stood there, in the night air, with my hands pressed to Rudolph's stucco. Everything was covered with salt—the windowsill, the streetlamp, the palm leaves, the cinder-block retaining walls, my hair, my shirt, my bow tie. I had climbed through it to this spot. Now I felt heavy and slow, glued there, at the window, by the sight of my Grace and by the warm salt air.

I remember thinking how I might confront Grace with my newfound knowledge. "I'm not even angry," I would begin. That was true. I felt lucky; I was seeing her naked. So ran my general spirit that night. I stood there, as close as I dared, watching for a full twenty-two minutes before sprinting back to the theater. I arrived, breathless, to meet the last of the customers on their way out. They shot me queer glances as I ran up to them. "Sorry," I panted, waving good-bye. "Raccoons. Raccoons in the garbage." That just came to me.

★   ★   ★

I've often tried to think of adjectives to describe the way Grace looked that night. At the time I settled on "innocent" and "beautiful." These were much like those B-words I came up with earlier—the first things in my line of vision. Years later, with Grace at my side, when I told this story at parties, I used words like "majestic" and "stately." She said that I made her sound like a cruise ship. Now I just say she looked "good" and that the sight of her like that—lounging, flipping through a magazine—was "welcome." I remember that the blinds afforded me a partial view, so that I had to change my perspective to see each part of her body. I got good at it, though, because I was there every night that week.

I didn't say anything to Grace about my discovery. I just begged out of several dates, in hopes that she might see Rudolph even more. She did. He was finishing his painting. I could see that from the window.

Each night I cut it closer and closer on the sprint back to the theater, until it finally occurred to me that I hardly needed to be there at all as the people filed out. At the drugstore below my apartment, I bought a tiny sign that said, THANK YOU, which I propped up on the snack bar before I left each evening. I began to stay later at the window, propping my ass against a pawpaw tree, until I finally didn't worry at all about returning.

★   ★   ★

One evening the moon was out, full and glassy white over the Gulf, and I got worried that someone might see me there at the window of Rudolph's house. So I left a little earlier than I had the night before, still long after the end of the late show, and walked back to the theater along the beach. It was late August and the night was as hot as they get. Grace had taught me to like walking by the water. She pointed out the things one couldn't see in the darkness, as well as the many things—the shells, the weeds, the debris—that became visible as I walked over them. That night I could see as far out as I ever had before. A lighted boat and not much else bobbed on the horizon. There was plenty out there, I knew.

I missed Grace and wanted her then. We had recently agreed to see more of each other when we returned to school in the fall. I had decided to tell her I knew about the painting. I would say, "I accept it. I respect it." This was yet another Foley. Honest Foley. Tolerant Foley. Good Foley.

When I turned off the beach, I could see right away that something was wrong inside the theater. Things looked wavy and out of balance. At first I thought someone had turned off a bank of lights in the lobby, but as I ran up to the doors of the theater, I found that the sidewalk was wet, as if someone had run a hose over it.

The lobby was flooded. The surface of the water shone with broken glass, popcorn and boxes of candy. In this mess, in the glint of broken glass, the patterns of jujubes, I could see the tiny splashes of Rudolph's dying tropical fish from one end of the lobby to the other.

At that point I was struck with a queer sensation, a little like being kicked in the neck. This sensation told me I had finally made it. I was bad.

*　　*　　*

After all the phone calls were made, after the police had come and gone and the cleanup had begun, Rudolph called me into his office to hear my story one more time. I was so far past sorry that I didn't care. The lobby had been demolished. Fire extinguishers emptied, snack bar smashed, cash drawer jimmied, fish tanks shattered with Rudolph's very own ballpeen hammer. I thanked God that I had left the projection room locked.

When he sat, Rudolph took a deep breath. I suddenly saw him as very old, like a grandfather is old. He had a bottle of scotch on his desk. He told me to sit and did not offer me a drink.

"How could you not have heard?" he said. "This is like a war happened in here." He leaned back in his chair. I told my story again: I had been up in the projection room, cleaning up after the show. I'd forgotten to lock the doors before I went back up.

"Four thousand dollars' worth of fish," he said. He held up four fingers. "Four thousand."

I shook my head. "I'm sorry." I was trying so hard to radiate sincerity that I could see myself—as if from some corner of the room—shaky, alone, nervously gripping the arms of the chair.

Rudolph got up then and closed the door to the office, and that's when he pulled the gun. I didn't see when he picked it up, but I felt it because he came up behind me, jerked me into a half nelson and pressed the barrel end of it against my temple. It felt absurdly big, as if the tip were the diameter of a doughnut. I cried out.

"Do you think she didn't know you were at the window?" he whispered. "Do you really think I didn't know you were there?"

"I wasn't," I said. He choked me. I put my hands in the air, a criminal now, or a victim. I couldn't tell the difference. He pulled tighter.

"Liar!" he said, twisting me a little. "She saw you!"

"I wasn't," I said, pulling at his arm. "It wasn't me! I don't know what you're talking about." I could hear him grinding his teeth.

He loosened a little and I bent my head to one side and slipped out. I turned to him. The gun was down. "It was you at the window," he said. "She saw you tonight."

"No," I said. "Not me."

"She told me you were there," he said. "I was going to go out and get you, but she said no. She said it was okay."

I wondered again when he had picked up the gun, thinking, If he'd had it while he was painting, he could have shot me through the window. I heard what he said about Grace seeing me at the window. It didn't register. I was too busy believing that I hadn't been there. He said nothing for a moment, then stared past me, as if he was reading a map on the wall. "I presume you know that you're fired," he said. I nodded, and then he slapped me.

*　　*　　*

I was the first person to ever split a movie theater. At least I thought of the idea. For a while I made a good bit of money doing it. My architectural firm called it "theater conversion." We built soundproof walls down the middle of old theaters, split their giant screens and realigned the seats as best we could. Theater owners loved it, since it doubled the draw overnight. Once, in a local paper, my firm was credited with "the death of the double feature."

The idea for splitting occurred to me the night Rudolph held a gun to my head. It happened like this. After he slapped me, he told me to get my things and go. It was numbingly quiet as I walked through the theater, down the aisle toward the locker room. My face was still burning, my ear still ringing. In among the seats I saw empty popcorn boxes—here and there, the random drinking cup. The vandals hadn't come in here and this part of the world seemed normal. Things could be picked up, the floor could be swept, the reels rewound and things would start again tomorrow. Like normal. The lobby, where Rudolph sorted through the wreckage and wept, was a ruined place, another world really, separated from this one only by a wall, by a line. One place, two worlds. Like that.

I had crossed lines again and again all summer. All I wanted that night was to stumble out, find my way back, recross that line, march along it for the rest of my life. This was the good-bad line I was thinking about. But as I kneeled to pick the last of my stolen change from the floor of my tiny locker, I wasn't sure that I'd be able to move ever again. So I knelt there for a long time, rattling nickels in the palm of my hand. I now recognize it as an attitude of prayer.

*　　*　　*

I didn't see Grace again until I got back to school, and even then she wouldn't talk to me. From the moment I saw her in the doorway of the biology building, I wanted to tell her everything. Not just about watching in the window, but everything—the stealing from the till, my summer-long callousness. Without hoping for more, I wanted her to know.

To her credit, she wouldn't have it. She refused my phone calls, left my letters unanswered and turned away whenever I approached.

Finally, after a year, I saw her at a party in New York of all places. I worked then at a Manhattan architectural firm, keeping my theater conversion idea very close to the vest. I had a decent, windowless office that I shared with an older student from Cornell. That firm had the first electric pencil sharpener in New York City.

I saw Grace as she came in, but avoided her, as she was with a date. Between drinks I reminded myself to get her phone number. "Are you in New York now?" I would say, just as casual as that.

But before I could, Grace came up behind me and said, "I hear you paid Rudolph back."

I turned to her, drew a breath. "No," I said. "Not true. I wish I had." Before I left St. Pete that summer, I stopped by the theater and gave Rudolph my bankroll—three hundred fifty dollars, the sum of my unspent stolen money. "I'm sorry," I said again.

Rudolph shook his head. "I have insurance," he said. "I'm covered." He was on his hands and knees in the lobby, pulling up the carpet.

"Keep it," I said. "It's yours."

He nodded then. "Where'd you get it?" he said.

"I sold my car," I said, using the answer I had made up that morning while packing.

"You didn't have to do that," Rudolph said, holding the money out to me. "Really, I'm covered."

I didn't take it. When I left, I hitchhiked into downtown St. Pete, where my car was stashed in an hourly parking lot, then drove north to school.

It didn't surprise me that Grace knew about the money. Rudolph had told her. She got the story wrong because he had lied and told her I'd paid for everything. I straightened her out.

"I never minded you watching me in the window," she told me later that evening. "I liked it. The window was dark. I could only see your face every once in a while. You looked like a ghost. First time it scared me, but then I was glad you finally saw me that way. Then I knew you wouldn't be jealous of Rudolph anymore."

I've never been sure how Grace knew that last bit or why it was so true. We began to see each other again that summer and I saw her naked many times during those months. Years later, after we were married, I even saw Rudolph's painting of Grace, when we went to visit him at his home in Pensacola. By then all the confessions had been made.

It's notable that upon my return to Gainesville, after the summer in St. Pete, I found that I was not entirely unpopular with the brothers in the fraternity that had blackballed me. I saw them all the time around campus, in classes, in bars, at various parties. Once I started talking to them, they were friendly. They regretted what had happened, they told me. Occasionally one of them would clap a hand on my shoulder and say how sorry he was about the whole thing.

After a while I just told them to forget it, that it had been like a trial, that I was better for it. The silly thing was, I believed what I said.

*Everything that touches you shall burn you, and
you will draw your hand away in pain, until
you have withdrawn yourself from all things.
Then you will be alone.*
—THOMAS MERTON

Philip Cioffari

# DANGEROUSLY THE
# SUMMER BURNS

The first thing Karen noticed about him
the night he opened the door of the
southside 7-Eleven was that he wore sunglasses. It was nearly midnight and she
thought he was only trying to be cool, until he pointed the gun—small and silver
and only slightly larger than the hand
that held it—at her face. For a moment
all she could think was *where did it come
from?* Then she remembered he had kept
his hand down at his side, in the pocket
of his coat perhaps—and that was the
second odd thing about him: how small
his hand was, like a woman's hand, the
fingers thin and delicately curled against
the revolver's metal, the barrel's dark
orifice directed at her throat.

Afterward, in the cramped yellow light
of the police station, she squinted at the

shell of the face Detective Canthrow was helping her to build. She had already decided upon the forehead, black hair in a wave, no part, combed back from a broad, nearly straight hairline, the forehead itself smooth-skinned, angular. The eyes, of course, remained a cipher. Detective Canthrow showed her a page of eyeglass styles. She pointed to a pair of black-rimmed glasses and he slid the strip containing those glasses into position beneath the forehead. It was like a child's game, sliding the pieces of a puzzle into place until the right one fit.

Half a face stared up at her from the broad, white surface of the table. Next, the nose. Small and rounded, the nostrils slightly flared. The lips thin, taut, as if keeping a secret. The detective inserted six different chin variations before she said *yes, that one.* The face stared back at her, complete, life-like; a thrill of recognition shivered through her, as if, turning a corner in some foreign city, she ran head on into a lost friend from childhood.

She wondered if the detective would show her pictures of hands— the hand that reached toward her in the bright-as-day fluorescence of the 7-Eleven's interior—but of course he didn't. What he said was a punk like that was more than likely the hit and run type. He might have already left the island, headed back up U.S. 1 for the upper Keys, maybe for Miami. She closed her eyes so that the face was no longer a facsimile on a table, but a real face preserved in memory, imprinted on the dark screen behind her eyelids; and disappointment weighed heavily inside her, at the possibility of losing him so soon.

*   *   *

At six, when her shift ended and Lou the manager came on, she walked along White Street toward the beach in the warm gray light of dawn. Lou had asked her if she wanted to take a few days off, just as he had asked her if she wanted the rest of the night off when she returned from the police station sometime after midnight. No, she had said both times, and no, she wasn't afraid, though what she felt was akin to fear, enflamed by a burning restlessness that unsettled her.

Through the slow hours of the night she had felt the gunman's presence in the store. She had watched the door constantly, the reflected glide of car lights drifting like moons, then disappearing, across the dark horizon of the plate-glass windows. At any moment she expected him to loom suddenly before the counter and ask her in his low, phlegm-edged voice to open the register, hand him the money. And now, as she hurried past wooden bungalows half hidden by the fan-like fronds of palm, by flowering bougainvillea and hibiscus, she imagined him watching her from the shadows of an alley, listening to her footsteps slowly fade in the stillness of morning.

At the beach she sat on a jetty that divided the Gulf of Mexico from the Atlantic, his presence filling the air around her like the heat of the sun rising from the sand and from the rocks of the jetty, riding sea-blown in the wind. This was crazy, she thought. There was no way he could be watching her, no place he could be hiding—the sea on one side of her and the white crease of sand on the other, deserted along its entire length.

She stayed until his presence, exaggerated by the sun's heat and sharp light, proved more than she could tolerate. It was only July but already this summer, according to the radio, was turning out to be the hottest summer in the island's history, the temperatures since early June in the nineties by mid-morning, close to a hundred by mid-afternoon. Usually she enjoyed these early morning hours on the beach, a winding-down period before going home to bed, and in the month she had been living on the island she came out every morning, even in the rain. In New York, when she had finished her all-night shift at the diner, there was no place to go to unwind, Central Park still unsafe at that hour, the rivers rimmed by highways already noisy with commuter traffic.

Too restless for sleep, she walked back along White Street to the civic center, a former church, clapboard and stucco in a modified Spanish style built by the island's first settlers, where she worked as a volunteer, helping out with the senior citizens and the homeless, whoever wandered in for food and company.

Sunlight fell through stained glass onto the bare, scuffed floor where a half-dozen elderly people, Hannah among them, sat isolated in a random configuration of folding chairs. Karen passed through them to the ladies room in back.

In the mirror her face stared out at her, tired and worn, despite the red blush from the sun. It seemed to her that in the last year her face aged noticeably from day to day. At first she had blamed it on the city— the foul air, the soot, the late-night hours—and that was one of the reasons she left. At thirty-seven she had given it the best years of her life, and what had it given her? A subsistence-level job, a cramped two-room apartment on Avenue B, a series of burnt-out relationships with men. So she had taken the bus south, until the road ended. *Here.* But looking at her face now in the mirror, she looked as old and tired as she had in New York. Her tan didn't change a thing.

She came out and pulled a chair next to Hannah, who sat with a scarf on her head, her hands folded prayer-like in her lap, her eyes staring up at the sunlight igniting vivid reds and yellows and blues in the holy pictures.

"How are you today, Hannah?"

"Hannah not too good," the old woman said. They had this same conversation nearly every day.

"What's the matter?"

Hannah sat silent for a long while; she squinted at the light without blinking, like a primitive sun worshipper long since gone blind. "The usual," she said.

"Do you want some tea? Do you want to play checkers?"

Hannah waited again before replying. She raised her hand to tighten the ends of the scarf beneath her chin. "Maybe," she said.

★   ★   ★

That night at the Red Parrot, Karen ordered a beer at one end of the semi-circular bar. The crowd swelled around her, shadowy shapes and motions gliding back and forth along the arc of the bar or stalled in silhouette in the open doorways. The usual Friday night frolic, and though the Parrot was a friendly place, Karen sat alone. The regulars had already learned she wasn't easy, that she had come down from New York with some kind of wall around her, so they stayed away. Occasionally a tourist would initiate a conversation, try to pick her up, but Karen would quickly lose interest.

She had heard it all before: the flattery, the bragging, the promises, the lies. Good intentions or bad, always derailed. In the eighteen months before leaving the city, she had given herself to no man. It was that isolation that finally drove her away, that clung to her here in Key West like the damp summer heat.

She was relieved when it was time for work. At the 7-Eleven, when there were no customers to distract her, she read through each of the local newspapers, looking for reports of theft, for some hint that the gunman had not abandoned her.

A half-dozen holdups had occurred in the past twenty-four hours: a liquor store, a bowling alley, a cosmetic shop on Duval, three convenience stores on different parts of the island—but the descriptions did not match the man who had held the gun to her throat. In a separate article the island's police chief offered explanations for the recent crime wave. He believed that widespread crime originated in the large cities and moved in ripples to the outlying areas. The island, he said, was caught in a crossfire between Miami and the drug capitals of South America. This particular outbreak he attributed in part to the unusually hot weather. "Heat can drive you to the breaking point," he was quoted as saying. "And when that happens, well, hell, who knows . . . ?"

When Lou came on, she went directly home. She hadn't slept in a day and a half, and the heat deepened her sense of exhaustion. The thermometer on her verandah read 89. Her fourth-floor view faced west and far off, beyond the clustered rooftops and the solitary turret of St. Paul's scorched red in the early sunlight, the Gulf etched a blue line across the horizon.

Inside her apartment she opened the windows, turned on the overhead fans. Even in the heat she couldn't sleep without a sheet covering her, the hem bunched in her fist as she drifted into dreams. *Open the register,* his voice commanded, his words rough-edged and, in an inexplicable way, tender. *Hand me the money.* She saw it happening again: the blue-white fluorescent glare of the 7-Eleven lights, the root-beer colored lenses, the pistol directly between her eyes, then at her throat, her heart; and her hand—stuffed with bills—moving slow motion through the air as if it were water, his palm open, fingers twitching, reaching to take what she had to give.

She was awake. Voices shouted on the street below; car horns warred with each other. Then she must have been dreaming again because she saw the Bronx apartment where she had lived so long ago with her mother. All the furniture had been removed, the rooms empty, bare-walled, heavy with a rain-colored light, the windows open wide to an alley's gray brick. The gunman watched her from the alley. *There's nothing left,* she said, *don't you see?* But he refused to leave. He followed her through the empty rooms, then into bed with her, touching her between her legs, and in her dream she heard herself moan, her pleasure deep and far-off, choked, like a cough she was trying to hold back. *No,* she cried, *no more, no more.* Then she seemed to be alone on the beach, the sun burning from a clear sky above the ocean, but he was watching as her face turned into a hag's face, ancient, bony, scarred, and then she was totally alone, growing older still, with no one to touch her but herself, and only the memory of him relentless as the whir of fans or the music of waves or a ringing phone that no one answers.

★   ★   ★

She woke wet and hot, staring into the shadowy flicker of the overhead fan, the motionless fronds of the palm plant on the verandah a dim green in the twilight. Saturday night. Her night off. She showered and, with the sky above the island filled with blue-gray light, the neighborhood around her dimmed with shadow and the last colors of the day gathered in a small pink arc above the Gulf, she walked down a cobblestone alley to the Red Parrot.

From her sanctuary at the end of the bar she overheard a man mutter that it was Midsummer's eve and she knew that must be important, but she didn't know why. When she turned to find the man who had spoken, she saw Detective Canthrow pushing through the crowd toward her.

He settled himself on the stool beside her, a large man with a broad, flat face and massive shoulders. Not the kind of man to maneuver easily in tight places, so that when he tried to smile he was breathing too heavily to manage it. "Been looking for you," he said.

"You've caught him?" she said with a quickness in her voice. He ordered a beer for himself and one for her. She assumed from that, and from the heavy dose of lime cologne he was wearing, that he was off-duty.

"Guy like that catches himself." He turned toward her so that she had a full view of the dark, thick hairs curling in the open V-space of his shirt collar. "He keeps at it till he gets nabbed, or till he runs into a storeowner quick enough to put him out of his misery."

She winced at the image of him—blood on his hand, his face, his glasses—lying like knocked-over merchandise on the drab white tiles of some 7-Eleven aisle. "That's horrible," she said.

The detective shrugged. "Anyway, they caught some guy knocking off a Mini-Mart in Marathon a few hours ago. We've got some pictures down at the station."

She stood up quickly and reached for her purse, but his large hand clamped down on hers. His smile came more easily this time. "You can finish your beer first."

At the station he showed her photos of the gunman: one full-face, and two profile shots: the dark glasses, the small rounded nose, the lips creased thin and taut. She stared at each of the three photos in turn, spread like placemats across the table. "No," she said.

"No?"

"It's not him."

The detective looked at her as if he didn't understand. "You're sure?"

"Yes."

"It's not him?"

"No. I don't think so."

His large hands swept the photos into a pile. He stood them on end and tapped them on the table's surface, before sliding them into a manila folder. "He'll show up. Sooner or later."

On the drive back to her apartment, he said: "I'm off-duty now. For the next couple of hours, I mean."

They drank a beer on her verandah, the palm fronds scraping the porch railing at the slightest hint of a breeze, an occasional car headed toward Duval rushing by on the street below. He was unusually soft-spoken for a man his size, for a hardcore cop in a Southern town. He told her the story of his daughter who died before her seventh birthday and his wife who walked out on him a year later without saying goodbye.

The story left her feeling even sadder than before, emptier, and she watched him sitting there in the wicker chair opposite her, his shoulders hunched inward, his eyes cast down, his hands gripping his knees as if to steady himself. In the silence, she said, "Summer's half gone already."

He raised his head and smiled. "Where you come from, maybe. Down here it's summer all year long." He stood up slowly and thanked her for the beer. "I've got the day off Monday. I'd like to come by, if that's all right."

*No,* she thought. *Not again. Not yet.* She didn't want to make room inside herself for his pain. But she shook her head yes, and he reached to touch her cheek with the back of his hand, his fingers so thick they felt swollen, the gesture reminding her of the gunman lifting the pistol to her throat, as much an offering as a threat.

**Steve Cushman** | ME AND DR. BOB

Me and Dr. Bob had lived across the
street from each other for seven years
and had never said more than a dozen
words to each other. Then one night,
around midnight, I was taking the trash
out and I saw him standing in the middle
of the road wearing nothing but a pair of
green boxer shorts and holding a small
black poodle in one hand.

"How ya doin?" I asked.

"She left me," he said, and then the
dog jumped out of his hands, scratching
his thickly muscled chest and running
off. Me, I went in my house and went to
sleep.

The next day, he was knocking at my
door. He had on a pair of blue cut-off
shorts and a green t-shirt. "You got any
beer?"

"Sure," I said. We sat out on my back porch and drank a twelve pack of Amstel Light. He said he couldn't believe that his wife had just left him after eighteen years of marriage. Or that she'd left Harry, the toy poodle he'd bought her three years ago as an anniversary present. It seemed the more he drank the more he talked. He went on to tell me he was an orthopedic surgeon and that he specialized in total joints. Said that he ate morphine like candy and that he'd had five affairs over the course of the marriage.

That was three months ago, and since that time we have become the best of friends. Sometimes when we're talking, he'll say, "I don't miss her at all," or "I hate this dog." But, I don't buy any of it. I've seen him sleeping in the middle of the street with the dog on his chest.

*   *   *

My wife died ten years ago, breast cancer at thirty-two. After she died, I took a month off work and while grocery shopping one day came across a magazine called *WoodenBoat Lovers*. I fell in love with the boats inside. They were all so beautiful and foreign to me. I quit my job as the sales manager at Palmer's Light Fixtures and moved to Washington state for a year to go to boatbuilding school. After graduation, I came back to my house, converted my three-car garage into a workshop and started building boats, mostly canoes and kayaks. It took me six months to build a boat that could float and another year to actually sell one.

I have a cat named Lucky. Lucky weighs seventeen pounds and when he walks sometimes his belly rubs against the ground. Lucky is black and white and mean. When he wants to go outside, he doesn't meow, just bites my leg. He kills snakes, lizards, and his speciality is newborn cardinals.

I have a basketball hoop up against the back of the garage with a blue and white striped net. Every Saturday night, me and Dr. Bob play basketball. I haven't beaten him yet. I'm tall, thin, have a weak right ankle, and no outside shot whatsoever. Bob is short and stocky, but he plays hard, all knees and elbows flying. Bob says his knees are bad from all those years of squatting in the weight room. He comes over, sweat pants, white t-shirt, and blood in his eyes.

Afterwards, we sit around and drink beer and swallow a couple of morphine pills. After Bob starts feeling good, he'll ask me if I'd like to drive his car, a red Jaguar. I tell him no, thanks, and smile, knowing the pain I'm causing him.

Teresa, a young Spanish girl, moved two doors down from us into the Pollys' garage apartment six months ago. Bob talks about her all the time. She runs and has legs like an angel. Deep dark tanned legs, strong calves, long black hair and small breasts.

Bob gets laid a lot; I don't. He brings women home a couple of nights a week. He says they're all nurses, and asks me if I'd like to come over and watch them have sex. I tell him no, thanks.

★ ★ ★

I have not had sex in five years. The last time was with a girl named Christy. She was beautiful, all long blond hair and green eyes, fair skin and thin lips. She was twenty-four years old and working the reception desk at Thomas Lumber, where I was buying the wood for my boats. I'd seen her in there before, you notice a girl who looks that good, but I'd never really talked to her. One day, she said to me, "So are you the guy who builds boats?"

"Yes," I said.

"I'd like to see them," she said. She was wearing black jeans, a white button-up shirt, and a pair of black boots.

"Sure, anytime," I said.

"How about tonight?" she asked. "I'll come over, cook you dinner, and you can show me your boats."

I smiled and said, "Okay."

I must've walked into three walls that day. She came over that night, made chicken carbonara, and it tasted awful. The bacon was too crunchy and the sauce was sticky. "Um, this is good," she said.

"Yes, it is," I said, smiling, feeling stupid.

"You have an honest face," she said. I didn't say anything. She slept on the couch, but a week later we had sex. She was crazy, a wild woman, she started yelling and carrying on. Her arms and legs were flapping all over the place. She gave me a headache by the time we were done.

A month later, she moved in. She showed up one day, with two suitcases and a kitten named Lucky. She told me she was going to school to be a phlebotomist, and that if she moved in with me she could quit her job at the lumberyard and finish school a lot quicker. I didn't really say okay, but I didn't say no either.

She started coming home with needles and wanting to practice drawing my blood. I let her at first, but then it started to hurt. The girl would stick the needle in my arm and dig around for five minutes looking for a vein. She'd eventually pull it out, blood flowing, and then start again.

School lasted about six months, and we stopped having sex after the third month. She was too wild for me. After graduation, she got a job at the county hospital. Three weeks later, she moved in with an overweight redheaded pharmacist named Mike. She left the cat, said Mike was allergic to cats. I missed her for a day at the most.

*   *   *

"I want some of that," Bob says, as Teresa runs by. Bob was last in his class at medical school, and it took him three years to finish up his last year of residency. Bob makes $300,000 a year, before taxes.

Bob wants me to come and work for him, be his assistant. "No, thanks," I say. I am happy here in my shop with my boats. Bob has bought two of my kayaks.

When we play ball, it's usually around six or seven, early enough so that we can see Teresa run. I watch her run, and she is something. When her feet touch the ground, it all seems so soft and smooth. Her hair bounces high in the air and falls onto her shoulders. After a couple of laps around the block, her hair starts to mat against her forehead from the sweat.

Bob says that his wife's tits weren't real. I tell him I don't care. He asks me if I ever saw the man who stole his wife, a dentist named Pidkin. I lie and tell him no. Sometimes, you don't have to add insult to a man.

Bob has a small man-made pond in his backyard. There are no fish in it. It's all overgrown and weeds are sticking out the top of it. Bob has not mowed his yard since his wife left. I started mowing the front yard;

the neighbors were complaining. Bob doesn't know it's me who cuts his grass. On the days I do it, he'll come home and start yelling, "Leave my fucking grass alone," at no one in particular.

Sometimes, me and Bob will stand in the kitchen and stare out the window, past the white cotton curtains, into the backyard. There's grass three feet high and we "ooh" and "ah" at what could be out there. "An infinite world of possibilities," Bob says. I shake my head and smile.

I've asked Bob to take the kayaks out, to go on a river trip. He hasn't used them since he bought them, and he says that he is waiting for just the right time.

Bob also talks about drinking margaritas and making love slow to Teresa. He brings over a book on margaritas. There are different recipes and photos of sixty varieties of the drink. He smiles and says, "This is it, this is the way to a Latin woman's heart."

"Could be," I say.

*   *   *

I've been working on my outside shot, and I think it's getting better. Bob played football at Florida State University. Bob wears Polo shirts and white slacks to his office. It's only ten minutes from his house.

I've seen Bob kiss the poodle on the lips. Bob's ex-wife's name is Betty. Betty and Bob Kole of Orlando, Florida.

Bob tells me that he's going to have his backyard cleared and then he's going to put fish in the pond. I tell him it won't work. "They'll die," I say.

Bob looks at me and shakes his head, "Simms, you're such a fucking pessimist." I think Bob is a dreamer.

The first night I did morphine with Bob was a month ago. We'd finished our usual game, Bob winning by twelve points. Afterwards, the two of us were sitting there, rubbing our knees and ankles. Bob pulled out the pills, swallowed two, and then sat there waiting for them to kick in. "Want some?" Bob asked.

"What is it?" I asked.

"Morphine," Bob said. "The greatest drug ever invented. I take eight a day."

"Sure," I said. Bob gave me two, and I washed them down with beer. It was a beautiful May Florida night, seventy degrees, slight breeze, Lucky and Harry eyeballing each other across the yard. The initial wave came across me, and I felt a lightheadedness and then my whole body felt the lightness, like I could float, if I could only stand. We sat there, stupid smiles on our faces and numb bodies. Teresa ran by, and we didn't move, felt too good to get up. On her second lap, we got up though and were standing by the road with two large glasses of ice water, waiting for her, to refresh her. She ran by us and Bob held his glass high and inviting. She laughed and kept on running. "We were close, Simms, damn close," Bob said.

"Next lap," I said.

She didn't run by again that night. She probably thought we were dirty old men. We're both in our mid-forties. We sat at the end of the driveway and waited for her. It started getting dark and I said, "What kind of work do you think she does?"

"Don't know," Bob said.

"Maybe she's an accountant or something," I said.

"She's too young. She's a college student," Bob said, looking at me. "Haven't you noticed the parking sticker on her car?"

"Oh," I said, and thought that Bob was full of surprises.

Bob fell asleep in my driveway, and his beeper started going off. I pulled it off his sweat pants and read it, "Femur FX-ER bed 12." I didn't wake Bob up, and Harry came over and slept next to him.

*　　*　　*

Tonight is no different, Bob wins again by ten. Teresa is running, and she has a guy with her this time. He's tall and muscular and is wearing a gray tank top. Bob is eyeballing him, and I say, "He must be an athlete."

"Yeah," Bob says, all serious-like. The guy has short blond hair and has on a pair of faded blue running shorts that look just like Teresa's. He doesn't have socks on, and he seems to be smiling a lot as they run. I think that we'd all smile a lot if we could run with Teresa.

On the second lap, with the morphine in us, we walk to the road. "Hey, stop," Bob says, holding out his arm like a football player trying to facemask an opposing quarterback. They run around Bob's arm, and Teresa says something to the guy. They keep running and when they get about twenty yards away, the guy turns around and looks at us. Bob waves to him.

The next lap they do stop. "What's up?" the guy asks.

"You play ball?" Bob asks, dribbling the basketball. I get a bad feeling about this and run my hand through my hair.

"Sure," the guy says, all smiling white teeth.

"Come on, Jim," Teresa says. "I want to run." I look at her and smile and see that the laces on her running shoes are loose. I want to tell her, to warn her, but I don't.

"Jim Boyston," the guy says, shaking Bob's hand.

"Dr. Bob Kole," Bob says, smiling at Teresa.

I decide to sit out the game. They start practicing, throwing the ball at the net. It takes about a minute to see that this guy can play. He does have an outside shot. Bob walks over to me, swallows two more pills, and winks at me. I sit in my white plastic chair and do all I can to hold onto my beer. They start playing, and it's friendly at first, mostly outside shots. Jim takes the lead. Teresa runs by again and shakes her head. Bob ties up the score with a head fake and a quick layup.

On her next lap, Teresa walks over and sits next to me. I give her some water from my cooler. Both guys smile at her.

"Thanks," she says, taking the glass of water. She drinks half the glass fast, and I see sweat on her neck. I can smell the sweat and the sweet perfume and sticky thick smell of her lipstick. I try not to stare at her. Jim has taken the lead again, and Bob is sweating pretty hard. I wonder why Teresa runs so much. I'm tempted to ask her, but don't.

Bob is hitting Jim pretty hard every time he gets inside. Jim is taking it, no problem. "So, what do you do in there?" Teresa asks, pointing at the workshop.

"I build boats," I say.

"That must be hard," she says.

"No, not really."

"Can I see one?"

"Sure," I say. We get up and walk into the side door of the shop. Jim and Bob stop playing for a second and look at us. They start playing again as soon as we're out of sight. From inside, we can hear the ball as it's hitting against the wall. We walk past the workbench, it's twelve feet long and covered with tools: c-clamps, hand saws, a Japanese saw, and an orange orbital sander. There are two partially completed canoes up on sawhorses. She looks around at everything, in a kind of amazement, a different world. The shop smells of sawdust and glue. In the back of the shop is my latest finished boat. A fourteen-foot canoe made of strips of red and white cedar. I lift the blue sheet that's lying over it, protecting it from dust and big cat claws.

The boat shines from twelve coats of marine spar varnish. "Wow," she says. That's what I say every time I finish one. "That's beautiful," she says.

"Thank you," I say, and use about every ounce of strength I have to not tell her how beautiful I think *she* is.

She runs her hand across the wood and feels the curves on the outside. Then she feels along the top, over the gunwales and inwales. Then she does something that completely shocks me. She bends over and smells the boat. I've never seen anybody else do that, and I know at that moment that I could love this woman.

She straightens up and is about to say something when we hear a scuffle outside. We run out there. Jim has Bob on the ground, and they are wrestling, both getting in whatever punches they can at such close distances. I pull Jim off and grab Bob. Bob's nose is bleeding, and I can see under his left eye the indention of a small ring. Jim looks spotless, except for a scrape on his left knee. "Asshole," Jim says, and he grabs Teresa's arm and they walk away. Teresa turns around and smiles at me as they get close to the end of the driveway.

"That son of a bitch," Bob says, as he notices the blood on his nose for the first time.

"That'll impress her," I say and laugh.

Bob walks around in a circle, trying to calm himself, to get control. I give him a beer, and he takes a mouthful. Then he says, "What were you two doing in there?"

"Just showing her a boat," I say.

Bob looks at me, curls his swollen lip and says, "Let's go."

"What?"

"Let's take those damn kayaks out. I feel like getting wet," Bob says, as he starts to walk across the street to his house. We carry the two kayaks out of his garage and back across the street to my house. Then we load them up on my green Chevy pickup. He takes the keys, and we start heading toward the coast, which is an hour away. We don't say anything on the drive, just let the night air come in through the windows. I think about Teresa, and how she smelled the boat. About how I want to touch her and smell her and taste her. I can feel the air get cooler, as we get close to the coast and start to taste the salt in the air. I wish I'd brought life preservers, but I didn't.

We unload the kayaks at the Canaveral National Seashore, an eighteen-mile strip along the east coast of Florida. The waves are high, four to six feet, and I know we probably shouldn't go out. I know I'd prefer to do this in the daylight.

"Let's go," Bob says again, like an army colonel, as he sits in his kayak and pushes off into the water. The two kayaks are identical. They're sixteen feet long and made out of redwood strips, except the tops which are made of 4 mm mahogany plywood. I climb into the other kayak and push off. For the first fifteen minutes, we are within thirty yards of shore and heading south. I can see Bob; he's about ten yards ahead of me. I see him paddling for all he's worth, not really using any kind of technique, but just using his muscle and all the stuff that's built up inside of him. I see four lights ahead. I can't tell if it's a hotel or maybe even part of the launch pad for the Space Shuttle.

Within forty-five minutes, my arms are killing me. My shoulders feel like mush. I can still see Bob, though he's put more distance between us, thirty yards or so. Then, I can't see him anymore, only hear his grunts and the paddle hitting the side of the kayak. He's going out deeper, building strength, to a place I don't want or need to go. I stop paddling and let the waves push me to shore. I don't think I can lift my arms; they are heavy. I climb out of the kayak and pull it onto the beach. I can no longer see or hear Bob. I think of Teresa and Jim and the love they are probably wrapped up in right now. And I think about me and Bob and how he's out there, pushing, paddling, doing what he thinks he has to, for reasons I don't think I'll ever understand.

*John Henry Fleming* | WIND AND RAIN

First let me tell you about the rain, Louis.
Last night it started to rain when I
walked home from the hospital. I didn't
even notice it for awhile because it was
thin and slow. Then the mist thickened
and began to roll over me. A few drops
ran down my cheek. By the time I came
out of the package store, the rain was full
and steady and the whole world looked
shut down and closed up.

When it rains like that I think about the
cop and what the cop said in his report.
He said maybe it was the rain that made
him believe he saw a gun in there. You
remember what was in there? I do. When
I went and claimed your car from the
police, the first thing I did was search
through the glove compartment. There
was an owner's manual for the wrong

model—for a Monte Carlo instead of Grand Prix. There were a few notes from Lila. I read them, hope you don't mind. Baby, Meet you here at 3, Love, Baby. None worth keeping; you probably just put them there to put them somewhere. There were a couple of paper clips in there. A broken pencil. A mileage log from the previous owner. Gum. Tic-tacs. A plastic bag with cookie crumbs. Your driver's license.

How could he mistake any of that for a gun? Can the rain change things that way?

Last night I sat on my bed and watched the rain. At the package store I'd gotten beer and Old Crow. I poured some of the Old Crow into my flask to take to work today. Then I took a nice big swig and felt it warm me. Mother doesn't like me drinking in the house, but she works cleaning offices now, doesn't get back until two A.M. I leaned back against the wall and looked at the rain. It was hard and steady, just the kind of rain the cop was looking through. I tried to test my eyes, to see things the way that cop did. I looked across the street and I could see the big cracks in Mr. Cullen's driveway, the water streaming through those cracks and over the lumpy places where he'd tried to repair them. I could see the car under the carport and could tell it was a Dodge Diplomat even though I couldn't make out the badge on the trunk. I could tell it was in pretty good shape for a car that old. I could see the striped awning over Cullen's living room window. There are eighteen stripes, and the water ran off each one. I could see through the living room, too, where the curtains weren't pulled together. Cullen was in his chair, watching TV. I couldn't tell what show, but there was lots of action and quick scene changes. An adventure show, maybe, or a kung fu movie. Next to Cullen was a lamp on a table, and on the table was something I couldn't see so well. I thought maybe it was an ashtray. I stared at it for a minute and tried to imagine it was a gun. I squinted my eyes a little. I focused on different parts of it and tried to reshape it in my mind. It was no gun. Even if I could make it look like one, I knew Cullen would not have a gun there. And anyone who knows you knows that you would not keep a gun in your car. Not now, but not then either.

I don't ever imagine things in the rain. It's under the bright lights here that I sometimes have problems. Sometimes when I'm here I think I see things that later I know I didn't. I think I see your fingers move. I think I see your eyes start to open, or your lips start to say something. I'll see it out of the corner of my eye and then I'll put down my magazine and move my face right up next to your plastic mask and I'll try to see it again. And sometimes I think I do. Then I'm not sure. I remind myself that the doctors say there's no way.

There's all that junk I put inside me, Louis. The beer and the Old Crow. That kind of rain can cloud up your eyes from the inside.

Maybe the cop really thought he saw something and that's why he fired his gun. Later, when he got back to work after his suspension, he'd have to know he was wrong. But maybe the cop doesn't think about it.

It was raining, and I saw everything clearly. I still do. And I think you do too. Your eyes aren't open, but you're not dead, so you must see something. Do you still see the rain that night, streaking the windshield and dulling the glow of the streetlights? Maybe you're still looking into the glove compartment, watching your hand grab the license, your frozen picture coming into view. I hope that's all you see. I hope you don't see that cop out of the corner of your eye, raising the gun toward your head. I hope you don't see the flash.

I told you once you ought to keep your real license in your wallet. What if a cop comes up on the street? But you said a cop can't ask you for your license if you're not in a car. You kept the fake license in your wallet just so you could go to bars with me, your big brother. And then you put the real license in your glove compartment. It's still there. I see it.

I see the cop following us after we leave the bar. I'm looking over the seat and I'm seeing his lights right behind you. It's raining pretty hard and maybe you should be driving slower, but that cop shouldn't be on your tail like that. He's trying to scare you, Louis. I see that now. I see the cop's headlights, and I see his grille, the grille of a Caprice Classic. I see the big, wide hood. The wipers going. You know what else? I see his face, too. Maybe there was a little light coming from his radio or something. But there it is. His big wire-rims. His pocked cheeks. I see him twenty years ago, too, a high school kid who doesn't fit in. Too much acne. Never got used to the way his own voice sounded after it changed. I see him reaching up to give a little siren blast. He likes the siren a lot better than his voice, though he's never gotten used to that, either.

I see you walking back to him in the rain. He shines his spotlight on you. You lean over trying to hear him in the rain, and your shirt clings to your skin. The water drips off your hair, your nose, your chin. You reach for your back pocket. Then you remember.

What's up? I ask when you climb back in the car.

I forgot my damn license.

I told you.

The cop has followed you back. He's shining his flashlight around inside. On your eyes, on me, on the back seat, then back to your eyes.

You lose something? you ask him.

That was a dumb thing to say, Louis. I know you can see all right, but you aren't thinking clearly.

The cop has on a hooded slicker. The rain is loud as it bounces off his hood. There are a few drops of rain on his glasses. Maybe those drops are right in front of his eyes. There are drops on the face of his flashlight, too, and maybe that changes the way things look to him. It's raining harder, now. Everything is splashing and making noise. The street and the roof of the car and the cop's slicker and the cop's flashlight. Like a machine grinding to a stop. In this kind of rain, most people sit in their houses and wait for it to end. They don't think anything that happens out in the rain can make any difference. They wait it out. Then they start their lives again. Maybe the cop thinks that, too. Nothing that happens now is going to count. When the rain stops and the water flows down into the street drains, anything that happens out here is going to flow with it.

We know better. The rain stays with us, and everything that happened in the rain happens again and again.

He said he saw something. Can a license ever look like a gun? Even with rain on your glasses and on the face of your flashlight?

Let me see your license.

You almost say something. Then I see your hand in front of my knees. The glove compartment is open. The flashlight beam is there. You feel around for just a second. You touch the notes from Lila. The owner's manual for the wrong model. The broken pencil. You feel your license.

Then everything stops. The rain falls over the car and stops everything inside it. The hand touching the license. The gun rising and flashing. Your head falling to my knee. My hand jerking up against the window. A dark streak on the window, not washing away in the rain. I'm thinking, What is that? What is it? The same thought the cop might have asked himself a second earlier. You could have answered it for him, Louis.

All of these things are now one moment, and that moment is stuck inside the rain that falls in us both. Everything's clear in there. I wonder if the cop ever sees it, too. Or does the cop still see the gun that isn't there? Does he wonder what it's like to be you, Louis, stuck inside one rainstorm and always living just that one moment, not remembering anything before or after, nothing ever changing?

I know you know all this, Louis. You don't need me to tell you what you see. But in all the times I've come here, I've never talked to you about it. Not once. And when I looked out at the rain last night with the Old Crow warming inside me, I thought maybe you'd like to know that I see it too. Part of the time I'm out here seeing other things, but most of the time I've been in the rain with you, and I thought you might want to know that.

The rain is why you're here, Louis. It's why I've been coming here up till now, even when everyone else began to fall away into their old lives. They went back in their homes to wait it out. We stayed out in the rain. For you it never stops. But I've been thinking about other things, too, and last night I started to put them together. I thought you'd want to know what I've been thinking. It's been so long since I said anything to you, Louis. I didn't think it would change anything. But now I'm going to tell you everything I know. It's not much, but it's something. You already know about the rain. Now I'm going to tell you about the wind.

A week after the shooting, I was back to work on the golf course. The superintendent said he was going to give me busy work for a while, stuff to take my mind off it. The irrigation man would fill in as his assistant. Any paperwork could wait. This went on for a few weeks, and I was beginning to think I'd lost my position. I didn't say anything, though.

One day I was out raking leaves. There was no wind that day, but there had been the night before, and the wind had blown pine needles and avocado leaves all over the greens. I was working ahead of the greens-mower, Enrique, clearing the leaves off so he could mow the greens evenly. Three-sixteenths of an inch all over. It was mid-afternoon, hot and still. I had to rake because the blower wasn't working.

The sweat rolled down my neck and got soaked up by my work shirt. There were only a few golfers around. Quiet day. Only the sound of Enrique's mower one or two holes back, the sound of my rake.

I'd been raking all day, not even stopping for lunch, so I could keep ahead of Enrique. I was doing the same kind of work I started doing there six years ago, and that was getting me worried. That irrigation guy was good friends with the superintendent. They both had agronomist's degrees from Gainesville. Here I was doing the work of a high school kid. No offense, Louis, but I'd already been through it. I didn't want to do it again. I'm older. I got experience.

My arms and back ached from the raking. I was thinking about my job. I was thinking about you. I didn't bring a flask to work then, but I'd had plenty the night before and plenty in the morning. It was still with me. My head wasn't right.

It was quiet and hot and then something came out of the clear sky and knocked me in the head. I remember the sound of it, like the crack of a baseball bat. And the echoes in my blood that made it seem for a second all my veins would explode at once. All I could hear was the crack and it was everywhere, and then it was only in one small spot on my head. I rubbed the tears out of my eyes and saw I'd dropped the rake. I reached up and felt my head. It seemed to swell under my hand. It throbbed, and the blood warmed my fingertips.

My eyes still closed, I heard an electric cart whir up beside me, right next to the collar of the green. Someone clicked on the brake lock. I blinked a few times and looked up. There were two old men there, and they were staring at me like I was something in the way of their golf game. Something they had to check the rule book about. A divot that hadn't been repaired or a tree limb in the way of their backswing.

Then the man stood up next to the cart and turned toward his friend behind the wheel. You ought to thank him, he said. His head kept your ball from slicing into the trees.

They both laughed.

That's when I first started to think about the wind.

Do you remember when I started work on the golf course? You were only a kid. You said, How do you play that game? I tried to explain it then, but I didn't know all that much about it myself. Now I do.

It's a stupid game, Louis, and here's how you play it. First you go into the woods and yank out most of the trees. Then you bring in truck-loads of grass from Kentucky or Bermuda or somewhere else and you carpet over the space you cleared. Next you get your mowers out and you mow the grass again and again until it's so short you can't even call it grass anymore. You call it green, because you can't tell it's anything else. Some of it you call fairway, which sounds a lot like freeway, which is what they ought to call it, because it's smooth and wide and the golfers drive up and down it in their little cars, weaving side to side like they own the road. Once you've got all the grass in and you've mowed it down to its color, then you build a few little mounds and you fill them in with sand, and they're like little deserts that get in your way, except you rake them real smooth, so they're more like the beach in front of the Breakers Hotel. Once everything's been torn out and sodded and raked and mowed, then you finally get to knock a little white ball around until it falls into a cup. And if it takes you a long time to do it, it's nobody's fault but your own, because everything's been cleared out and mowed down for you. Everything's exact. Only the wind can change where your ball goes. If there's no wind, then you've got no excuse. If you hit the ball and it curves, it's only because you didn't hit it right, and if you hit the ball and it lands on somebody's head, it's because that's where you aimed it.

This is what I figured out with those two old golfers standing right in front of me, my head throbbing, and blood on my fingertips. I thought, Any excuse they've got has been cleared out and raked up and mowed away. The grass is exact and the fairways are wide open. The only thing left is the wind, and there was no wind. If there'd been wind and the guy had taken the same shot, the ball would have sailed over my head or maybe a little to the right and I wouldn't have thought any more about it. If the guy had taken a different shot and the wind had pushed it into my head, the guy would have that excuse. But there was no wind. The guy had aimed the shot exactly at my head, and once he'd struck the ball, there was nothing to make it change its course.

It was all clear to me as I watched them smile at each other. The ball was sitting on the collar of the green between me and them. My head was bleeding. I took a step and picked up the ball, then walked over to the man who'd spoken, grabbed him by the back of his white hair, and jammed the ball through his teeth. When the ball fell to the grass, it was spotted with blood.

The board of directors couldn't understand it. I hadn't even hit the man who'd swung the club. I'd hit his friend. I don't know why I hit his friend; it didn't seem to matter. It still doesn't.

The board called in the superintendent and asked him about it and the superintendent told me he couldn't answer them. He told me he explained my situation to them. They said they understood, but that they couldn't keep an employee who endangers the golfers, especially ones who've done nothing wrong.

I said, So if I'd hit the other guy, I could've kept my job?

The superintendent shook his head.

Because I can still go hit him.

The superintendent just stared.

When I walked out of there for the last time, I thought, If there'd been a breeze everything would be different. None of this would have happened.

Bad things happen where there's no wind, Louis. I know that now. You know something? There was no breeze that night in the rain. Can you see that? There's lots of rain and I guess you can call it a storm. But there's no wind at all. I know that because I see how the rain comes straight down. It bounces off the top of the cop's slicker, off the top of his flashlight, off the top of his gun. Exactly off the top.

I left my job knowing something about the wind. I was going to learn more.

I never told you any of this before. I never thought it would matter. Now I have to. I have to tell you everything.

After I left the golf course, I looked around for a while, but I had to take something quick. This room you've got isn't cheap, and Mother doesn't make nearly enough cleaning offices. I had to have something. There was this man down at the City Sanitation who remembered Father. Father was the first man he'd hired, he said. And somehow he'd heard about what happened to you. Newspapers, maybe. He sent a note to Mother, and Mother told me about him. It was nice of him to remember, she said.

I didn't want to talk to him, but I had to, and he offered me a job loading garbage. I know you've done better, he said. But your father managed on it for a long time and he never complained. He was a good man, he said.

I remember the first time I smelled Father. You were just a baby, and I'd been blowing up balloons all day and throwing them into your playpen. I remember the taste and the smell of those balloons. Like a hospital, clean and dry.

By the time Father came home, I was out of breath and a little dizzy. I could still smell the clean smell of the balloons until Father crouched down next to me. Then I smelled him. I'd never smelled him before. I moved my face away and frowned. Father didn't say anything, but he might have noticed because he left the room then to take a shower. I tried to make an animal out of the balloon he'd blown up for me. It popped in my hands and I smelled him again.

Once I noticed that smell, I couldn't forget it even when I tried. Even when Father took a shower, I smelled it. When I was almost old enough to start working myself I thought, I never want to smell like that. I didn't mind the smells on the golf course—the grass, the machines, even the chemicals. All those things were better than the smell of someone else's garbage.

I never asked you, Louis. Did you ever smell Father that way? I smelled it on him even when he lay in this same hospital breathing through a tube like you. We both went to see him, and I wondered then if you smelled him, too. But I couldn't ask. Now I wonder if you can smell me. For the last few months I've taken a long hot shower before I came in here, hoping you wouldn't be able to smell the garbage on me. Now I've changed my mind.

I'd take showers for myself, too. Every day I'd come home from loading garbage and I'd stand in the shower for twenty minutes, soaping up and shampooing, trying to get the smell out. I checked myself after I'd dried off, smelling my arm and blowing into my cupped hands. I smelled something. I wasn't sure.

Out on my route, too. After I dumped a can of garbage into the hopper, I'd put my nose right up to my arm and sniff. There, I'd think, that's me. I'm a garbageman. Everyone knows it, just like they knew it about Father. If they forget, all they've got to do is get near me. They'll smell the rotten vegetables they threw out last night.

I had a girlfriend for a little while. She moved in with us when I was between the two jobs. Her name was Melody and she was sweet and understanding. I didn't deserve her. When I took the sanitation job, I couldn't tell her right away. It hurt too much. But she figured it out. From Mother, maybe. Maybe from the smell.

One day I asked her how she liked the way I smell.

I don't mind it, she said. It just smells like you've been chopping bell peppers.

I had to kick her out. I couldn't stand that she smelled me. She might have smelled bell peppers all right. But someone else had chopped them.

I hated myself, and I tried to make it worse. All day long at work, I'd hold my arm up to my nose and smell it. I'd smell my work shirt, too, and my trousers. Before I emptied the garbage into the hopper, I'd stick my nose into it and take a big whiff. It made me feel good to hate myself. Smell that, I said to myself. Nothing changes. It's the smell you're going to smell all your life. The smell of garbage. I started to bring a flask to work. I thought if I drank enough by afternoon, I'd forget to stick my nose in the garbage and I wouldn't hate myself so much. Sometimes it worked.

Then one day I stopped in to see you on my way to work. I'd never done that in the morning before. That day I just sat there and looked at you from across the room for a minute and that was it. I didn't say a word to you. But when I got to work I still had that hospital smell with me, and it reminded me of those balloons I'd blown up as a kid. I didn't think much of it until I got out on my route. Then I took a big whiff of that first garbage pail, and this time it didn't smell like garbage. It smelled like rotten vegetables, sour milk, grass clippings, wet newspapers, shampoo bottles, diapers, even plastic bags and cardboard boxes. But not garbage. That one smell had become all those separate smells. I smelled every can I emptied that day and none of them smelled like garbage. They smelled like whatever was put in there—bell peppers or potato skins or splintered wood. Every can had something different in it. Some cans had almost the same smells in them. But none were exactly the same.

After that, I began to pay attention to all the individual smells. I stuck my nose in the garbage like before, only now it wasn't for self-pity. Now I wanted to pick out all the smells. I wanted to know what was in there by its smell. I got good at doing it, too. The other loaders saw me and started testing me. They'd have me close my eyes, and they'd put a piece of garbage up to my nose. Once they held up a dead gerbil. Once a carton of rotten eggs. I didn't mind. Almost always, I could tell what it was by the smell. I'd get worried when I couldn't. Sometimes there was no wind and I'd be smelling the same thing all day. That can dull your nose. It's all becoming one smell again, I'd think. Then the wind would pick up and I'd be okay.

That's how I got good at smelling. I can smell just about anything. I can smell the difference between royal palms and coconut palms, between sea grapes and sea oats. I can smell what kind of animal is hiding in the bushes. I can smell a woman's perfume from half a mile away. When there's a breeze coming in off the ocean, I can smell what kind of fish are running offshore. Let me tell you. I can smell. And the important thing about smelling is to pay attention to the wind.

Here's what I've found out, Louis. The wind is talking to us all the time. Most people don't listen, though, because they don't know how to smell. But smelling is the only way to understand the wind. You can't talk back to the wind, but you can listen to what it says, and if you know how to smell, you'll know that it says a lot. The wind doesn't make its own smell. It carries the smells of everything else. That's how it talks. It might take the smell of a pine tree's sap and carry it down the street to an old man sitting on the porch of a nursing home, looking out at traffic. Then that old man smells those pine trees and remembers when he was a kid and used to chase lizards and squirrels up those pine trees, and after, when he'd hop down and look at his hands, and they'd be covered with sap and little pieces of bark stuck to the sap, like he'd grown a new skin. He'd think, Mama's gonna be mad at me because that ain't never gonna wash off. But now he looks at his old, trembling hands and he sees that it has washed off. He leans back in his chair and smells the sap, remembering what it felt like on his hands, remembering until the smell fades because the wind has taken it somewhere else. The wind has been talking to him and he has listened. It was saying something sad, but something he wanted to hear anyway.

A boy might be walking home one night and he's mad at himself because he lost all his money shooting pool. He's had a few drinks so he's looking at his feet to make sure they move the way he expects them to, and then he smells something, stops, and looks up. He sees that he's in front of his girlfriend's house. He has smelled what he smells when her mother opens the door for him, her mother's house-dress that smells a little like floor wax, all the little knickknacks her mother collects that smell like they sat in the Salvation Army story for a year before she bought them, the paint on the mantel that's just beginning to chip. And from all the smells of the house he finds the ones he knows belong only to his girlfriend. The cup of her palms, the inside of her forearm, the shoulder scar from her vaccination, the curls in her hair, and most of all her breath. He reaches out for these smells especially, and he grabs onto them and holds them for as long as he can. Standing before her house he smells all this and he is happy. The wind has brought these smells to him. It is speaking to him. He is just drunk enough that he might go up and rap on her window.

When these things happen, you might start to wonder if the wind is good or evil. But the wind doesn't care one way or another. It talks, and it wants us to listen. And the more we listen, the more it will talk. Not everything it tells us is good, but it's always something we ought to hear.

The only time we should be scared is when the wind stops talking. When the wind is quiet nothing changes. The sky stays the same. The earth stays the same. People stay the same. They smell the same. They smell just like their fathers. When the wind is still, a man can swing a golf club and the ball will go exactly where it is aimed. A man can raise a gun and his hand won't blow to one side or the other. He can fire the gun and the bullet will go exactly where the gun is pointed. Nothing will change its direction. The time between makes no difference. It doesn't count. Nothing will change what happens.

When people want to hurt each other, they throw things at each other—rocks, spears, golf balls, bullets. You take aim and then you let your rock fly, hoping your aim is exact and the rock will hit the other guy's forehead exactly between the eyes, knocking him out, making the blood roll down into his eyes so he can't get up and do the same to you. So the rock gets thrown and everything's looking good. But when things are in the air they belong to the wind, and the wind doesn't work on calculations. The wind likes to blow things around, mess things up, throw off your calculations. It sees a tree full of leaves and decides the leaves are in its way so it blows them all off the tree. Then it sees somebody's piled up the leaves and it decides to mess up the pile. It sees a quarterback put the football up and decides to blow it over to the defensive back. The wind can stop people from hurting each other, too. The wind might see the rock heading for the guy's forehead and decide to blow it off course. Then it just glances off the side of the guy's head. The guy gets mad and throws a rock back at you, but that rock misses completely. Because of the wind. You end up shaking hands with the guy, and you both say, Forget it, we aren't good enough rock throwers to make it worth our time. But really it's the wind. It's not that the wind is trying to teach anybody a lesson. The wind doesn't care about that. It doesn't care about anything. It just likes to push things around. And that's a good thing for us. If there weren't any wind, there'd be a lot more people hurting each other every day. There'd be nothing to throw off their calculations. Golf balls would never miss. Bullets would never miss.

These are the things I've learned about the wind. It changes the direction a bird flies. It changes the look of the sky by blowing the clouds around. It changes the look of the earth, too—sometimes it carries leaves off of plants, and sometimes it carries their seeds and makes them grow somewhere else. And the wind changes people, too.

It carries smells to them and makes them think about things. It talks to people that way. It reminds them that things can change, that things will always change.

That's why I'm here, Louis.

Before I came in here, I asked the doctor, Can he smell anything? He didn't know who I was talking about at first. He'd forgotten about you. I reminded him, and I asked him again. Can he smell anything? He said he wasn't sure. He said maybe. I said thank you.

Then I came here to tell you all this. Maybe you haven't heard a word I've said. Maybe you can only hear the sound of the rain and the sound of the gun. But the doctor said maybe you can smell, and if you can smell then the wind can talk to you even if I can't. The wind changes things. The wind can stop the rain. It can blow it away. Then people will come out of their houses again and pick up where they left off. And you can smell the people and what's in their houses, and the trees and plants around their houses, and even the garbage they put out in front of their houses and the garbagemen who come to pick it up.

I'm going to try to show you what I mean. I'm going over to the window and I'm going to open it up. I never opened it before because I didn't think it would matter. I didn't think it could change anything. But there are trees out there, Louis. Oak trees and pine trees. There are birds flying between the trees. Blue jays and sparrows. There are squirrels, too, and the squirrels are running in the grass. There are mushrooms in the grass. And blue and yellow wildflowers. There's a parking lot next to the grass, and there are cars pulling in and out of the parking lot. There are people walking to and from their cars, and those people have all sorts of smells—their skin and their clothes and their sweat and their deodorant and shampoo and everything they've had for breakfast and lunch today. I'm going to open the window and you're going to smell them all. The wind is going to bring them to you. Then maybe the rain is going to stop for both of us. Then maybe things will change.

"Marco," called my daughter Lucia with a giggle.

"Polo," answered her sister.

Amanda's splashing and squeals of laughter as her sister lunged at her in the pool made me give up on the newspaper I was trying to read. I looked at my daughters, thin and summer brown, their dolphin-smooth skin glistening in the water. The sun made the water shine so brightly it hurt my eyes. A heady sweet smell drifted towards me from *Mami's picuala* plant. I don't know what it's called in English, but the vine blooms most of the year with sprigs of flowers that blossom white, turn pink, and become crimson once they mature.

"You know . . . ," said my mother.

She stood in the shallow end of the pool, with firm legs and protruding tummy, not unlike a toddler.

." . . some fresh *pan cubano* would be really nice for dinner. Feel like making a little trip to the *bodega*?" she asked.

Just as predictably as Polo follows Marco, I knew what my mother would say next.

"Don't go to the Pulling Road store, go to the one on Kelly. I know it's a longer drive, but their bread is better. The afternoon batch comes out at three. *¿Qué hora es?*"

"It's a little after that now. Let me throw some clothes on over my suit."

Sluggish from the heat and the Florida sun I left the pool, giving behave-yourselves orders to my daughters, who were now involved in a sword fight with fluorescent-colored foam noodles.

★    ★    ★

I lingered in the *bodega,* chatting with Humberto, the owner, about my children and my visit home. Living in another part of the state, I tried to visit my family as often as possible. I liked watching the girls delight my parents, and getting pampered in return. After months away, I'd start to yearn for what my American husband called "a heavy dose of Cuban"—the foods, and sounds, and people not present in my Anglo life.

I bought several loaves of bread, some spices, and huge heads of garlic. We'd have *pan con ajo* this afternoon; bread dripping with olive oil and fresh crushed garlic. Chased with a cold beer—Cuban soul food. I envisioned my father. I knew he'd take a few bites, grin at the girls and say, "No vampires around here tonight, eh, *niñas?*" I like the comfort of patterns, traditions, the same corny jokes told over the years. Like warm baths, they soothe.

Cradling the long bread loaves, I turned from the register towards the exit door and bumped into someone. I stepped back, momentarily blinded by the glare from the storefront windows. And I saw him . . . I hadn't seen him in years. Tia Gloria divorced him a long time ago.

He wasn't as tall as I remembered him. For a long time I'd wished him dead. I would picture him bloated and chalky, with circles of rouge on his face as he lay in his coffin.

Then I saw the girl—she was in front of me, ethereal, made of gossamer so that I could see right through her to him. I wanted to move forward and put my hand in front of her, instinctively, protecting her from him, the way I shield the girls from a sudden stop in traffic. There she stood, with her smooth, straight long hair and thin tanned body, wearing the blue and white print dress.

★   ★   ★

Her mother had taken her to Hartley's Variety store on Ninth Street. They'd walked through the bolts of fabric together.

"Nothing too expensive. Remember it's your first dress, you'll make mistakes. And pick a cotton, no knits; they're tricky to run through the machine," her mother had said.

She'd painstakingly followed the directions on the Simplicity Easy-to-Sew pattern, carefully cutting and pinning the material. As she sewed, she kept a measuring tape draped around her neck, the way she'd seen her mother do. The short-sleeved, round-collar shift had turned out well.

"*Ay, qué lindo,*" her aunts said when she showed it to them.

So she wore it to the party. It wasn't a party, really, not like somebody had sent out invitations. It was just the family getting together. They did this often, usually on a weekend, and it was great fun. One of the aunts had made a big batch of seafood rice, somebody else brought salad, everybody brought beer. This party was at her godparents' house.

She was almost twelve. Her breasts had started to bud. The week before at her grandmother's house, she'd stood in front of the living room mirror, arms above her head gathering her hair in a pony tail. Her cousin Leo, younger by two years, had walked by, tweaked the few strands of hair under her arm, and teased: "Hey what you got there? Not enough for an art brush." She'd chased him out of the house and through the backyard, trying to hit him with her hairbrush.

This Saturday night, in the dress she'd made herself, she felt grown-up. Besides, lately at these gatherings her mother had allowed her to stay in the living room or the kitchen with the adults, instead of shooing her outside with all the younger kids to play their stupid "bang-bang, you're dead" games. So she laughed at jokes she didn't quite understand, and bobbed her head in agreement when the women nodded at something one of them had said. She listened intently at how much *bijol* to put in the seafood rice to make it yellow. And, on the last trip to Miami, which company the women had decided was the best to use for shipping medicine to sick relatives back in Cuba.

"Even from here, *mija*, we have to take care of Titica before she gets another attack of asthma. You know she was always such a picky eater, and now there's nothing to eat. Nena's last letter says she's nothing but skin and bones. *Vieja tu sabes,* one bad gust of wind and she'll be blown away."

"Si, an-ja, that's right," their heads nodded as they murmured agreement.

Then the music started. Ignacio, her godfather, placed a Cuban music LP on the record player. The laughing and eating and talking continued. Somebody started keeping time to the music by tapping a fork on a beer bottle. Her Tio Roberto started thumping his hands on the kitchen counter as if it were bongo drums; someone else tapped on a metal pot lid, and the adults started singing along with the record.

"*Oyeme Cachita, dime una cosita,*" went the song, a cha-cha. Several of the women got up and started to dance. Somebody moved the coffee table from the center of the small living room.

"*Ven, ven,*" her aunt, whose name really was Cachita, said, as she pulled her up to the floor.

She loved the music and tried to move her feet in the right pattern. Her Tia Cachita got behind her, like a shadow, put her hands on her hips and prodded her through the moves. One, two, three . . . cha-cha-cha. One, two, three . . . cha-cha-cha. She got the hang of it, and her aunt let her go. She moved her body rhythmically, swaying her hips to the music.

"*Dale, dale. Ya lo tiene, ya lo tiene.*"

As the song finished, so did she, triumphantly, with a triple shake of her shoulders. A big smile spread across her face when everybody clapped and her mother kissed her cheek.

It was getting late. Pedro and his wife wanted to go home. They'd gotten a ride with someone who wasn't ready to leave. Her godfather offered to drive them back. After all, the party was at his house. Her *padrino* Ignacio was one of her favorite uncles. He always paid her small compliments, telling her that her outfit or her hair looked nice. He often asked her to help him with his English, and she felt proud that she knew the answers as they read over the grammar book together. His wife, Gloria, her aunt and godmother, was her mother's sister. When they were heading for the car he called out to her. Did she want to come along, keep him company?

The drive to Pedro's house was chatty and noisy, as the men joked and talked above the music playing on the radio. But on the drive back, her *padrino* was quiet. They were a mile or so from Pedro's house, on a two-lane highway that led back to her godparents' house. Scrub pines and palmetto bushes lined the dark road. Her godfather turned off the car radio, and then took a turn that wasn't the usual one. She started to say so, and realized he was pulling the car off to the side of the road. She thought something was wrong with the car, that her *padrino* was listening to the engine. She listened too, but only heard the sounds of frogs and crickets from the woods, and the hum of the engine. She turned to talk to him, but he reached across the length of the front car seat, and pulled her towards him.

"You've learned to dance, *bonita*, now I want to teach you to kiss."

His mouth was so close to her lips she could feel the heat of his beer breath on her face. She pushed his chest back, shook her head, noticing the beads of sweat on his forehead.

"Come on, *mami*, *ven*, I won't hurt you, why would I hurt you?"

She kept pushing away. He had both her thin wrists in one hand. The other hand he started to run up her dress between her thighs. His fingers pulled the elastic at the legs of her panties. She was sobbing, pleading to be left alone, to be taken back. His damp cheek was rubbing against her face. She freed one hand, and tried to open the car door. Suddenly he stopped.

"*Esta bien, esta bien,*" he said abruptly. "I'll take you back, stay in the car, I'll take you back."

He was driving again. She pushed her body close to the door, as far away from him as she could get, her hands and legs trembling.

"Stop, it's all right, I'm sorry."

As he approached the driveway of his house he slowed the car to almost a stop.

"*Basta, ya,* no more crying," his flushed face close to hers again. "Don't tell, say we got lost, that you got scared, but don't say anything."

And she didn't. She was afraid her mother would be mad at her. What would she say anyway? How could she say it? Her father would be furious with her. She wasn't quite sure what it was, but she knew she must have done something horribly, terribly wrong.

Pleading homework and headaches she spent most of her time in her room over the next few days. It was a Wednesday afternoon, and as usual she was home alone for a few hours before her mother arrived from work. The radio played as she did her chores. She made the beds, picked up the newspapers, rinsed out the breakfast dishes. Walking from her parents' bedroom, a bundle of clothes in her hands, she found him in the kitchen. He'd come in through the back door, which was rarely locked. She started to rush past him towards the door, but he grabbed her arm.

"Wait, I just want to talk, *ven aca,* come here, I just want to talk."

His hold on her arm was crushing. She found her voice, and yelled. She called for her grandmother, three houses away. Her screams loosened his hold, and she ran past him out the door, through the neighbors' yard. Crying and running, she screamed for her *abuela.* She burst through her grandmother's door, her lungs burning, demanding she make him leave. And between gasps, and sobs, and the shocked ashen look on her grandmother's face, she told.

She awaited an explosion that never came. The only noticeable difference around her home was that the tone of life was more subdued. There was a dry-mouth stillness in the air. Her mother treated her more delicately; her father would stand beside her as she watched TV and gently stroke her head. They didn't ask her anything about it, not one question. Nobody yelled, nobody argued, nobody talked about it—not openly.

She overheard whispered conversations. Walking out of her grandmother's house, she heard two uncles speaking on the back porch. "He was drunk," one of them said. "She's a good girl, *la niña*, she doesn't tell lies. What is the family to do? Gloria believes him. You can't tear apart a marriage, you can't tear apart sisters."

A few nights later, passing by her parents' bedroom, she overheard her mother talking with her aunt. The bedroom door was open just enough to give her a finger-thin view of the women as they sat on the bed. She stopped just past the door, pressing herself flat against the wall, and listened.

"It did not happen, my sister. He loves her. She misunderstood. I cannot believe this happened. *La familia* is the most important thing. *Ay, mi hermana*," her Tia Gloria cried, "I can't bear problems in the family."

"*Esta bien, Gloria, esta bien*," her mother said.

It's all right, she heard, it's all right . . . and nothing was ever mentioned. Over time she quietly fell into certain patterns. She avoided anything that had to do with her godparents' house. She never left doors unlocked when she was alone. She learned to keep a cool distance from Ignacio at family gatherings; and she became cautious of most men.

⋆    ⋆    ⋆

And here he stood. I carried him with me for a long time. I'd be moving to the rhythms of everyday life when suddenly, out he'd pop—my secret menacing jack-in-the-box, his face flushed and frightening. But the cogs that stopped the music, the things that triggered him out of my memory, were usually things I wanted. A look of lust in a man's eyes, a lover's touch or the warmth of his breath, could suddenly freeze me.

*Come on mami, ven, I won't hurt you, why would I hurt you?*

My aunt finally left him. It turned out the scar she had on her upper lip hadn't happened when she slipped on the wet patio floor. Tia Gloria wasn't as clumsy as she made people believe. She found courage to leave one day, but his effects were still visible. My aunt resembles a piece of delicate clothing, maybe a scarf or a blouse, that's accidentally gone through the sturdy wash cycle. She came out physically wrinkled, emotionally mangled—never as good as the original.

It wasn't easy making his face stop appearing on the faces of men I wanted close to me. I took the fears and emotions that made me fragile and exercised them. Like a body builder I pumped through them, past the ache and sting and rawness, until I was strong. Until I took away his power.

I looked at him—straight at him. He was surprised to see me; his mouth opened as if to speak. But I was amazonian. I could crush his carapace with one foot the way I would a roach. I stared at him, like an animal staking its territory, my eyes so still, so steady, he had to look away. And only then, without a word, did I slowly leave the *bodega*.

★ ★ ★

Amanda and Lucia were still in the pool when I returned, playing in the deep end, their bare arms and legs splashing in the sun. *Mami* was on the opposite side of the pool. She sat at the edge, her feet resting on the first scalloped step in the water.

"*Ey*, there you are," said my mother.

I stripped down to my bathing suit and sat next to her, dipping my feet in the cool water.

"How have they been?" I nodded towards the girls.

"They've been in so long they've grown scales."

I played with the water, cupping it in my hands, letting it drip on my legs. I wanted to tell my mother about the *bodega*. I needed to tell her, the way I'd needed to talk to her about that night so long ago.

"*Mami*," I said, looking at the water, and not at her. "*Tu sabes que* Ignacio was at the *bodega*."

"Oh?" my mother glanced at me. "Your father and I, we don't see him since Gloria's divorce. Every once in a while, around, it's a small town. Did you talk to him?"

My mother's voice had a quiver I recognized. It's that slight nervous edge it gets when she asks a question she really doesn't want answered.

I shook my head. "I don't have anything to say to him." I stopped playing with the water. "Mama? How come we never spoke about it?"

There. The lid was off the jar. I'd twisted and turned it, wringing my hands over it for years, never prying it off. Now—one swift turn and there it was, open.

"*Ay, mija.*" my mother took a breath, holding it for a long time, dropping her shoulders as she let it out. "I . . . we, *Papi* and I, we didn't know how to talk about it. It was different then. *Dios mio*, not like now when all you need to do is turn on the TV. And we were different, barely speaking English, working to eat, to build a life. We only had each other, the family needed to work together to survive. *Tu estabas bien*, you seemed O.K., you were—*ay, niña mia*—weren't you?"

My mother's eyes needed me to agree. I looked away, and played with the water again, concentrating on how it fell out of my hands and on my legs. This time, the long held breath was mine.

"No. Not really, not completely. I never told you, but I saw a counselor, a therapist, about it, about him."

"*¿Cuando?*" my mother asked, her face frightened.

"Years ago, not long after college. When I had my own money—my own insurance actually."

"You never said anything, why didn't you tell me?"

I shrugged my shoulders. "No reason, lots of reasons," I whispered. "I don't know," I said louder. "I didn't know how. First I was scared, and I didn't want to worry you. Then I was angry, really angry. At Ignacio for being such an asshole, at the family for pretending it didn't happen, at me for thinking it was my fault. It was all jumbled up; I just had to untangle it all."

My mother took my hand and patted it, crying. "It was never your fault, it's my fault, I . . ."

I pulled my hand away and snapped, "No, *mami*, that's just it . . ."

I took my mother's hand again and lowered my voice. "It's not your fault, nor mine. I don't blame you and I'm not mad. None of that. *Nada*. It is O.K. Now, it is all right. Oh, Christ," I sighed.

I walked to the patio table and grabbed some tissues.

"Here mama, blow your nose." Handing her the tissues, I sat down again. "*Mami*," I said gently, "I just needed you to know. That's all. I just wanted, and needed you to know it all."

"Hey, Mom," my daughter shouted at me.

I looked at Lucia as she climbed out of the water and stood at the edge of the pool.

"Watch, Mom, watch me dive," she shouted.

Readying herself, she adjusted the wet bathing suit that clung to her emerging woman's body. Lucia tucked a strand of her straight wet hair behind her ear. Her slim muscled legs bent, and she dove into the shimmering water. As she moved, I realized how closely she resembled the young me.

A warm breeze gently swayed the *picuala* plant. Like a giant perfume mister it released its scent, and the fragrance from its white, pink and red flowers wafted across the pool. At the girls' invitation *Mami* and I jumped in the water. We were all there: my mother, my daughters and me. Only the gossamer girl was gone.

Jeffrey Greene | THE BLIND GAMBLER

*His biographers generally agree on the essentials: Caspar English was born blind in London in 1883, the only son of a French-Jewish gem cutter and a schoolmaster's daughter who emigrated to Brooklyn in 1885. Virtually ignored by his father, he became morbidly attached to his mother, who kept the frail, sickly child in almost complete isolation from other children, teaching him every card game she knew using a specially marked deck of playing cards. By the age of eight he could identify each of the fifty-two cards in a fresh deck by touch alone, describing complex sensations of smell and taste that had no analogue in the visual lexicon, since he had never seen a color, a number, or the shape of a suit. Around this time, a ne'er-do-well uncle taught him poker and a few simple coin and card tricks, and by his early teens he was confounding professional magicians and gamblers three times his age.*

*His father's death in 1900 coincided with his discovery by P. T. Barnum, who was impressed enough to call him "a Marvel of Nature" and install him among his stable of human oddities. By most accounts a social misfit and a chronic insomniac, English was still living in the same Brooklyn apartment with his mother when she died of pneumonia in 1905. His uncle, who had been earning a precarious living on the fringes of the Irish underworld, offered his services as manager, surrogate father and all-around bad influence, and within two years English left Barnum's employ and struck out on his own, first at private parties and night clubs, and by the height of his career, around 1913, in packed concert halls in the Americas, Europe and Russia. In 1910 he met Ivana Karyakin, a Russian immigrant and former puppeteer, who became his full-time assistant, both on and offstage, taking the professional name of Saffron. According to most accounts, she drowned with him during a poker game at the Glades Hotel in Belle Glade, Florida on the night of September 16, 1928.*

*It is unfortunate that none of English's biographers seems to have read* My Cracker Journey, *by Iris Wilkins, published in 1976 by the small Bone Valley Press in Fort Pierce, Florida. Out of print for a number of years, it is an engaging memoir of Ms. Wilkins' childhood in Belle Glade in the 1920s and her later experiences in Cuba during the Batista regime. She describes in harrowing detail the hurricane that killed some two thousand people, the majority of whom were Haitian and Bahamian migrant farm workers. Now eighty-five and living in Annapolis, Maryland, Ms. Wilkins is one of the few people alive to have met Caspar English in the twilight of his career, and her eyewitness account of what was probably his last poker game illuminates a personality that has been both fictionally imagined and scientifically studied, but never fully understood. I quote from the chapter titled "The Dividing Line of My Life":*

"September 16, 1928 was a Sunday. Two days before, weather reports from West Palm Beach, forty miles to the northeast, had confirmed that a powerful hurricane (this was before they began naming them) had caused extensive damage and loss of life in Puerto Rico and the

Greater Antilles, but they predicted that the storm would pass by Florida without making landfall. By Sunday noon, however, the townspeople, who had experienced a devastating hurricane two years before almost to the day, began to see ominous signs that the weathermen had made a serious error: fast-moving clouds, fitful surges of rain, rapid changes in wind direction. To make matters worse, it had been a rainy summer that year and the lake was very high, already straining the four-foot-high earthen dike erected to prevent the natural flow of water into the Everglades. Belle Glade is bordered on the north by Lake Okeechobee and on the south by the Everglades, and the only high ground as far as the eye could see was up the nearest tree or in one of the two hotels. There were no vacancies at either the Belle Glade or the Glades, and the lobbies of both hotels were filling up with people, black and white (the Whites Only rule had been temporarily suspended), who, mistrusting their migrant huts or woodframe houses, sought shelter in the town's sturdiest buildings.

"From 1917 to 1925 my father was the biggest catfisherman on Lake Okeechobee, owning forty boats and eight refrigerated freight cars, but overfishing killed the industry in less than ten years and by 1928 he had been forced to sell off everything to cover his debts, including our house, and had moved us into the top floor of the Glades Hotel. A big, handsome man with the hard blunt hands of a fisherman, Tom Wilkins always believed that a confident appearance was half the battle in business, and although he'd had little luck so far raising a stake to invest in the growing sugar cane industry, he liked to present himself to his friends as if he were on a leisurely sabbatical, waiting until the signs were right to make his mark in farming, which he was loathe to admit he knew nothing about. Through our brief experience with wealth to our present genteel poverty, my mother had stood by him, not just because she loved him but because loyalty was one of the traits expected of a well-bred woman in those days. I never realized how little my father appreciated her until the night of the hurricane.

"One of the ways he maintained the illusion of our prosperity (which fooled no one but himself) was to continue his long-established tradition of hosting a weekly poker game in the hotel room. My father was rather too fond of gambling, and although my mother disapproved, she continued, even after taking control of the purse strings, to graciously welcome my father's friends. The games were friendly, an occasion for whisky, cigars and story-telling, and often ran far into the night, but the sums lost and won amounted to tens or hundreds, never thousands, of dollars, though the stakes might have been higher if my father had had his way.

"The men began arriving around seven, bringing their families with them because of the hurricane, and our rooms were almost festively crowded by the time the last player arrived. All the regulars were due that night except Sheriff Collier, who was too busy supervising emergency preparations to take his usual place. My younger brother, Ham, went off to play with Frank Stranahan's son Walter, but as long as I kept quiet I was allowed to watch the game. By the age of fifteen I knew all the variations of poker and loved to stand behind my father and observe how he played his hands. 'Father John' MacPherson (I don't know how he got that nickname; he was certainly no priest), who in happier times had been the foreman-in-chief of my father's fishing crews, was the last to arrive, accompanied by a man and a woman he'd met at the town's one bar and invited to join the game. John was a little tight already, and he grinningly introduced the couple as 'Caspar English, the world famous blind poker player from London, England, and his lovely assistant, Saffron.' After leaving a 'successful engagement in Miami,' the pair had stopped for the night in Belle Glade on their way to Tampa, and having overheard Father John talking about the game, the 'famous' Mr. English had wondered if there might be an open chair at their table for himself and his 'indispensable Saffron.' My father always liked a full table and welcomed the new arrivals with a wink at the others, for it was clear that no one in the room had ever heard of the blind gambler, nor was his assistant lovely in any obvious sense, at least not to a sighted person.

"Caspar English was a disturbingly thin man with dyed black hair and a pale gray face almost too sparely fleshed to form expressions, his thin lips pursed around an ivory cigarette holder and his prominent, nearly translucent beak of a nose giving him the distinguished profile of a corpse. He was over-dressed for the climate in a black and somewhat threadbare three-piece suit, a somber tie, white gloves and a black bowler hat, and except for his fingers, his gestures were stiff and minimal. His fingers were long, slender, antenna-like, as if all his senses were concentrated in his tapered fingertips, which seemed burnished to a shine by contact with innumerable decks of playing cards. He wore rimless dark glasses and walked with the tentative care of the blind, using a cane adorned with the carved head of a playing card king, but once he sat down and removed his hat and gloves he seemed very much in his element. Saffron was a small, undernourished woman in her thirties, with a sun-starved pallor, tired brown hair and a Slavic face saved from utter plainness by her large, pale blue eyes that never seemed to look directly at you but missed nothing going on at the table. Under her light raincoat she wore a rather low-cut, parrot-blue evening dress. I don't remember her saying more than a word or two the entire evening; she just seemed to fade into the woodwork as soon as she took her place beside English. They were like two bedraggled birds of an unfamiliar species blown off course by the storm, but such was the hectic, almost carnival atmosphere that night, that these refugees from the show business gutter were taken in and accepted without question.

"As I've stated elsewhere, my mother was a beautiful woman, tall and fair, with the wide-set green eyes of her Scottish ancestors and a proud head of thick auburn hair that seemed to distill a fragrance of its own. She also had a lovely voice, and when she asked the pair if they would care for a drink, Caspar English cocked his head as if listening to a moving passage of music, his dark glasses catching the lamplight. 'So kind of you, madam,' he said in a dry, whispery voice. 'Sherry is our preference; failing that, brandy.'

"'Excuse my bluntness, Mr. English,' my father said. 'But I for one have never played poker with a blind man before. Should we deal to your assistant, or to you?'

"'To my assistant.' He accepted the sherry put before him with a slight bow, and holding the glass under his nose he deeply inhaled the bouquet, took a tiny sip, then set the glass down exactly where it had been. 'Saffron is my eyesight,' he said. 'She will convey to me through a series of tapping signals the notation of the cards in my hand, as well as those face-up on the table. She is not a player, and all decisions to raise or fold are mine alone. So that no one at the table harbors the slightest suspicion regarding my blindness, I have found it a good policy to remove my glasses once before we begin. I apologize for any unpleasant feelings this might occasion.' After a theatrical pause, he took off his glasses, revealing with a slow turn of his head what no one had seriously doubted in the first place: his milky-gray eyes were tiny, almost vestigial, deeply sunken and turned up in their sockets. Some of the smaller children gasped, and were immediately shushed by their mothers. I felt an uncomfortable mixture of pity and disgust, and, with some shame, as if I were committing a sin, an immediate dislike of the man. I was sure my mother had a similar reaction, though for different reasons. There are subtleties of human expression—not just of the face, but the whole body—that even an observant man may miss, but rarely a woman, especially one who, in the presence of her husband, has become the object of another man's covert interest. He had no eyes to see with, but it was clear to both of us, and perhaps to every woman in the room, that Caspar English was acutely, rapturously aware of my mother's every move.

"He put his glasses back on and drew a large wallet from his coat pocket. 'I assume you're acting as the bank, Mr. Wilkins,' he said, handing the wallet to Saffron.

"'They're my chips, is all,' my father said, amused by the man's stage manner. 'How much would you like to buy?'

"'Five hundred, if you please.' She handed the bills to my father, who counted out the chips and pushed them across the table.

"'One-dollar ante, gentlemen,' my father said. 'Five-dollar limit on bets. No big city stakes here, Mr. English.' He shuffled, then handed the deck to Gonzalo Mendez de Canzo to cut. Gonzalo, who was one of the biggest cane growers in the area, cut once and passed it back. 'Draw poker. Jacks or better to open.'

"Waves of rain lashed the plywood-covered windows, palm fronds flailed and scratched at the walls, and every so often a strong gust of wind would shake the whole building with a vast, scary *whump*. I could only watch the game between chores, because my mother had put Ham and me to work assembling candles and drawing buckets of water from the tub faucet. In spite of the increasing violence of the storm it was fascinating to watch Saffron pick up English's cards one by one, look at them, then tap a fast three- or four-beat code on the tabletop and hand the card to the gambler, who would place it in his hand from right to left and remember it from then on. He must have had an amazing memory, since, to avoid the very real possibility of another player learning his system and guessing what was in his hand, one supposed he had several codes for each card in the deck and changed them at random every few hands. Everyone knows that winning at poker requires more than luck; one must be able to read faces, sense whether or not a player is bluffing. How English accomplished this I don't know, but I suspected Saffron of translating expressions as well as the cards into code, although it's also possible that the blind man's hearing and sense of smell were keen enough to make his own educated guesses as to his opponents' emotional states.

"By now the winds were probably gusting at over a hundred miles an hour, attacking the walls and windows with an unnerving barrage of small and large objects. On top of the sick fear that kept rising in me, I was becoming alarmed at how quickly my father's pile of chips was diminishing. It may have been the imminent threat of death, as well as a misplaced pride of the sighted, if I may put it that way, that made my father and his friends play more recklessly than usual, but for whatever reason, Caspar English was quietly winning hand after hand. My father had already dipped into his wallet for reserves and seen them dwindle, and like his friends he was drinking hard. The wind seemed to beat at the walls and windows with giant fists, and the sounds it made—from insane shrieks to eerie, protracted moans —seemed less like wind than the battle cries of some immense oceanic life form carrying a grudge against humanity as big as the sea. The blindness of the windows made everything worse, and as the winds slowly increased to what I later learned was a hundred and fifty miles an hour, the idea of my own death entered my body for the first time.

"My father threw down his cards and glared at the blind man, who was calmly sipping his sherry, his face bland to the point of boredom as Saffron scraped up yet another winning pot. Looking at his old crony Father John, he said, 'Looks like we've let a sharp into our midst,

John. How am I gonna tell old Jack Collier that the guy who cleaned me out couldn't even see the cards?'

"'Now you know that isn't fair, Tom,' Frank Stranahan said with an uneasy smile. 'The hand may be quicker than the eye, but I haven't seen any funny business from Mr. English. He's just lucky, that's all. And lucky streaks always end, sooner or later.'

"'It better be sooner or I'll have to go begging among the migrants downstairs,' Father John said. 'Where'd you say you blew in from, Mr. English?'

"'Miami.'

"'Before that, I mean.'

"'Havana. I never denied making my living at cards, Mr. MacPherson. I thought that was understood.'

"'Oh, we understand, all right,' my father said.

"The dark glasses glinted in the light. 'Exactly what do you mean, Mr. Wilkins?'

"'Nothing, just deal the cards.' Gonzalo broke in, trying to diffuse the tension in the room.

"My father drank some more whisky, then, leaning back in his chair and spreading his arms in a noncommittal gesture, he smiled and shook his head. 'Nothing at all, Mr. English; I'm just amazed by your luck. Anybody would be. Let's play.'

"They played, and one by one they were cleaned out; first Gonzalo, then Frank. My father left the table only once, to get the money my mother was saving for emergencies. She quietly took him aside and argued against it, but the single-minded stubbornness that had served him so well in business was his worst enemy in games of chance, and he was too angry and frustrated at being beaten by a blind man to even consider quitting. He was half-drunk, too, and like his friends he knew that he had condescended to this man who was now humiliating him, which made him even madder, and my mother saw that he wouldn't stop until he'd won his money back or the hotel blew down, whichever came first. I think she was as furious at him as she was frightened by the storm, but even then she didn't make a scene in front of our guests. She gave him the money.

"They played quick hands, my father oblivious to everything but the cards. Fear had sobered up Father John, and he started to his feet every time the building shook, his eyes showing too much white. Saffron appeared to be shrinking, drawing herself into an invisible shell, but the only sign of fear in Caspar English was a sheen of sweat on his forehead and threads of black dye trickling from his sideburns. Around 9:30 the wind ripped the plywood off the window in my parents' bedroom and blew out the glass. My father ignored it, so Frank, Gonzalo and my mother tried to cover it with a tall wardrobe, getting themselves drenched in the process. But they had no tools and it wouldn't stand up. Outside was a deafening, coal-black chaos from which they quickly retreated, pummeled by the wind as they fought to close the door against it. They got it closed, but it seemed inadequate to hold back the forces pushing and pulling at it. At that moment Father John left the table, stepped up to my mother, and said quietly, 'He's cleaned out, Emily.'

"The storm made everything else seem irrelevant, so I couldn't immediately grasp what had happened in the two or three minutes since the window blew out. The three people at the table, illuminated by the single oil lamp, were still and silent. My father, his chips gone, an empty glass and a nearly empty bottle of whisky beside him, was staring blankly at the three Jacks in his hand. My mother approached slowly and stood behind him, breathing hard in her soaked dress. Saffron was sitting with clenched fists in her chair, as if expecting the walls to collapse at any moment. Caspar English might have been a dead man propped up in his chair for all the emotion he showed. Part of me registered that his eight-high straight, laid with precise symmetry on the table, had won him the hand, but I still couldn't believe that my father would have gambled and lost what little money we had left in the world.

"Caspar English picked up a blue chip from his huge pile and fingered it thoughtfully. 'Well, this would normally be our cue to leave,' he said. 'But since we're registered at the other hotel, the storm has put us in a somewhat awkward position . . .'

"My father reached for the whisky bottle without looking at it and knocked it off the table. It shattered on the floor. He looked down at it, then across the table at English, his eyes desperate. 'Of course you can stay here,' he said. 'On one condition: that we play one more hand, double or nothing.'

"My mother stared at him in disbelief, but Caspar English seemed amused at the prospect of being turned out in a hurricane. 'Mr. Wilkins, please,' he said, smiling contemptuously. 'If you're asking me to accept our continued sanctuary as collateral, well then . . .' He shook his head sadly at such a woeful breach of hospitality.

"'You're busted, Tom.' Father John said. 'Just let it go. You and Emily and the kids can stay at my place until we figure something out.'

"'Good advice.' English said. 'You're lucky in friendship, sir, if not at cards.'

"My father suddenly reached back and took my mother's left hand. 'Give me your wedding ring, Emily,' he said. 'I promise I'll make it up to you.' She angrily refused, and he tried to take it by force; there was a brief, embarrassing struggle before she gave up and let him have it. When he heard the ring land on the table, Caspar English shook his head. 'It pains me to say this in your wife's presence, but really, Mr. Wilkins . . . a ring for all I've won? Hardly a fair exchange. However . . . there is one form of collateral I'd be willing to accept.'

"'Name it.'

"English paused, his face orienting to my mother's position in the room like a rat lifting its nose to catch a whiff of cheese. He adjusted his glasses, smoothed his hair, fingered the stem of his empty glass. 'She has a beautiful voice, your wife,' he said quietly. Father John spat an outraged curse, and for Saffron this seemed, on top of the hurricane, to be about the last straw, but my father said nothing; he just stared at the blind man, as one stares at a rattlesnake that is too close to back away from. My mother waited for his indignant refusal, then her shoulders slumped and she closed her eyes, as if unable to bear the sight of him. 'I'm prepared to bet all my winnings against one draw of the cards,' English went on. 'If you win, you take everything on the table. But if I win, Mrs. Wilkins—and the money—leave this room with me.'

"For what seemed a very long silence, broken by gusts of wind-driven rain like volleys of birdshot against the shutters, my father sat there, staring at nothing. Then he slowly turned his head and looked at my mother. 'It's our last chance, Emily.' he said hoarsely. 'You see that, don't you?'

"She looked gently at Ham, then at me, but her eyes hardened as she looked at her husband. 'All right, Tom,' she said in a voice trembling with anger. 'But don't expect me to call it back if you lose.'

"'Iris, there's a new deck in the drawer over there; get it for me, please.' I did as I was told. We could hear people yelling in the halls outside, and the wind on the other side of the bedroom door was like a horde of maniacs trying to break in, but in the still space of that room we seemed outside of it all, in a kind of fluid suspension. My father ordered me to shuffle the cards, which I did with clammy hands and pounding heart, then he passed the deck to English, who passed it back without cutting. Fanning the cards face down across the table, my father said in a strangled voice: 'Go ahead.' Fitting a cigarette into the holder, English lit it and puffed slowly, taking his time. He reached out, his fingers walking over the cards, then he picked one from the middle and placed it face down in his other hand. Running his fingers caressingly over the card, his mouth twitched in a sour smile and he threw down a six of clubs. Saffron leaned over and whispered the number to him. Heartened by the low number, my father drew a card from the end and triumphantly threw down a ten of spades. Saffron called out the number, then did something unexpected: she smiled. The men began applauding my father and slapping him on the back as he reached across the table, encircled the great pile of chips in his burly arms and pulled it to him. His face as impassive in defeat as in victory, Caspar English slowly drew on his gloves, conferring in whispers with Saffron.

"My father, in what I'm sure was meant to be a grand gesture of reconciliation, picked up the wedding ring and held out his other hand, inviting my mother to let him put it back on her finger where it belonged. But she spoiled his triumph. Disdaining to take the ring, or even to look at him, she turned instead to Caspar English.

"'I trust you'll stay with us until the storm passes, Mr. English,' she said.

"He opened his mouth to thank her but never spoke the words. It was just after ten, and the hurricane, in crossing Lake Okeechobee, had driven so much water before it that the northern end of its seven hundred square miles was laid bare like a tidal flat. An eleven-foot-high wall of water broke through the mud dike like a wave through a sand castle and swept through Belle Glade, South Bay and Pahokee at God knows how many miles per hour. We heard it coming, a ground-shaking bass roar thrumming underneath the wind's keening treble, and we felt the building shudder as the water hit it. We were thrown off balance as pictures fell from the walls, glassware shattered and the shouts in the hallway turned to screams. For a moment it seemed as if the building was going to stand up to it, then my stomach dropped as I felt it float free of its foundations. We were moving, the room rocking like the deck of a ship. I barely heard my father shouting above the roar of water: 'Grab anything that floats and hold on!' I lost my balance and fell forward, cutting my hand on the broken whisky bottle; my mother reached for me and I felt the sleeve of my dress tear loose in her hand. The oil lamp slid off the table, and just before the flame went out I saw my father and Caspar English, still sitting in their chairs, gripping the table at each end, then the room went black and I felt the poker chips raining down on me. People I couldn't see were screaming, wailing, praying, and then with a jarring concussion the building hit something—another building, probably—and broke apart. The walls and ceiling caved in and warm water flowed in from all sides; the next clear memory I have is of being swept along in pitch darkness, holding on to what I think was a wooden beam from the ceiling. I seemed to be alone, but even if my mother had been a yard away I wouldn't have seen her, so isolating was the screeching wind and stinging rain, the blackness broken only by blinding flashes of lightning that revealed nothing but a wilderness of raging water.

"I was trying to face the wind and kick my legs in order to stabilize the beam so it wouldn't roll me underwater, but it was too long and heavy and I was wearing out fast. What saved me was a raft-shaped piece of somebody's roof about four feet square that jammed right into my back; I let go of the beam and grabbed for it. It was easier to control, but there was a continuous spray of water blowing in my face that got into my ears and nose and down my throat, half-drowning me. At one point my legs got tangled in the branches of an uprooted tree and held me there. It seemed like a lucky break until lightning revealed, like a flashbulb in Hell, a ropy mass of cottonmouth moccasins in the branches about five feet above my head. I kicked away from the tree in a panic and didn't stop drifting until morning. Somehow I held on, sleepless, my arms and legs cramping, feeling a snake or an alligator in every piece of driftwood that bumped me, in every waterweed that grazed my bare legs. But the snakes and alligators had problems of their own and nothing bit me, not even a mosquito.

"The sun rose on a world I couldn't recognize, mainly because I'd been blown a couple of miles into the Everglades. The hurricane was gone, along with my old life and everyone in it. I think the worst part was wading back through the sawgrass, sugarcane and custard apple thickets, which had caught and held more bodies than I could count. It was a democracy of death by drowning: there were men and women of every age and station, some dressed for dinner, parties, or church, others in their nightclothes, some naked, little children face down in the water, cows, pigs, chickens, dogs, cats, deer, wading birds, possums, raccoons, and, strange to say, alligators, hundreds of them, their white bellies exposed to the sun, as helpless before the flood as everything else. I saw the body of a man lashed to the floating corpse of a cow; he must have tied himself to it in the night and either drowned or died of a heart attack. Lumber and debris floated everywhere. There wasn't a building left standing, nothing standing at all except four palm trees. Of the roughly six thousand people who had lived here, scattered over three small towns and a few farms, four thousand dazed survivors wandered back, and after they'd tended to their own needs, they began burying the dead.

"Frank Stranahan, his son Walter, and I were apparently the only survivors from our room that night. I was put to work tending to the orphaned children. The men and older boys built coffins out of the wreckage, while others in flat-bottom boats went searching out into the Everglades, finding bodies and tying them to ropes trailing in the water. They would come back towing flotillas of a dozen corpses at a time. Most of the bodies had to be cremated in giant pyres, the Florida heat having made a decent burial impossible. One morning an aunt of mine who'd survived came and told me they'd found—and already burned—the bodies of my father and brother. They never found my mother.

"I was sent to Miami to live with my uncle's family. They treated me well, but I wasn't happy there and at nineteen I married a man twice my age who ran an import business. I'd married him to get away from home and he had married me for my youth, but we came to love each other and stayed together, more or less happily, until his death thirty years later. We traveled regularly between New York, Miami, and Havana, raising two children on the wing, and for many years I wouldn't talk to them about the events of 1928. Two or three times a month I had dreams, sometimes nightmares, about the hurricane, in which my mother was always alive, telling me where she had been all these years and what had happened to her when the water came.

"In 1953 we were living in Havana, my husband's interests having prospered there, and now and then we indulged in a little gambling at a casino we liked called *El Sueño Colorado*. Instead of one crowded, noisy room, like most casinos, The Red Dream consisted of several smaller rooms connected by narrow hallways, and the blackjack and draw poker tables were in the very back. My husband and I were playing roulette with some friends, but I grew bored after a few turns of the wheel and went wandering by myself through the various rooms. In the last and quietest room, while having a martini at the bar, I noticed that one of the standing dealers was a foreign woman. She was pale, stout, well past middle age, and looked vaguely familiar, though it wasn't so much her face as the way she dealt the cards that finally jogged my memory. But we only see what we believe in, and for twenty-five years I'd believed that Saffron was dead.

"Feeling my eyes on her, she looked up and her eyes flicked over me without interest, returned to the players, then slowly, almost reluctantly, she raised her eyes and searched my face again. After a minute or two she gestured to a dealer at an empty table, who came over and took her place. She approached me slowly, walking with a pronounced limp. Her hair, skin, even the color of her eyes seemed to have faded with the years. She ordered a sherry and sat down beside me.

"'I remember you,' she said, in an accent I now recognized as Russian. 'I thought you were dead.'

"'I thought I was, too,' I said.

"'No less than I did,' she said. 'When the flood came, part of the ceiling fell on me, breaking my leg in three places. Then it floated off me, and I grabbed hold of a timber and got swept out into the swamp. It was two days before they found me, delirious and horribly sunburnt. As you can see, my leg didn't set right. I don't think they ever found Caspar's body.'

"'I'm sorry.' I said. I remembered as if it were yesterday the smile transforming her face when my father drew high card, and realized, rather belatedly, that she had loved Caspar English.

"'It comes back to me so often,' she said. 'You, too? I'm sure it was bad for you, Miss Wilkins, but can you imagine how it must have been for him? A blind man, swallowed by an angry God, then vomited out into that terrible night. I see him—sometimes, in my dreams, I *am* him—rolling like a log underwater, bumped and jostled by drowned bodies and nail-studded debris. Or maybe he caught hold of something, an uprooted tree maybe, and died some other way. I don't know why it should matter to me how he died. Caspar used to say—trying to justify himself, I suppose—that God must love gamblers, they're so much like Him. Except He plays with lives instead of cards.'

"'My father was a gambler,' I said with unintended bitterness. 'He was killed, too.'

"'I'm so sorry,' she said, sipping her sherry. 'I didn't know your father, but he seemed like the kind of man who shouldn't gamble. I was sorry for your mother, though. Did she make it?'

"'No,' I said. 'They never found her.'

"'A pity. She was a real lady; I admired her as much as I hated her.'

"'Hated her? Why?'

"'Caspar English wasn't a good man, Miss Wilkins, but he was all I had, and we needed each other. He never stopped being a poker player, not even with me, so I'm not sure if he ever knew, or cared, how I felt about him. But I could tell he was drawn to your mother, to her voice, her strength, her smell. He wanted her, and he had smelled your father's desperation. He knew if he got him down far enough he would stake everything on one turn of the cards, even his wife. And I knew she was the type of woman who would honor her husband's bets, whatever the cost. She had the kind of beauty even a blind man could see, and I knew what would happen to me if your father lost.' She paused, then leaned close to me and said in an undertone: 'We cheated, you know.'

"I could only stare at her, appalled.

"'Not on every hand, of course. We had to lose just enough to make it look right. It worked like this: the players paid attention to the blind gambler, not to his plain assistant. They were so busy trying to figure out how he did it that they overlooked me. I have a "talent" for being ignored by men, which is why your mother wouldn't have been any good at my job; she was too striking. The card was dealt, and while I was tapping the code—for the other players' cards, not his; he could read them by touch—I was marking it with the nail of my other hand, ever so slightly. You'd be surprised how little time it takes to mark a whole deck. The marking was for my benefit, and I had sharp eyes back then; I could read the other players' cards as they were dealt, then rap out the code to Caspar, so he always knew when to bet and when to fold.'

"'Was this your standard practice,' I asked indignantly, 'or were you just fleecing the Belle Glade rubes?'

"She laughed. 'Everybody was a rube to Caspar. High-class city people weren't any better at spotting the set-up. But when your father asked for that fresh deck, it threw me off. There was no time to mark the cards. I don't know, maybe your father got lucky. But I'll tell you something, Miss Wilkins: in eighteen years I saw Caspar English lose maybe three hands he didn't intend to lose. He knew the cards like no man ever knew them; they were more real to him than people. This is just a guess, but I think at the last minute he changed his mind. He heard and smelled things that other people couldn't. Maybe he heard that wave coming before we did and figured he had just enough time to do one decent thing before the Deluge. Which would have been his *only* good deed, as far as I know. Caspar's mother filled his head with God, and no matter how many people he cheated he always believed in his own damnation. Maybe he thought: everyone in this room will be dead in a few seconds, and nothing can change that, but God will know what I did and judge me accordingly. Me, I'm not religious; I don't give a damn whether or not he threw the game, or why. It was worth losing the pot to keep things as they were.'

"Her faded blue eyes, glazed with memory, briefly met mine in the mirror behind the bar, then she finished her drink and stood up with a grimace of pain. 'Well, it all seems rather quaint and distant now,' she said. 'A little bad weather between the wars. An atom bomb is so much worse than a hurricane, don't you agree?' I nodded, feeling a bit numb. 'That's a lovely dress you're wearing,' she said, 'and the necklace is just stunning. I guess we haven't done too badly, have we? I mean, for people who've lost everything. Goodbye, Miss Wilkins.' Dipping her head in a terse farewell, she limped back to her place at the blackjack table.

"I finished my drink and rejoined my husband. I didn't tell him about Saffron. There are some things you can only share with the dead."

William R. Kanouse | ALLIGATOR JOE & PANCHO VILLA

I've one Pancho Villa story and this is it.
I'm working as a stringer for a Florida paper during Nixon's time of troubles and
I'm dispatched to Delray Beach where
a woman has shot a celebrity alligator in
cold blood because it had eaten Putty,
her rottweiler pup. Putty's returning
from obedience school one day and she
gets away from Ms. Tull and jumps into
the inlet water and is quickly drowned
and then eaten by the reptile. The next
day the gator lounges on the spongy
grass outside Ms. Tull's condo and greed-
ily waits for her other dog, a gray poodle,
to make a false step. She calls the state
game commission and they send out a
trapper, Johnson Mandel, who hangs a
sharp hook with lung meat pronged to
it onto a cypress branch. A day later the

gator goes for the meat but gets away. Ms. Tull takes her cue from Mandel and posits a carcass of irresistible old meat on a wooden pole and jams the pole into the ground, this approximately ten yards outside her back door. Sure enough the gator goes for the bait, and Ms. Tull plugs it three times which creates a furor because Alligator Joe's popular with the golfing element, old men who like to watch Joe sunbathe on the green of the water-traversed sixteenth hole. I ask her a few questions, and she tells me when Pancho Villa raids Columbus, New Mexico, in 1916 her mother hands her a rifle and hides her in a storm cellar, directing her to shoot Pancho Villa between the eyes if he gets near her. "I just shot me a Pancho Villa-type character sixty years later. Time stands still." I recall staring into her cobalt blue eyes, speculating that she had known many men in her lifetime.

No charges were ever brought against her.

*Karen Loeb* | FAUNA IN FLORIDA

There's nothing between you and an alligator except a lot of humid air and a
whole lot of bad wishes from both of you.

*   *   *

Gotta watch out that alligator   watch out
watch out.

*   *   *

Feeding time's at 5 P.M. at Sawgrass Lake.
The cars on I-275 that skate along one
side of the park form a background hum
like piped-in restaurant music that you
can never get away from. The alligators
slither along the bank of the skinny lake
which looks like a stream and some of
them swim on over to the bridge where
the ranger throws things like chickens
and skinned animals that are probably

rabbits into the water and the jaws scissor open and grab the animal which is already dead meat. Then the alligators dive below, drowning their meal just as if it's alive and kicking.

*   *   *

Gotta watch out that alligator   watch out   watch out.

*   *   *

Everyone wants to see the 'gators. Some of them go to Busch Gardens and stand behind fences and glass gawking at the slithery boggy-looking reptiles. Every year some kid falls into the pit somewhere.

*   *   *

Gotta watch out that alligator   watch out   watch out.

*   *   *

You're not really a part of Florida till you've seen a 'gator in the wild. A woman laments she's been in St. Pete 12 years and never saw one yet. All you have to do is sit by a lake and observe. Not any special alligator-infested lake. Just a fresh water lake, a pond really. You know the kind—the ones that are dug out to make an apartment complex look pretty or to make a housing development more appealing. If you wait long enough, you'll see a 'gator. That 'gator might be coming or going. Those things migrate all over the city, and there aren't any fences to keep them in. That's what seeing a 'gator in the wild is: seeing it over by Mirror Lake one block from city hall. Some people in the apartments take fistfuls of marshmallows and call out, "Here, alligator," and throw the marshmallows into the water and wait for the smack as the jaws open and close. Sometimes they even name the alligators. Sammy. Josie. Alexander.

*   *   *

Gotta watch out that alligator   watch out   watch out.

*   *   *

A woman living out on 4th Street got up one morning and stuck her bent-up toes into her terrycloth scuffies by feel—the morning light didn't get to her bedroom because of the huge bougainvillea bush with its killer thorns she had by her window to keep out intruders. She tied her terry bathrobe and scuffed along the hall into the bathroom. No, you guessed wrong. No alligator had worked its way up the toilet pipe. None was floating in the bathtub covered with bubbles. She eventually made her way to the front door to get her newspaper. She opened the door and bent down and reached out her arm by habit and almost lost her wedding ring and charm bracelet which she never took off which had ten golden heads attached by gold loops, one head for each grandkid. Their birthdays were stamped on the heads. The girls had ponytails and the boys had crewcuts. She almost lost these things because there was what looked like to her a real-life gray-green four-footed slimy-mouthed alligator waiting for a meal. His two front feet were on the plastic wrapper of the paper. Well, the woman got her door closed, and a special detachment of the local police arrived. The Alligator Relocation Squad moved right in to the neighborhood with giant nets and ropes and stun guns. If you can keep the tail from wagging and the mouth tied shut, you're pretty much home free is how they look at it. After they got the 'gator all trussed up, they stood around with Polaroids and took each other's pictures, and of course the paper came and did a little feature on it in the city section. Then they put it in their relocation vehicle, which looked suspiciously like a paddy wagon and they took it across town, making sure it was still a little stunned. Then they untied it and left it on the edge of some pond in a neighborhood very much like the woman's on 4th Street.

*     *     *

Gotta watch out that alligator     watch out     watch out.

*     *     *

One theory goes that there's only a certain number of alligators in St. Petersburg, and they get antsy, and spend their time migrating from lake to lake, pond to pond. Some of the most popular watering holes are Lake Maggiore, Mirror Lake, Crescent Lake, and the lake at Eckerd College which probably has a name but no one uses it. But there are hundreds of others and they all are safe harbors for reptiles. You can't even trust a rain puddle, some people say. Sure, some 'gators reproduce, but they're not what you would call prolific. They don't have the same energy as rabbits or mosquitoes.

*　　*　　*

What will you do to see an alligator? What will you sacrifice? One artist did it this way. She was looking for a whole slew of alligators to paint. She went to Busch Gardens. Wasn't good enough for her. There was the matter of a fence keeping her back, keeping her from getting close in where she could see detail, as she put it. She spent weeks going to different enclosures, but always the 'gators were too far away. She had seen plenty in the wild over the years, and knew it wouldn't be good to get too close, because then she'd want to run instead of paint. But she had to get her 'gators. She had been painting fish, and it was time to move on to alligators. Pretty soon, it was all she could think of. She had dreams about alligators rooting around her closets and soaping up in the shower.

She talked about alligator-watching parties. One friend she had left gave her binoculars, but it wasn't the same. She discovered that people didn't want to talk alligators. They were too busy dealing with other fauna, rounding up palmetto bugs and running from wolf spiders. "Real things," someone told her. Finally, one night she was watching TV, trying to take her mind off alligators, when what should come on but an ad for an alligator farm, a place that grew alligators like corn, and harvested them for fancy restaurants to put them on the menu under the label of "Delicacies." Next day she called them and figured the direct approach was the best, so she told them she was an artist and just had to see their alligators.

"We got postcards," the man on the phone said.

Well, it was clear he didn't understand, but he told her to come on ahead, that feeding time was around 2 P.M. She got there in time for the alligator siesta hour. Their bellies were full and all you had to do was imagine the snoring and pretty soon the air sounded like hundreds of buzz saws.

The men who worked there were all pretty skeptical, especially when they saw her camera. "What are you, some kind of tourist?" one of them asked.

She just smiled at them and figured it wasn't the best time to begin an explanation of photorealism. "Can I see the 'gators up close?" she asked.

"Sure," the man said. "We can give you close. Just follow me."

She spent the next two hours snapping pictures of alligators lounging on rocks, sleeping three deep, or sleeping with snout sticking out of the water. It was like walking around in her exercise class when she had to leave early: she had to step around all the alligators, they were so many under her feet. Just in case she did step on one, or one hadn't eaten its fill, the man followed her with several pieces of equipment and a running commentary on what she should do in case.

"In case the 'gator open his jaw, don't step inside."

"In case the 'gator wag his tail at you, don't bend down and pet him."

"In case you get a notion to pick up one of them baby 'gators, don't."

"And in case a 'gator start chasing you, don't run away. He can outrun a human every time, and when he catch you, you'll have less strength to fight him. Might as well let him catch you, then hit him on the snout, hit him right there on the snout. He'll get stunned for a minute and let go. Now of course, m'am, I don't know a living soul who'd willingly let a 'gator catch him, but it's just something to ponder as we walk around here."

The artist couldn't avoid hearing the man muffling a laugh as he gave her his advice.

*   *   *

Alligator fact: The Yearling Restaurant near Cross Creek, home of Marjorie Kinnan Rawlings, serves alligator meat, broiled, fried or steamed.

Alligator fact: Eduardo Alligator was a logo for alligator purses in the 1940s. Eduardo was stamped inside the purse. He wore a straw hat, and carried an alligator purse in one hand, and a cane looped over his paw in the other. He was standing on his two back feet.

Alligator fact: Alligators were on the endangered species list for years, but have made such a comeback, they are being grown on farms like corn.

Alligator fact: They migrate through city streets, and everyone leaves them pretty much alone.

Alligator fact: Alligators can outrun a human for a good distance, as the man on the farm said. If an alligator is chasing you, use the same advice farmers give for bulls: climb a tree.

*   *   *

Gotta watch out that 'gator      watch out      watch out.

*   *   *

This is a story about alligators. So there's no room left to talk about sharks, except to say that when you look out on the Gulf of Mexico and see whitecap waves, a few of them could be shark tails and fins you're seeing. Sharks come in close to shore and scope out the bathers. The view from a helicopter shows dozens of sharks weaving in and out of people doing the Australian crawl, the side stroke, the butterfly and the dead man's float.

Alison Lurie | THE POOL PEOPLE

Clary Graber's husband had warned
her against staying with his mother for
three weeks, but Clary decided to go to
Key West that April anyhow. She was
determined to get four-year-old Kate
out of gray drizzling Boston. Her
daughter had had a runny, wet cold off
and on ever since Christmas, and a
worrying little cough. It was dreadful to
see her snuffling around the apartment
day after day, pale and limp and whiny,
not her normal self at all. But outdoors,
in the sun . . .

"Sure, it might help," Ron said. "But
you're going to be irritated and bored
out of your mind down there, darling."

"I don't see why; we all had a good
time last year," said Clary, who sometimes congratulated herself on her

93

ability to get on with her mother-in-law, unlike many of her married friends.

"Yeah," Ron grinned. "For four days."

"And I think it was really nice of June to invite us." Clary didn't mention that she'd suggested the visit herself. "Besides, you're going to be in Brussels most of next month."

"Okay, if that's what you want."

*   *   *

Even after a week in Key West, during which she often had to admit that Ron had had a point, Clary knew she'd been right to come. Kate's sniffles had dried up almost overnight, and in a few days the cough was gone too and she was full of energy and joy. It was marvelous to watch her in June's pool, paddling about at the shallow end in her ruffled swimsuit and orange life jacket, sailing leaves or a yellow plastic boat full of plastic Ninja Turtles.

It was the first time that either Clary or Kate had really swum there. Ron always insisted on going to the beach; he didn't care for his mother's pool. It was an unusual shape: long and trapezoidal, and Ron said that when he did laps he kept banging into the sides. He disliked the noise of the pool machinery, and the way the water bulged and seethed and churned below the surface at the deep end, as if it were coming to a boil. It gave him a queasy feeling, exactly like June's cooking, he said.

Clary saw absolutely nothing wrong with June's pool. Because it was so deep, and heavily shaded most of the day, it hadn't become stale and warm at the end of the season. The water remained limpidly cool, with a shifting pattern in its depths, white reflections on aquamarine like delicate wire netting. Its constant flow was silky, sensual, caressing; and the hum of the filter peaceful, almost soporific. Clary thought that what Ron had really wanted, as usual, was to get away from his mother.

Ever since they'd met, Clary had felt sorry for June Graber. Some people might have said that was ridiculous, because June was healthy and remarkably attractive for fifty-eight, and she was also extremely well off, having been married to three very rich men. But you had to feel sorry for somebody whose son made jokes about her behind her back and who didn't appear to have any real friends.

It was true, June knew a lot of people in Key West, but she didn't seem to know them very well. According to articles Clary had read, the town was supposed to be full of interesting types, but June didn't seem to have met any of them. Her acquaintances were all well-to-do retired people, mildly and monotonously interested in travel, real estate, home improvement, tropical gardening, and their own ailments. These people also had less than no interest in children; they tended to become anxious as soon as they saw Kate. It was written all over their faces that they were afraid she would damage their rice-paper screens or their hand-blown crystal, or that Kate herself would be injured by their spoilt and irritable pets. Of course it would have been more sensible to leave Kate at home with a sitter, but in Key West during the season sitters were a vanished species; all the local teenagers were working in shops or restaurants.

After a couple of disastrous encounters, Clary decided that it would be easier, not to mention less boring, to take Kate away whenever June's friends came over, and stay home when June was invited out. Kate didn't mind being alone; she carried on long conversations with her plastic turtles, and with two imaginary friends called Davy and Big Bill who lived in the pool.

Clary recognized the names, which were those of the carpenters who had been remodeling June's Key West house last year. Kate had made friends with them, following them about and feeding them animal crackers, her favorite food. Davy, who was small and dark and handsome and sometimes wore a purple t-shirt with the slogan GAY IS GOOD, told Kate long stories about his dog. Big Bill, a large, slow-moving, muscular young man with three children of his own, made her a set of blocks out of ends of lumber, carefully shaped and sanded.

Kate's current Davy and Big Bill were not exactly like the ones she had known; they were blue, and you could see right through them. Some days they were in the pool, she explained to her mother, and other days they weren't.

Clary, however, had no friends in Key West, imaginary or otherwise. The only adults she had spoken to now in days besides her mother-in-law were Rusty and Joy, two handsome, deeply tanned, slightly spacey Key Westerners who came twice a week to clean and service the pool. But she was reconciled to being bored. A more serious disappointment was her mother-in-law's lack of interest in Kate. June had always been, or pretended to be, dotingly fond of her granddaughter, and Clary had assumed she'd want to spend time with her. She had imagined how, during this time, she herself would be exploring the shops and art galleries, or out on the reef, snorkeling through a cool pale-green universe of brilliantly hued coral and sparkling fish. Instead, she literally couldn't go anywhere alone.

"It's so long since I had a small child," June had explained when Clary first suggested that she might take Kate somewhere. "I'd feel much more comfortable if you came along too."

Another thing that Clary hadn't fully realized was that her mother-in-law was a compulsive talker; she had thought of her, simply, as lively and voluble. But in the past there'd always been other listeners around; now Clary was the only one. The moment June entered the room she began a monologue, even if Clary was reading to Kate or watching the news on TV. She followed her daughter-in-law from room to room, out to the pool and back, talking and talking, and if Clary was going anywhere June always volunteered to come along.

The only time June was quiet was during and just after her daily swim. She did laps every morning for twenty minutes in a silvery or aqua dressmaker suit, her carefully streaked and set gold hair bunched under a white rubber cap, her leathery bronze shoulders glistening. When she came out and lay dripping on one of the chaise lounges she seemed for a little while to be a different person, with a different, peaceful, sated expression.

"Oh, that felt wonderful," she might murmur, or "I wish I could stay in the water forever." Then for up to fifteen minutes she would lie silent, her eyes closed.

Occasionally June spoke of films or TV programs, but her usual topics were goods and services. Each morning she drove back and forth across the island in her rented Buick Le Sabre with the air-conditioning turned to high, prowling the end-of-season sales. She returned at lunchtime with news of reconnaissance, attack, skirmish, and defeat or triumph in her battle for the most desirable food, drink, clothing, and household furnishings and services. ("Would you believe it, there's not such a thing as a down cushion/salad spinner/scissor sharpener on this entire island. . . . I tried Sears first, and this absolutely imbecile salesgirl said she'd never heard of them. And then I went to Strunk's, I'm positive I saw some there last year, only the man denied it. He was incredibly rude, and I told him so, I said . . .")

June's most extended narrative concerned the remodeling of her house. Its basic theme was the delay, deception, and waste of expensive materials that had taken place during construction. These were, June declared in a favorite phrase, "mind-boggling." ("I used to wonder, when I was a kid, you know, how you boggled a mind," Ron had remarked once. "I figured you did it with some kind of mechanical gizmo, kind of like a toggle switch." Clary hadn't laughed; she'd had her own troubles with workmen.)

Now she heard the saga again, with additions and elaborations. There'd been nothing but trouble from the first, according to June. The job had been delayed literally for months because of objections from Historic Preservation of Key West, and their ridiculous rules about everything from the colors of paint you could use to the seven feet you were supposed to leave on each side of your lot, though half the houses in town were jammed up smack against the property line. But if you were a local, as far as June could see, whatever you wanted to build was just fine. She got so furious at one point that she threatened to sue Historic Preservation, which she might as well have done, because after her lawyer talked her out of it the old biddies on the board raised even more objections, and her architect had to redraw the plans at a frightful cost (figures supplied).

Several times during the summer June had had to come down to keep an eye on things.

"The heat was frightful, totally exhausting, but I truly believe that if I hadn't been here they would never have lifted a finger," she announced. It was just after lunch and she was sitting by the patio table, chain-smoking, while Clary tried to read the *Times* and Kate, humming softly to herself, colored a paper napkin. Overhead high shredded clouds drifted across a pale light-suffused sky; leaves rustled down one by one from the banyan and sapodilla trees; and the bare blunt fingers of the frangipani invisibly unfolded sprays of creamy stars.

"You cannot picture how slowly they were working," June continued, breaking the calm.

"Mm," Clary said. In fact she could picture it. Key West was a leisurely, laid-back place: the speed limit, even on the highway to the airport, was thirty-five miles an hour. June Graber, however, was used to life on the fast track. She didn't decelerate in Key West; maybe, after nearly sixty years in Manhattan, she didn't know how.

"Of course the contractor was never around when I wanted him," she told Clary, stubbing out her Kent and lighting another, "and those two carpenters of his were impossible. Half the time they were just pretending to be working. I'd look out of the window and I'd see Big Bill carrying a piece of pipe around the side of the house, and five minutes later I'd see him carrying the same pipe back.

"And then, if I asked that big good-looking oaf what he thought he was doing, he wouldn't answer. It turned out he had a hearing problem, but even when I came up close and positively shouted he just kept nodding stupidly and repeating 'Yes, ma'am. Right you are, ma'am.' And on top of that, he was a born-again Christian. For a while he was actually trying to convert me." June laughed shrilly. "He kept leaving these smarmy evangelistic tracts around the house, and once he told me that if I would let Christ into my heart I would find peace. Can you imagine the nerve?"

"Mm," said Clary. I wish to God you *would* find peace, she thought, and then, ashamed of herself, added, "Awfully annoying."

"Awfully. And I very soon found out I had to watch them every minute, or else something was sure to go wrong. Well, for example, one day I was having a sprout sandwich here on the deck, and I glanced up and saw that Davy—you remember him, that tough-looking little homosexual—was getting far more paint on my aralias than he was on my fence." June indicated the leggy, rustling shrubs that edged her backyard.

"The contractor had asked me please not to talk to the crew, to come to him if I had any problem. But really, he was never there half the time, and if I saw somebody doing something stupid right under my nose, I was going to mention it. I had no intention of paying for sloppy work and the waste of expensive materials. That's exactly what I said."

"Yes, I remember your telling me," prompted Clary, hoping to urge June toward the end of this familiar episode.

"So when I saw that Davy simply splashing paint everywhere, naturally I spoke up. I said I'd never seen such carelessness. I'd been watching him for fifteen minutes, I said, and he wasn't worth sixteen dollars an hour. Well, I don't know if I told you—"

"You told me," Clary murmured.

"—he became incredibly offensive. At first he didn't even answer me, he simply slammed down his wet paintbrush right on the tiles, you can still see the mark if you move that pincushion cactus, and stood up and started to walk away.

"So naturally I followed him. 'Where do you think you're going?' I asked, but really quite calmly and nicely. 'I'm paying you for your time,' I said, 'and I'd really like you to listen when I speak to you.' Well, then Davy turned round. He pulled his arm away and screamed at me. 'Oh, go to hell, lady!' he positively screamed." June looked at Clary for a reaction.

"Very rude," she said, feeling as if she were repeating lines in a play.

"Yes. That's exactly what he said, shouted really, and then he climbed on his motorbike and rode off. Can you imagine?"

"Mm," Clary said. If only June would stop talking for just a moment, she thought. And we'll be here for nearly two more weeks.

"Well, of course I was furious. I told my contractor he had to fire Davy, but he persuaded me to give him another chance. What a mistake that was, but I guess I have a soft heart." June placed her manicured hand on washed aquamarine silk above the relevant spot.

"Of course, after Davy came back he was terribly sulky for a while, but I tried to overlook it. And then later I found out he'd had the nerve to tell people *he'd* decided to give *me* another chance, because I was obviously under the influence of negative forces from some previous-life personality.

"Absolutely. He said that. He was one of those New Age types; he always wore a crystal round his neck on a chain." June made the same face she had made at a restaurant the night before over some doubtful soft-shell crabs. "My private opinion is, they were probably all three of them on drugs."

"Mm." Clary raised and turned the pages of the *Times*, but June didn't take the hint.

"Right before I left for New York in July," she continued, "I came back to the house unexpectedly at lunchtime, and what did I see?"

"Yes, I know, you saw—"

"Just let me tell you," June interrupted. "I saw Big Bill sitting on the edge of my pool, dangling his beefy legs in the water and eating a sloppy-joe sandwich. Davy was there too, lying beside him smoking, and his long greasy hair was wet, which proved that he had been swimming.

"Well, I made a big effort: I controlled myself and didn't say anything till I saw Mac, and then I told him I'd prefer it if the crew didn't eat on the job or use my pool. Just that, very politely. I didn't contradict him when he pretended they hadn't been swimming, or say anything about not wanting bits of bread and tomatoes and cigarette ashes and long greasy hair in the water I swam in every day. I think that was perfectly reasonable," June finished, on a note of inquiry.

"Mm, certainly," Clary agreed, looking at the pool as it rocked in the sun-dappled shade like a cool, pure trapezoid of ice-blue Perrier.

"But that's the kind of help you get down here." June sighed. "The cleaner we had last winter . . ."

Briefly June was diverted, but soon she resumed the saga of the house. After she went back to New York, she said, everything began to go wrong. She could tell from the photos—thank God she had absolutely demanded photos with the weekly statement. The bedroom windows had four panes instead of nine, and the closet shelf divider was completely off-center, and they'd used this hideous gray grout between the salmon-pink tiles in the bathroom and hung the mirror horizontally instead of vertically. Naturally she insisted that everything be done over.

"And then, can you believe it, Mac expected me to pay for their errors. It simply didn't make sense. I sometimes think that he was deliberately allowing things to go wrong, maybe subconsciously. A friend of mine, she's a therapist, and she said it sounded to her like Mac was a passive-aggressive personality who was working out his hostility to more successful members of society by screwing up my house along with his own career."

About this time, June said, it became nearly impossible to get hold of Mac on the phone. Even if she called him at 11 P.M. after the rates went down, he'd have his machine on. Or else his wife would answer, and Clary couldn't imagine how rude she was. "'Mac has to get up in six hours to work on your house, and I'm not going to wake him now for you or God herself.' That's exactly how she put it, she was some kind of feminist nut."

Clary, with difficulty, suppressed any comment; but one was supplied by Kate, who was now playing on the deck under a red hibiscus. "She goes, n' she goes, n' she goes on," Kate sang, pushing a plastic truck laden with plastic turtles along a track between two boards.

Warming to her subject, lighting another cigarette, June described the final battle. She related how she had paid to have her Key West phone turned on so she could reach Mac on the job, and how often he wasn't there. "I'd call and Big Bill or Davy would tell me that he was at the lumberyard. And then I'd call back an hour later and they'd say he was at City Hall. Well, eventually I blew up. 'God damn it,' I said, 'I'm tired of hearing your lame excuses. Do you know what these calls are costing me?'"

Perhaps predictably, when June phoned the following day her Key West number did not answer, though she tried it for over an hour, becoming more and more upset and furious. Finally she called her next-door neighbor, an elderly woman with arthritis. She was sorry to bother her, June said, but she had to know what the hell was going on at her house.

Reluctantly, the neighbor agreed to investigate. While the phone charges rapidly piled up, she went slowly next door and came slowly back to tell June that nobody was home. After further persuasion, she went out into her yard, climbed onto a bench, and looked over the wall. She returned to report that the fellows who were working over to June's place probably hadn't heard the phone or the bell on account of they were in the pool. Wishing not to cause trouble, she neglected to mention that they were in the pool without any clothes on, though this came out later.

"Yes. Buck naked, in my pool. Can you imagine!" (June spoke, it struck Clary, with a mixed thrill of horror and sexual excitement. She was reminded of something embarrassing a drunken elderly man had said to her at a Key West party a year ago: "Age calls to youth. I've got a giant crush on you, Clary, just like June's got the hots for those good-looking workmen of hers.")

As soon as she hung up, June Graber continued, she started dialing her Key West number again, and she kept at it for over two hours, until Mac finally answered.

If anything could have made the situation worse then, she said, it was his attitude. He didn't apologize or try to pretend he didn't know what had been going on; instead he laughed.

"'For Christ's sake, Mrs. Graber,' he said. 'it's nearly ninety-five degrees out today, that's goddamn hot, and the guys were on their lunch break. Anyhow, if you're not here, what difference does it make?'

"Well, I answered that question. I said it wasn't merely that his crew had deliberately contravened my orders. He'd also allowed someone who could very well be infected with AIDS to use the pool. 'You're not going to deny that Davy is a homosexual, I suppose,' I told him."

Mac did not try to deny this, June said. Instead, could you believe it, he started to act as if she were at fault and not him. He claimed that there was nothing wrong with Davy, and that anyhow you couldn't get AIDS from swimming in the same pool as an infected person.

"'Yes, that's what the so-called experts tell us,' I said to him," June declared. "'They tell us the water is safe to drink and the wax on apples doesn't cause cancer and a whole lot of things like that, and later you find out they were lying. I'm taking no chances,' I said.

"Well, then Mac changed his tune. 'All right,' he said to me, but very unpleasantly, you know. 'If it bothers you so much, I'll tell the guys to stay out of the pool.'"

June took a breath, preparing for the climax. "You know what I said to him! I said, 'I don't want you to tell them anything. I want all three of you off my property this afternoon.'" She smiled, reliving her victory. "I told him, 'I don't ever want to see you or those lazy bums you've got working for you again.' That's exactly what I said." She blew a self-congratulatory cloud of smoke.

Of course, June added, Mac had tried to argue with her. "But I simply wouldn't listen, though it meant I had to fly back down to Key West and find another builder (what a frightful job that was; I'll tell you all about it later). And then Mac had the gall to send in a final bill for over three thousand dollars, when I'd already paid far more than the work was worth. The way I figure it, he was lucky I didn't sue him for contaminating my pool."

June smiled, ground out her cigarette, and looked round. "And what did you do this morning, Katie?" she called to her granddaughter.

"Played with the pool people," Kate said.

"They came today? Now that is rather annoying." June frowned. "Monday and Thursday are their days, you know, Clary, and I really can't have—"

"It's not your regular pool people she means," Clary said. "Not Rusty and Joy."

"Uh-uh," Kate agreed, walking a plastic turtle across the deck toward her grandmother. "Davy and Big Bill."

Uncharacteristically, June was silent. She had gone pale under her leathery tan, and her expression was one of strain, even panic.

"Kate hasn't really seen Davy and Big Bill, I'm sure," Clary reassured her. "She's just remembered them from last year, and used their names for her imaginary friends. You know, back home she has an imaginary rabbit. It takes baths with her. Are Davy and Big Bill rabbits too, darling?"

"Nope. Like ordinary people, 'cept they're blue."

"You see, June, they're blue." Clary laughed. "And they don't come in from the street like ordinary people, do they!"

Kate shook her head. "Live in pool," she explained, pointing downward into the water. "They said, when was my Grammy coming to swim at night again! We want to play with her. That's you," she told June. "You're my Grammy."

June sat frozen; she opened her mouth but seemed for once unable to speak. Either she disapproved of imaginary friends, Clary thought, or she was furious at Kate's term of address. She had already said several times that she didn't want to be called Grammy, Grandma, or Granny. ("It always makes me feel like some pathetic little old lady. Why can't Kate say 'June,' like everyone else in the family?")

*　*　*

The following day it turned very hot, and when Rusty came to clean the pool Clary brought him iced tea.

"Thanks," he said, leaning against the shady side of the house. "Nice and peaceful here. You'd never know—" He paused.

"Never know what?"

"Well." He took another long swallow. "All that bad business last fall."

"You mean the way those workmen behaved to Mrs. Graber." No doubt everyone in town's heard that story by now, Clary thought.

Rusty gave her a hard look. "Hell, no. I mean the shitty way she behaved to them, excuse me. And what happened afterward."

"Really?" said Clary. "What happened afterward?"

"Well." He looked across the deck to where Kate was digging in a flower bed. "After she fired those guys, and wouldn't pay what she owed them—you know about that?"

"Yes," Clary said. "At least, that is—" She frowned.

"Well, they were up the creek. It wasn't so hard on Mac. He had a couple of repair jobs lined up, and some savings. But Big Bill had a wife and three children under six, and he really needed the money. So when this character he knew asked him to drive a load of never-mind-what to an address in Atlanta, for a thousand dollars, he said okay. You never heard any of this?"

"No."

"Hell, maybe I shouldn't—"

"Go on."

"Well. Okay. Big Bill, he made it the first time, but on the second trip he ran into a police roadblock just north of Summerland Key. He freaked out and turned the truck round and started back, and a couple of cops started after him. Pretty soon he got to speeding, and when he came to the construction on the bridge he lost control and crashed through a barrier and was DOA at Keys Memorial Hospital."

"Oh, that's awful." Clary set down her iced tea; her fingers felt frozen. "I'm really sorry—"

"And then Davy. You heard about that?" Clary shook her head. "He didn't have any family responsibilities, but he was paying out over eighty dollars a week for AZT. He tried to get on the county program, but they had a six-week waiting period. So he got antsy and took off for San Francisco, where he'd heard the situation was better, only he ran into more red tape there. Sold his bike and was sleeping in a park. Round about Thanksgiving he decided he couldn't take waiting around to get sick and die, so he jumped off some big building they have out there."

"Oh, awful," Clary repeated. "But I really don't think June—Mrs. Graber—knows any of this, or she wouldn't be so—" She paused, unable to think of a neutral term.

"She knows," Rusty said. "She knows, all right, because I told her when she got down here just before Christmas."

⋆   ⋆   ⋆

On Clary's arrival in Key West, June had declared that she was going to give a cocktail party for her. Clary had thanked her mother-in-law politely, but now that the gift had been presented she wasn't enjoying it much. Under an orange-stained, rapidly fading sunset, two dozen well-preserved aging people in strangely youthful and colorful garb— fire-engine-red slacks, Hawaiian shirts, yellow Bermuda shorts, and purple ruffled sundresses—stood around the illuminated pool with drinks in their hands. As dusk fell the water glowed brighter and brighter, an almost supernatural turquoise; but they turned their backs on it, absorbed in news of local real estate transactions and their own homes, plants, pets, and ailments.

June, in pink silk patio pajamas, wove continually among her guests, urging them to try the conch fritters. Clary stood by the shallow end watching her daughter sail leaves and hibiscus flowers in the water and listening to a discussion of restaurants in Bermuda, where she had never been and had no wish to go.

Suddenly, at the other end of the pool, there was a commotion. June Graber, or so it appeared later, had taken a step backward and fallen in. There were screams and splashing, increasing to a crescendo as several of June's guests, most of them over sixty and more or less woozy with alcohol, jumped in to save her, some on top of each other.

Almost at once the slippery trapezoid of water was full of thrashing multicolored bodies, the air of confused, hysterical cries. Other guests waded in past Kate, or threw green and magenta-flowered chair cushions that, though intended as life preservers, acted as weapons.

It was fully dark when all the would-be rescuers were helped from the pool, or sloshed themselves out of it, bruised and dazed. June Graber was removed last. Apparently she had hit her head on something and sunk almost at once. Though several volunteers, and later an ambulance crew, tried to revive her, they all failed.

Clary didn't witness these vain efforts; at the first glimpse of that heavy, sodden pink thing, she had hurried Kate into the house.

★ ★ ★

Back in Boston, once the shock had worn off, Clary and Ron's main concern was for Kate. A child's first experience of death was important, and had to be handled tactfully.

"You see, darling," Clary concluded. "That's why you always have to wear your life jacket when you're around water, because you can't always be thinking about being careful all the time. Grammy wasn't thinking about it, so she walked backward and fell into the pool."

"No," Kate said.

"How do you mean, no?" Clary hugged Kate anxiously.

"Grammy didn't walk backward. Big Bill grabbed on her leg and pulled, and then Davy pushed her down in the water."

"Oh, no, honey," her father protested.

But in spite of anything her parents could say, Kate stuck to her version. When they continued to press her she burst into tears, and it took the best efforts of both Clary and Ron to calm her.

"Kate doesn't really understand about death yet; she's just too young," Clary said later. "When I put her to bed tonight she told me that your mother is living in the pool in Key West."

"She said something like that to me too," Ron agreed. "I think maybe it's just a way of denying that she'll never see June again, because the loss is still too painful."

"Ye-es." It was painful for Ron, Clary thought—far more than she would have guessed. But really June didn't mean anything to Kate. It was just as well that they had never been close.

Clary pictured June's house in Key West, now on the market, since Ron had refused to go there ever again. She could see the backyard clearly in her mind: the shutters would be closed now, the deck furniture under plastic covers. But the outside spotlights, intended to deter burglars, would have come on automatically at dusk, bathing the palms and hibiscus in their unnatural glow. And the pool would still be full; the real estate agent thought that looked better to prospective buyers.

The water is as cool and clear and silvery green as ever, Clary thought: rippling out from the inlets with the same slow silky bubbling and churning, the same low continuing hum. And there are the same leafy reflections on the surface. And the same shifting lattice patterns on the bottom—as if someone were slowly shaking a spectral net in which, down at the deep end, shadowy blue figures were moving.

*Wendell Mayo* | JAGGED TOOTH, GREAT TOOTH

Three days after Hurricane Agnes, Hester
and Charles Bonn, retired and newly
transplanted to southern Florida from
Tampa, joined the people at the Venice
Public Beach to search for fossil sharks'
teeth. Their searching was silent, covered
over with the gentle lapping of waves. In
the gray hours of dawn, the water in the
Gulf was drawn out as far as the eye could
see, under a sky that was overcast and as
gray as the water, its aspect seamless and
without perceptible horizon. Yet even this
calm part of the day was not without process: the water walked onto the beach,
then ran out in smooth, overlapping
sheets, where the folds in the water became indistinguishable to the human eye,
indiscernible in the flatness of the Gulf.
The eye could follow the surface as it

heaved without breaking its smoothness, as it surged and came forward, as it fell back and lost itself in the overall aspect of the dim day.
The pupils of Hester's and Charles's eyes had become so wide that
these apertures seemed as limitless as the Gulf itself, and the reflec-
tion of the vast expanse of water in their eyes as unfathomable as the
sea. Their grief, too, was as smooth and unfathomable. They had
outlived their only child.

Hester and Charles stood at the edge of the water, then they sat,
squat like children in the moist sand on top of a little ridge of black,
silver and brown bits of matter left out by the high tide. Their hands
sifted through the water, the debris of driftless ages, the bits of fossil,
quartz, bone, and scale, all swept together by the storm into one place.
Their hands pushed through the matter; their legs shifted, pulled up
against their bodies, then stretched straight out before them. Their
hands moved between their legs, scooping and sifting the matter toward themselves, then lifting it in dripping chunks to eye level.

Charles turned the sand over in his hands. Great White, he thought.
What are you? Where are you now? Jagged tooth, great tooth . . .
Tommy? Tom? Gone too? Only petrified, broken teeth of the Great
White remain. Where?

He picked through the damp chunk of sand, slapped the mass back
and forth, hand to hand. The mass caught the new sunlight; he picked
out the black, fossilized tail of a stingray, then the amber-colored
lower mouth plate of a puffer fish, both very small and only fragments;
yet he kept them both, just as he kept all the fragments he found. He
believed that someday two of the fragments might miraculously fit
together; perhaps he might one day find the upper half of the stingray's tail, the upper mouth plate of the puffer. It was the conceivable
that had always fascinated him, not simply the actual play of life, but
those possibilities that were genuinely plausible in the mind, so that
when and if they had ever happened, the very contemplation of their
possibility would vindicate his thoughts. His whole life he had looked
for the coincidental to manifest itself in important ways: like the
stranger, a thin, red-haired man he saw three times in three different
places in a single day in Tampa, a man who had looked precisely as he
himself had at the age of thirty-three.

Charles ran his hand over the smooth knobs of Hester's knees. He felt her kneecaps stiffen and lock; he followed her calf with his hand, thinking how supple and fleshy her legs were. He closed his eyes and remembered the delicate, blue veins running from the crook of her knee to her calf, like the rivulets splaying through the Great Delta of the Nile.

"Do you still grieve?" he asked her. He looked at her blue eyes, thinking how blue didn't grow old, how all of it changed, but how blue, watery eyes, eyes like those of a baby, never grew old.

"You know I do. But not like at first. Not in many years."

"You know what I mean."

"Yes, I know. You mean that there will be no children." Hester turned away and picked a Tiger, a Mako, and a Dusky, all from one hand, and held them up for Charles to see. "Some nice teeth, although they're not very big."

Charles stood and waded into the surf. It split around his legs, then it rose and fell along his calves; he stooped and ploughed his hands and forearms down into the debris under the surf. He felt his arms under the sand and thought, Have no fear, Hester.

"I'll find a big one for you today," he said. "Promise . . . perhaps an extinct White."

"I know you'll never stop trying," she told him.

As the day wore on, the beach filled with people. Charles watched a sandy-haired boy with orange boxer trunks and a girl wearing cutoff jeans and a t-shirt tied in a knot under her chest. He saw them position their towels on the sand nearby. A balding young man walked slowly toward them. Behind the balding man, a red setter zigzagged in and out of the surf, drawing strands of seawater up with its jaw. Charles wondered at how the water seemed connected to the dog's jaw, to the dog's teeth; then the dog shook itself, and instantaneously the connection between water and jaw was broken. Soon more boys and girls, more men and women, were everywhere on the beach: in the water, digging in the wet sand, walking on the pier, and walking under the pier in its long, sharp, rhomboid-shaped shadow.

A young man waded near Charles. The water came to about his navel. The man's hair was wet and black and pasted over his forehead in serrations shaped like the tongues of flames. Charles watched the man slapping sand and sea stones from hand to hand. A young woman stood behind the young man, farther into the Gulf, with water up to her chin. Although her hair was tied back tightly, a lock of black hair slanted over her right eye like a crow's wing. When the water swelled, it covered her jaw, then the water surged up, over her head a moment; the black wing of hair floated, then, as the water fell back, it pasted itself back to her forehead. He felt an odd sense of apprehension. He recalled the day in Tampa that the Port Captain had phoned his office to tell him that Tommy had been lost in a storm far off the coast of Cuba. He watched the water cover the woman's face once more. He thought, Go no farther. Not now. Please.

★   ★   ★

Charles Bonn's eyes scanned a postcard: Sea Pleasures and Treasures: Prehistoric Sharks' Teeth . . . Hester was speaking:
"Charles . . ."
from the Shark
"Charles, do you remember that woman in the water?"
Tooth Capital of the World
"Charles . . . the woman with water up to her neck?"
Venice, Florida
He folded the *Venice Crier* on his lap and sipped his coffee. He glanced at the spiraling branches and deep green leaves of the banyan tree spread over the patio.
"That woman, yes," he said. "What did she want?"
"You saw when she came over to me. Her eyes—she frightened me—they were so white. Her jaw and teeth were clenched so tightly. All of a sudden her face relaxed a little, all of it except the tight lines of muscles that ran down from her temples, along her ears to her jawline . . . She said to me, 'I need to ask you something.' I couldn't say anything. I didn't know what to say. She was dripping and so tense. That man was standing nearby, the one with dark, wet hair. I guess he was her husband. He was looking for sharks' teeth. I didn't think that he paid much attention to the woman or me. Then she gestured to the man with her eyes. She said, 'He wants me to have an operation, but

I don't know if I should.' I couldn't look at her; I'm not sure what she meant."

Charles pushed the *Venice Crier* from his lap to beside his plate, and he smiled. "What could she have meant?"

"I can guess."

"I don't want to know."

"Anyway, I looked at her. I was sitting in the surf, sifting the sand the whole time she stood over me. I only glanced at her when she first came over, but I never looked at her as she spoke; when I looked up at her, she had turned away from me to the man with the black hair, who was glaring at both of us. She looked back at me, her voice brightened in a strange, nervous way, and she smoothed her hair with her hands. 'Having any luck?' she asked me. So I told her, 'Plenty of Lemon teeth'—and that's all I said to her, except that she asked me where I lived and I told her the Banyan House, about a mile from the beach, and that was when the man moved—"

Charles shifted in his chair; he sat pulling apart a leaf from the banyan tree shaped like a large hand. He began tearing the leaf along the veins in it. "So, he moved," he sighed and turned the salt shaker between his fingers several times.

"Yes, he moved. He made this move, almost as if it were involuntary, like an impulsive lurch. The woman had a tiny curl of black hair between her fingers and she was pushing it into one corner of her mouth and pulling it out—over and over—and her eyes were darting back to the man and to me—" Hester made a gesture with her hands like that of a magician, "and she just waded off, like that. She waded out until the water covered her neck and she stayed there."

"Thoroughly mysterious," Charles said. He rose from his chair, took a few steps to the center of the patio, knelt, and picked up another leaf from the banyan tree. Hester followed him, bringing her tumbler of gin and tonic. Charles thought: Why can't you let that be for a moment?

Charles nodded at the tumbler. "For Christ's sake, Hester, it isn't even lunch."

She looked at him with her blue and watery eyes, eyes with water not from tears, though they had been full frequently in past years, but watery from the effects of the gin, the stupor she seemed to retreat to, the watery film that he could see from this side of her life, and that she lived behind. She set the drink behind her on the edge of a redwood planter filled with white, red, and orange portulaca.

"I saw her too, Hester." He leaned back into a deck chair. He closed his eyes. He felt the sun begin to sink into his skin. Sea Pleasures and Treasures, he thought. Then he opened his eyes and ran them along the limbs of the great banyan tree that spread overhead. The tree, he knew, was Indian, and he thought how lonely it must be in southern Florida. He followed the dark, varnishy branches as they ran up in helical shafts from the horizontal trunk, until each joined another, turned horizontally, and intersected other branches; he could not follow one branch for long before it joined another and its geometric source became lost in the maze of dark limbs. Tree of Life, he thought.

"Look what the woman gave me," Hester said and she pressed a hard, fist-sized object into his palm. It was a huge specimen of one half of an extinct White's tooth, split almost perfectly, vertically from the tip of the tooth to the root. Great, great, great White, he thought, ageless, but just half of it was usual, always in fragments. "Hester," he whispered. He watched her take her drink into the house. "There will be no children."

\*　　\*　　\*

Charles sat under the banyan tree, not particularly astonished that the woman who had stood in the water up to her neck had followed them from the beach to the Banyan House. Hester had a genius for attracting strangers and now this one stood with Hester at the far end of the patio. The woman's hair was loose and tangled and fell in clumps and knots on her shoulders. And he too noticed the lines running from her temples along her jaw. Her lips were parted slightly, as if the last words she had spoken to Hester, who stood very near her, had never really come out. As Hester crossed the patio back to Charles, the woman continued staring past her to Charles, as if in a moment of panic she wished to call Hester back to her by relaying an unspoken message to him; her expression seemed to say, tell Hester to forget the whole thing.

He spread his entire collection of fossilized teeth, including the broken specimen of the extinct White, in front of him. He was fascinated that every specimen he had collected was broken or had some piece missing, that each was incomplete, that each, in all probability, had some bit remaining somewhere else.

"What does she want?" he asked Hester.

He pushed the pointed tip of one tooth against his index finger until it pricked him. What name is this? he thought. Atlantic Sand shark? Black Tip? How can I tell them apart? These bits and pieces. He picked up another tooth. This one? Extinct . . . one of the requiem family?

"Isn't it obvious, Charles?" Hester blinked her eyes rapidly. He noticed the sun streaming through the banyan tree, patching the patio with dark shadows shaped like hands and limbs. "Charles." Hester's voice was urgent. "Her husband wants to fix it so she can't have children."

"I'm sorry," Charles said, moving his index finger over the break in the extinct White tooth.

"She wants to know if I think she should have the operation."

"She wants to know from you?"

"Well, why not me?"

Charles looked back at the woman. The woman was chewing on a lock of her hair. Now she smiled at him in a way that scared him. "Maybe there are good reasons—"

"Like what?"

"Maybe there are things we don't know. Perhaps she's—"

"Crazy?"

Charles looked back to the woman. Her face was clouded now, and her cheeks concave, each with a perceptible shadow. "Hester . . . I'm just saying that it's none of our business."

"You mean none of *my* business—isn't that what you mean?"

Hester picked up her drink from the table near Charles, walked over to the young woman, took her arm, and led her into the house. Charles surveyed the broken bits of teeth spread before him on the table. Not gone, he thought to himself, some of these species are not gone . . . times like these, Hester, it hurts, wave after wave of smooth pain, not like when Tommy first died, his body, black-tipped fingers, his ghost in my dreams gliding in dark, warm waters. Down deep, so deep; see, Hester, those black tips on the fingers of my dead son? Black Tip shark . . . not extinct, living . . . How's that Mr. Cartmell? Charles opened Cartmell's guide book to sharks' teeth: "The teeth of the requiem shark families, Dusky, Bull, Black Tip, Spinner, and Brown, are all very similar in appearance. It is extremely difficult, and sometimes impossible, to tell one from another. It takes an expert who has made an intensive study of sharks to do so." He wondered: Dusky . . . Brown . . . Black Tip . . . dangerous to man. What about women? What about that, Mr. Cartmell? No, I know how it is. How does that go, Mr. Nietzsche? "I am afraid we are not rid of God because we still have faith in grammar."

*   *   *

Charles walked along the beach alone. It was the eventide, and unlike the day before under the gray seamless sky, the ocean was green and it rose to meet the sky, vacant and pale blue, in a great joint. Above him, the dunes were dotted with thick blades of grass. He saw a man and a woman bicycling toward town. The pier was suddenly illuminated with dozens of points of light, and more people appeared to him strolling on its boardwalk. When he turned back to consider the two halves of the sea and sky joined at the horizon, the great seam had vanished, or, as he thought, as far as he could see, the division was no longer there. Night had fallen.

Later, in front of the Banyan House, he saw Hester and the young woman sitting on the sofa in the front room; he saw them so clearly that he felt as if he were intruding. He saw their facial expressions, how they changed as they talked; he saw their mouths move; he even imagined the gradations of tone and volume in their words, which he could not hear, but only see in their making. He could not tell if they had become friends. He knew he would not ask Hester this. It was not his way, or hers. But the two women seemed at ease, even happy with every gesture, every movement of attentiveness and speech. After a short time, the young woman got up from the sofa and appeared at the front door with Hester; the young woman walked past him without a word, and Hester, as they had agreed earlier, followed him back down the lane to the beach.

Charles and Hester sat on the flat, warm lap of dark sand at the Venice Public Beach. The sky was clear and a quarter-moon was up. He turned to her and saw that her hair was like a head of kelpish tangles, and that her skin was the pallor of a fish's belly, but not the pallor of the dead, the pallor of a cold light that emanated from within her.

"What does she want from you?" he asked her.

"How can we sit here," Hester replied with a distant tone, "taking in the night, dreaming—if that is what we do—when every day the history of the world is broken into tiny bits by the sea and buried in ridges of debris on beaches like this one?"

He couldn't think of anything to say. Then he said, angrily, and in an absurd way, "Of all things, do you know what I read on the men's room wall at the change house the other day? This: 'God made time so that everything doesn't happen at once.'"

"Make sense, Charles."

"*You* make sense. What did the woman want from you?"

"I wish you hadn't made me sit under the banyan tree with you yesterday when she came to visit. It was . . . embarrassing. Like we were both waiting for her to crumble, or to leave; it was like we were throwing her out."

"I didn't make you do anything. She left on her own. What did she want tonight?"

"The same. She wanted me to tell her what to do."

"It's unfair of her to ask you."

"Why not? Why not me?"

Charles reached for her hand; it was cold and limp; she slipped her hand out from under his. "We have had our child," he said and she turned away; he paused a moment, then he whispered, "There won't be another." He reached up and took her by both shoulders. "Say it, Hester; say it like you used to when he died: 'Tommy is dead . . .'"

Suddenly, he felt her hand in his pocket; she withdrew the broken White tooth, made a tight fist around it, and smiled. Her own teeth were showing in the weak moonlight; as he adjusted his eyes to her face, he realized that her gaze was tenuous. "It's not for you to say!" she said. Then her smile was gone; she rose and walked away.

*　　*　　*

He did not follow her that night. He had followed her after Tommy's drowning. He had followed her after the funeral. Time after time, he had struggled to keep up with her flights from him and from the sharp pain until there was nothing left, not even pain. Now, he lay on the beach, listening to the waves come in, and gradually, with the incoming tide, the sound of the waves filled his thoughts. He reached into his pocket and turned the other teeth over and over with his fingers. It seemed vaguely unfair that in their ancient day something had formed these teeth so perfectly, only to have them turn to rock, to mix with the stone and rubbish of dead things and to become almost indistinguishable from things that had never been alive: they had become transformed from their smooth geometry in life, to broken, jagged, randomly etched bits of the past.

But now was not the slow passing of millennia; it was a single night, a miniscule night, not the great joint of blue sky and green sea, not the huge, dull, steel-colored dome of sorrowful mornings, but a small night: a high sliver of a moon and tiny fixed stars that shifted their positions only when one forgot that they were there—or slept—and saw them at a later time with new positions in the night sky. The sounds of the small night were terribly unlike the sight of the two women talking at the Banyan House: he lay on his back in the dark; he heard the water talking, but he could not see it; its source seemed entirely subsumed by the lashing sound of the surf. Yet he felt its invisible dark source all around him. He grew angry again and he could not think. Go no farther, he thought; then he slept and time passed.

When he woke, he became aware once more of a seamless, gray dawn over the Gulf. He had spent his whole life trying to distinguish all shades of gray—and now this: the same color returned morning after morning. And now, once more, he had the maddening urge to make the connections that had always seemed plausible, but impossible: to run into his double in Tampa, to find the other half of the extinct White tooth, to discover how water was somehow connected to jaw, to understand how everything could somehow happen at once. But nothing changed. The dawn presented its seamless self; his hands, then hers, would forever be breaking the sand, sifting through it, and tossing it back into the chaotic surf. Ray tail, Puffer, Tiger, Black Tips. Tommy. No change. Taste. Sight. No change.

It was fully morning when he saw Hester, then the young woman, wade into the water several yards from where he lay. He watched them move out into the Gulf until the water had covered them up to their jawbones. Their mouths were dark and beautiful; they sucked and spewed water from them: gray streams of water after each wave slapped their faces, after each surge of water wetted and wafted their hair in the water, then slid back and left the dark, tangled masses about their necks. He saw Hester rise up from the water, and with one powerful push from her lower body, lift the tooth over her head, bring her arm back, and cast the dark, broken fossil out, up, far into the fathomless Gulf. He lay still a few seconds, replaying the arc of the fossil against the sky, hoping that in some way, even if only in his imagination, the jagged tooth had torn the veil of gray, the smoothness of his grief. But it had sailed far out and had vanished, and he lay on the sand tumbling the teeth in his pocket.

Jill McCorkle | MIGRATION OF THE LOVE BUGS

My husband and I live in a tin can. He
calls it *the streamline model,* the top of
the line, the cream of the crop when it
comes to moveable homes. *Ambulatory
and proud of it.* That's Frank's motto and I
guess it makes sense in a way, since he is
the only one of six siblings who's still alive
*and* walking, not to even mention that he
spent his whole adult life setting things in
concrete—house foundations and drive-
ways, sidewalks that will remain until the
New England winters crack them once
too often and that new cement outfit that
just opened comes in to redo the job.

 We're in Florida now and the only concrete we own are the cinder blocks that
keep our wheels from turning. "Can't we
at least put our tin can up on a founda-
tion like everybody else's?" I asked our

first day here. "You know, pretend it's a real building rather than a souped-up vehicle?" He was in what he called his retirement clothes, pastel golfwear, though he has never touched a club. He was surveying the flat, swampy, treeless land as if this was the Exodus. Even that day, our belongings not even unpacked, I was thinking that if this was the Promised Land, Moses for sure dealt me a bad hand.

"I like knowing we can move at a moment's notice." He turned to me then, eyes wide. There was an exuberance about him that I found as foreign as the landscape. He didn't even look like my husband to me. He looked so small in those lightweight Easter-egg clothes. Where was the concrete dried gray on his knees? The bandanna in his back pocket? The heavy brogans I had decreed must always stay outside of our apartment door? "After all these years, Alice," he said and took my prize possession from my hands, my mother's silver tea service that I had carried on my lap all the way from Somerville, Massachusetts, "we're free to do anything we please." He kissed me quickly and then ceremoniously carried the silver service inside the tin can. I stood and watched this frail pastel imitation of my husband walk away with my only piece of inheritance and willed myself to wake up. I had never seen such an expansively bright sky, never felt such intense heat. I felt lightheaded, as if my whole world were encapsulated in some kind of vaporous bubble that could pop any given second. I closed my eyes tightly and waited.

"Alice!" Frank called. "Come see!" I opened my eyes, only to find the tin can in place, blinding me, and a swarm of sticky flies clinging to my pale arms. The Promised Land, Armageddon—who knew they'd be one and the same? "We've got a view of the driving range." Frank called in a voice so enthusiastic you might think he was Columbus and I was on board the Pinta. "I've for sure got to get some clubs, now."

★    ★    ★

There is no one in this neighborhood with naturally dark hair. The woman next door, her skin prunelike from what she refers to as her *southern upbringing* and what I (when alone with Frank) refer to as her *melodramatic melanoma-begging* life, has jet black hair that stains the fine teeth of the rattail comb that she uses to part and pincurl her hair. "I can't imagine living up there where you were," the woman says every time I see her. Her neck skin is like an accordion. *I can't imagine having hookworm,* I think but bite the words quickly. Frank claims every day that he has never been happier, and it makes me feel helplessly sad. It makes me question everything I've ever believed in.

*   *   *

"This is the life," he says after a round of golf lessons and a couple of martinis with the accordion's malnourished spouse. "You've got to give it a chance, Alice," he pleads. "The change is good for us." I want to tell him that I don't like change and never have and that he, the person who has bought me White Shoulders cologne every Christmas for years, should know that better than anyone. But instead, I tell him that I *am* giving it all a chance, that I am enjoying all this reading time that I never had before. Just this week I read an article about these very bugs that are driving me out of my mind, the ones that cling and stick to your skin whenever you walk outside. The article said that these bugs have created a boom in the market for car-headlight nets.

I'm not sure where the bugs started out, maybe in Canada, maybe on some cool lake in Maine, the White Mountains or the Green Mountains, or around the Cape. The article didn't discuss their origin, only that they are slowly migrating through Florida. Their destination is always south of wherever they are. It's a very slow migration because their life story is so brief: hatch, have intercourse, produce, and die. It sounds like a normal enough life, except that these bugs only get one turn each at steps two and three. And since they're chronically on the move, no two steps happen in the same place; there's no time in their short, migrant lives for settling down.

When Carl was born, Frank stood outside the hospital nursery window for hours on end. Mothers were treated differently in those days; having a baby was like being sick, like having something removed surgically. We took a taxi, Frank's face turning stark white each time I gripped the front seat and bit my lip. "It'll be okay, it'll be okay," he kept saying, his hands and hair damp as we bumped along the icy streets. I passed out while staring into the pale gray eyes of a nurse and woke with a terrible headache, my whole world disoriented until I remembered where I was and what must have happened. Within minutes Frank was there just like in a scene from a movie, flowers and candy and a fuzzy stuffed bear. Suddenly there was a new picture, a new life, new plans of *some day.*

Imagine if Frank and I, like the bugs, had dropped dead at that moment. We would have missed everything that we have come to know as our life. Or maybe there wouldn't have even been a Carl because it took years for us to have him. The article didn't say what happened to the unsuccessful, the infertile bugs, if there is such an error of nature. You wonder. Do they get to try again or do they just go ahead and die under the false assumption that they were successful?

"Mom, are you okay?" Carl asked when I called to say we were where we were going, only bound by cinder blocks and a doormat that said welcome to the tin can. I could hear his wife, Anne, in the background. "Say hi to Nana and Pop," she was saying, and each time she spoke, we'd hear the small echo of Joseph, eighteen months old and miles and miles away. They live where Frank and I used to talk about living some day, in Brookline. It was something I never expected to *really* come about, just as I never really thought we'd end up here. There's a park across the street from their building with a rose garden and swings for the children. Just a little over a month ago we were sitting there, Frank going on and on about *here,* this place, and how the weather would be so much better, so much healthier for both of us. I was already homesick just listening to him.

"Have you been home?" I asked Carl. "You know, by our building?" I felt like I needed to yell into the receiver. "I'm wondering if they ever fixed that broken windowpane in the front door?"

"Well. I haven't gotten out . . ."

"What do you mean, *our* building?" Frank asked. "Give me that phone." He laughed and took the receiver, Carl's voice trailing on about how it wasn't always convenient to just hop in the car or on the train and go. "Your mother is fine," he said and patted my arm. "Sure. Sure. She's going to love it once she gives it a chance." I caught a glimpse of us in the storm door, only to be alarmed by what I saw—a couple of dried-up sardines stuffed in a tin can.

* * *

I have to take a broom and sweep those sticky bugs off our screens at least once a day. I read in the paper that they have been nicknamed the "love bugs" because that's all they get to do. It's a real mess since they're all just looking for a place to either procreate or die or possibly both. I can't help but think if the bugs *knew* what was going to happen, they'd choose a celibate life and potential longevity. Don't they have enough sense to look around and see what's happening, to witness the great fate? I sweep them to our cinder-block stoop and then into the hibiscus, a lush bush with flowers so fiery red I keep expecting it to speak to me. I feel disgust and I feel pity as I sweep the carnage, some of the carcasses still joined at the thorax. The article theorized that they are heading for Cuba. I can't imagine why they'd choose Cuba. I'm sure that when they arrive it'll be nothing like what they expected. Millions and zillions of bugs to have died in vain. If I were a love bug I'd have to stop midflight and ask just whose idea was this anyway?

* * *

We had rented our apartment in Somerville for forty years, and the rent was frozen for us, safe and stable. For years I watched others move in and then out; with each tenant exchange and new coat of paint the rent increased. I knew all the neighbors, smooth-faced college students or young families replacing people like ourselves who had either died or one day just packed up and left. I had strolled Carl up and down that street, waved to all the neighbors on porches and at windows. "You don't even know that many people anymore," Frank said just six months ago, and I explained that, no, I didn't know them like I had known various relatives and people who had been friends for forty years. But I recognized people; there were young people who looked up at my window and waved, a young woman next door who was always asking me what smelled so good in my kitchen. I knew that if we left, we could never afford to come back; the rent would sky-rocket and what I had called home for forty years would be as unattainable as the moon.

*   *   *

The landlord already had the painters there in the hallway when I went in to look around one last time. There were clean white patches where Carl's picture had hung over the television set in our bedroom; there were bits of dried concrete in the corner of our closet where Frank threw his work clothes. There was an old ball of yarn that had belonged to our cat years before and had somehow fallen into a small space at the back of Carl's closet. Fitting, since it was in his closet that he had hidden the cat after sneaking it into the apartment. That was when he was only seven years old, and the cat slept in that same closet until Carl was a senior in high school. Finally the old cat went into the closet one Sunday afternoon and refused to come out. Carl was out at the movies with a girl in his class. Frank asked me to go down to the market and get him some bicarbonate, and while I was gone, he took the cat away so none of us would have to see it die.

I felt panic rise in my throat as I surveyed the apartment, pacing room to room and back. There was a mark on the living room ceiling made by a rocketing champagne cork on the day Carl and Anne got married. There were smudges on the kitchen doorframe where all of us held on while leaning into the living room to hear the conversation, or to announce dinner was almost ready. There was masking tape around one window pane in the bedroom, Frank's solution to the winter wind he had likened to a dog whistle. The painters were waiting. They would lay on a fresh coat of paint that would hide all traces of us. I excused myself a moment and then opened the window over the bathtub and leaned out onto the small flat section of roof where I had deserted a dying geranium. In the distance I could see the train, hear the familiar rumble as it made its way into the city, where it would spill all the people and scoop up some more. I thought of all those times I'd complained, my arms filled with shopping bags, while I stood and waited for the rush of wind that announced an approaching train. I wanted another chance; just one more trip into the city and I would return stoically, no complaint uttered.

My young neighbor, pregnant and cheerful, was watering her patio tomatoes. "We will miss you," she said, I assume speaking for her husband and unborn child, maybe for the whole building. I mouthed a thank-you and turned quickly, sat on the edge of the empty bathtub, my hand gripping the faucet. I grieved that I had never counted the baths taken there, never made little marks on the inside of the door with each passing day. I was sorry that I had not taken longer baths, that I had not simply lain back in my world and stared at the full green weeping willow which hid the building next door.

"Alice." Frank was there in the bathroom door, a young wild-haired painter behind him. "I was getting worried." He turned then to the young man and said something about *women things.*

"You know that we can never come back," I told him, and he shook his head, hugged me close. "If we leave, we can't ever afford to come back."

"Sure we can, honey," he whispered. "But we won't want to. Wait and see."

*   *   *

Frank and I were both born right near where we lived all those years; we figure we walked the same streets, shopped in the same stores, saw all the same movies at the same time, but we never met until we were in our twenties. He had just come back from World War II and I was taking some business courses in night school. I went to a party at my cousin's house and there he was. He was already in the same concrete business where his father worked for years before him, and he was spending his day off setting my cousin's children's swingset in concrete. He was kneeling there, his big hands pouring cement, face flushed with the brisk March wind, his thick hair a deep auburn in the late afternoon light. "Once it dries, that swing is set for eternity," he told my cousin when he was all finished. "Won't budge an inch."

*   *   *

I tell Frank about the love bugs and he gets a good laugh, says that if I'm going to waste my time thinking about such, I might as well go ahead and join Ida, the accordion-necked woman, at the bridge table. I do and by the end of the afternoon, I have heard about every stage of her daughter Catherine's life and everything about Catherine's children and Catherine's Christmas Shoppe up in Georgia. "You can buy yourself an ornament at any month of the year," Ida says. "Walk inside of Catherine's shoppe, that's shoppe with two *p*s and an *e*, mind you—sophisticated, huh?—anyway, walk in there and you get a shiver like it might be December and you're in a snowstorm, carols playing, bells ringing." I stare at Ida's face, at her mouth moving in a slow drawling way, her lipstick caked like clay on her dry lips, and I long for winter, the hiss and whine of a radiator, the rattling of ancient glass windows, windows made long before anyone had heard the word *thermal*. I wish it were Christmas in our apartment, and Frank had just tiptoed in and slipped that bottle of White Shoulders under the tree, leaned in the kitchen to say, *You'll never guess what I just got for you.* I wish I were standing in our neighborhood drugstore the first time I ever smelled that fragrance. It was a drizzly autumn day, four-thirty and already dark. I sprayed my wrists and then stepped out onto the busy sidewalk, my umbrella raised as I walked home, nothing on my mind other than the chicken I was going to cook for dinner and the calculated minutes until Frank got home. Carl was just an unnamed abstraction that we had talked about for ten years; he was the child we had finally accepted we'd never have.

Ida is still talking, her voice like a buzz, while I see myself up on a chair, reaching to throw old wool blankets over the curtain rods to close out the whistling air, while Carl at ten months holds onto the coffee table and pulls himself up in a wobbly stance. I want to feel the sting of cold; to pull a wool hat down close around my face; to huddle into a seat on the train, Carl pulled close on my lap while we draw in warmth from the strangers collected there, alive to the flashing lights and popcorn smells, the surfacing to daylight and the cold gray sky, the river frozen like a sheet of glass, lights thrown in crazy patterns onto the trees in the Boston Common.

★   ★   ★

"Then you walk out and it's ninety-odd degrees, what do you think?" Ida asks. She is staring and I nod at her. Returned suddenly to a much older body, a much quieter life, weather so eternally hot and humid that I feel like I might fly out and fling myself into the grille of a car. If I am going to sweat like a pig, then let me do it in Fenway Park or Filene's Basement. Let me have a purpose and a little dignity. "I said if there's something you want and can't find, Catherine could send it to you." Ida pauses and takes a sip of her fruity drink, some concoction I have refused. (It is always happy hour in the ambulatory senior citizens' park.)

"I like birds on my tree," Ida says. "Every year Catherine sends me a few new birds. You can't wait until December to get your ornaments. Any time of year is good. I want some woodpeckers, you know sort of a comical bird, for the grandbabies." I watch her neck, imagining strains of "Lady of Spain." All of a sudden I feel the hideous speckled nausea that comes just before fainting. I have to wipe my face with a tissue I dip in my ice water. I have to breathe deeply.

"My son and his family will be here," I finally tell her, though this is something we haven't decided for sure. Frank says we will not be making the long trip home, so we are hoping they'll come. Still, I know that if I were Anne and settled there in Brookline, her parents and siblings close by in New Hampshire, I would not drive to Hades to see anybody. "I have a simple tree, a biodegradable tree, popcorn, cranberries. I don't buy ornaments."

"Well." Ida is speechless for a fraction of a second. "Did I tell you about our son Harvey, the artist?"

*　　*　　*

"I still can't get over those bugs," I tell Frank late one night. Our bedroom is the width of the bed, and its ceiling curves with air vents. "I mean, what are they doing? Why don't they just stay put?" I know that he knows what I am insinuating but he just squeezes my hand.

"I know what's got you worried," he says, referring once again to what has *him* worried, hurricane season and what Carl calls *The Mobile Home Tornado Theory.* "First sign of a storm and we'll just move our cinder blocks aside and drive inland. There's nothing holding us down."

"Sounds easy enough," I say, knowing that he's describing what we've already done. Frank wasn't running *to* this new place as much as he was running *away* from our old one. *First sign of a storm* (or old age—legs that can't make the apartment stair climb, bones too brittle to risk icy sidewalks) *and we'll just move.* It makes me ache to picture our home at night, the familiar shapes and shadows of our belongings. Maybe Frank had a similar vision at one time, a picture of one of us sitting there alone, nothing to break the silence but the distant hum of a passing train. Maybe he felt the unknown survivor should begin letting go by degrees, throwing off old treasured relics that would only become burdens when the other one was gone. He knew, for example, that I would never stare out at this golf course and see any bits of our past. He would never look at the cheap flip-down table and be reminded of my elaborate holiday dinners. He didn't take time to see that the memories would be there all the same, that they might even be heightened by the strangeness of an unfamiliar place. I suppose he thought when one of us died the other could simply move away from the grief. His plan of action was as simple as taking a dying house cat from its home. Or maybe he didn't see any of these things; maybe an instinct to run had come to him out of nature without realization or explanation.

★   ★   ★

"As for the bugs," he says, "what's foolish is that they don't stop and stay right here for a while, in the lap of luxury." He says the word *luxury* with a slight shake of his head, as if in awe, this impossible dream that he has convinced himself just came true.

"They have a terribly short life," I say.

"Yeah, and the men bugs have really got it bad." He rolls into me, his hand on my hip. In the faint glow from the streetlight in front of Ida's double-wide, he almost looks the way I remember from the first time we met; it was the same day he poured concrete around the legs of the swingset in my cousin's yard, a cluster of children watching. "The men bugs only have three stages of life. At least the women get that extra one."

"Birth? That's the bonus?" I ask. "You're saying you'd like to give birth."

"Well, can't be much to laying a little egg."

"Try a seven-pound-and-ten-ounce egg, try that," I say, and then he pulls me close and I try to imagine us in our bedroom with the full-size window and lace panel curtains; the window overlooks a sidewalk that Frank's daddy poured not long before the market on the corner opened. The market has fresh fruits and vegetables that the clerks arrange on tables out on the sidewalk; even in the rain, you can stand under the bright green awnings and fill your bag. Carl is a baby napping in a crib; he is a teenager sprawled in front of the TV set with that cat stretched out on his chest. I close my eyes when I feel like crying but Frank doesn't notice; he jiggles me and laughs, pulls me closer, and I imagine Carl in his small apartment, Anne beside him. I imagine them halfway listening to each other, halfway listening for the baby's cry, and, once again, the bathtub drained, another night unnumbered. Maybe they are too tired to hold each other, too tired to tell about the day, to say our neighbor said this to me or you'll never believe who I bumped into when I went into the city or when I was on the train. They tell themselves that some day they won't be so tired.

\*   \*   \*

When I returned home from getting Frank his bicarbonate that Sunday afternoon, he was staring out the window, the cat nowhere in sight. I went to the kitchen to put away the things I had bought, noticing immediately that the cat food was gone, the bowls, the rubber mouse. There was a quietness as we sat and waited to hear Carl coming up the stairs. "I just didn't think it was right," Frank finally said when the three of us were sitting there. "House cats are deprived of nature." Carl shrugged, lowered his head to hide any response. "It's just a cat," he finally said and left the room.

\*   \*   \*

Frank is snoring quietly now, his warm arm draped over my stomach. I want to wake him, to tell him that there's no such thing as paradise;

there is no Promised Land. At journey's end, it is all a mirage, a picture of the journey itself and all we left behind. Wherever we are, here or inland or a hundred miles south, that's all that there is. There is nothing that can make the end easier for whoever is left behind. That's what I want to tell him but I don't. He is sleeping so peacefully, so satisfied with the accomplishments of his life; yet, even as he sleeps, he is preparing for some day when at a moment's notice one of us must take flight.

Peter Meinke | THE CRANES

"Oh!" she said, "what are those, the huge
white ones?" Along the marshy shore two
tall and stately birds, staring motionless
toward the Gulf, towered above the bob-
bing egrets and scurrying plovers.

"Well, I can't believe it," he said. "I've
been coming here for years, and never
saw one . . ."

"But what *are* they?" she persisted.
"Don't make me guess or anything, it
makes me feel dumb." They leaned forward in the car and the shower curtain
spread over the front seat crackled and
hissed.

"They've got to be whooping cranes,
nothing else so big!" One of the birds
turned gracefully, as if to acknowledge
the old Dodge parked alone in the tall
grasses. "See the black legs and black

131

wingtips? Big! Why don't I have my binoculars?" He looked at his wife and smiled.

"Well," he continued after a while, "I've seen enough birds. But whooping cranes, they're rare. Not many left."

"They're lovely. They make the little birds look like clowns."

"I could use a few clowns," he said. "A few laughs never hurt anybody."

"Are you all right?" She put a hand on his thin arm. "Maybe this is the wrong thing. I feel I'm responsible."

"God, no." His voice changed. "No way. I can't smoke, can't drink martinis, no coffee, no candy. I not only can't jump over a tennis net, I can hardly get up the goddamn stairs. It's enough."

She was smiling. "Do you remember the time you drank six martinis and asked that young priest to step outside and see whose side God was on?"

"What a jerk I was! How have you put up with me all this time?"

"Oh no! I was proud of you! You were so funny, and that priest was a snot."

"Now you tell me." The cranes were moving slowly over a small hillock, wings opening and closing like bellows. "It's all right. It's enough," he said again. "How old am I, anyway, 130?"

"Really," she said, "it's me. Ever since the accident it's been one thing after another. I'm just a lot of trouble to everybody."

"Let's talk about something else," he said. "Do you want to listen to the radio? How about turning on that preacher station so we can throw up?"

"No," she said, "I just want to watch the birds. And listen to you."

"You must be pretty tired of that."

She turned her head from the window, holding his eyes with hers. "I never got tired of listening to you. Never."

"Well, that's good," he said. "It's just that when my mouth opens, your eyes tend to close."

"They do not!" she said, and began to laugh, but the laugh turned into a harsh cough and he had to pat her back until she stopped. They leaned back in the silence and looked toward the Gulf stretching out beyond the horizon. In the distance, the water looked like metal, still and hard.

"I wish they'd court," he said. "I wish we could see them court, the cranes. They put on a show. He bows like Nijinsky and jumps straight up in the air."

"What does she do?"

"She lies down and he lands on her."

"No," she said. "I'm serious."

"Well, I forget. I've never seen it. But I do remember that they mate for life and live a long time. They're probably older than we are! Their feathers are falling out and their kids never write."

She was quiet again. He turned to the back seat, picked up the object wrapped in a plaid towel, and placed it between them in the front.

"Here's looking at *you,* kid," he said.

"Do they really mate for life? I'm glad—they're so beautiful."

"Yep. Audubon said that's why they're almost extinct: a failure of imagination."

"I don't believe that," she said. "I think there'll always be whooping cranes."

"Yes." He leaned over and kissed her, barely touching her lips. "Tell me," he said, "did I really drink six martinis?"

But she had already closed her eyes and only smiled. Outside the wind ruffled the bleached-out grasses, and the birds in the white glare seemed almost transparent. The hull of the car gleamed beetle-like—dull and somehow sinister in its metallic isolation from the world around it.

Suddenly, the two cranes plunged upward, their great wings beating the air and their long graceful necks pointed like arrows toward the sun.

Patrick J. Murphy | THE FLOWER'S NOISELESS HUNGER,
THE TREE'S CLANDESTINE TIDE

There were roaches in the house. His
mother tried to explain them away.

"They're not roaches. They're palmetto
bugs. It doesn't mean the house is dirty."
And, of course, it didn't. The terrazzo
floor was bare and clean. But the palmetto bug was a roach. Albert had looked
it up in the school library. They were
definitely roaches.

"See?" He held up the book. "I was
right." But his mother wouldn't even
glance down at the page.

"You can't believe everything you read."

So, late at night, while the others slept,
Albert rose quietly and stepped through
the house, his fingers brushing pale walls,
to the kitchen. He waited for a moment
by the switch, then turned on the lights.
Some of the creatures were by the sink,

some on the floor. He watched the legs churning, the brown carapaces moving quickly until soon the counters were bare, the terrazzo undisturbed. Albert imagined the roaches hiding in darkness, peering out.

*   *   *

It was his first year in Junior High and the first year he walked to school alone. He had a backpack filled with his books and the plastic bag containing his lunch. It was still early and the heat just beginning. The houses around him were all the same, variations on three basic models. Their yards were covered in white sand, waiting for grass. The roads were straight, geometric constructions, and numbered sequentially. Albert walked, feeling the sweat beginning on his back and already sliding in drops down his chest. He watched the numbers pass.

He was in no hurry. The school he attended was new and constructed of raw concrete. The halls were crowded and the students rushed from class to class driven by the sound of bells. The teachers were only present for fifty minutes and then gone. The other boys were larger and violent and sometimes waited until gym, sometimes not. He tried to avoid them, going each time a different way, staying with groups, becoming nearly invisible.

When Albert thought about it, there was nothing about school he liked. He wanted everything back the way it had been—thirty students he knew well in one class that stayed together the entire day.

At sixty-third street he crossed the canal, a broad, straight swath of water running to the next major street, where it dived into a culvert and reappeared on the other side. The entire southern section of the state was crisscrossed with such canals, part of a drainage system feeding into the Everglades.

Albert stood on the bridge for awhile, staring at the lightly ruffled water, the rocks piled to either side. He imagined himself in a canoe like the Seminoles had used, drifting down to be lost at last in the wild tangle.

Two days ago, he had ridden on his bike to the Everglades' edge. It wasn't far, as each new development was built on its ever-receding border. There had been asphalt streets coming to a sudden end and only the canals continuing, accompanied by a straight white road of coral rock, rutted from rain.

He avoided the deeper ruts, and watched the canal gradually broaden. Scrub grew on its banks and finally small trees: pond apple, guava, wild cherry. The white gravel disappeared, replaced by a darker earth. Snakes slid out of sight. Vultures flew in windswept arcs against the blue sky. Cloud towers piled on the horizon. Occasionally, one dirt road intersected another, and Albert pictured a grid of roads all ending up in the trackless Everglades.

He followed the canal until that, too, disappeared, becoming a flat sheet of uncontrolled water drifting past islands of sand and trees. Lilies grew in rafts and moved with the wind on the surface and sank roots down. Alligator gar and mud fish swam the middle depths.

Albert watched. The heat and the wide sky and the clear water seemed to drug him. He felt sleepy and yet fully alert. He imagined Seminoles poling their canoes between the islands, disappearing into the green tunnels between the trees.

At seventy-second street he met a few of the others, a gradually gathering group. Some of the students had already made friends and shouted greetings or pushed one another roughly. Albert tried to remember if there was anything he had forgotten. Assigned homework, upcoming tests. He didn't know why he had a hard time keeping track. Other kids always seemed more prepared, though he knew they weren't any smarter. There was a secret, he thought, that he alone was never told.

The halls were loud and lined with lockers and somehow damp. He drifted with the crowd, mostly larger and taller, keeping an eye out for a few of the boys he knew would cause him trouble. He climbed to the third floor and then down to the second and slipped just before the bell into his homeroom class. He took his usual seat near the back. He sat and looked out the window at the roofs of the houses in the distance and beyond them the pale grayness of the Everglades.

*   *   *

His mother was talking again. "I don't see why everything has to be so obscene." She was glancing through the movie section of the paper.

His father sat on the couch, smoking a cigarette. He was a roofer and had been to Vietnam. Albert wondered what he'd been like during the wildness of the war.

"It's not bad enough they have violence," his mother said. "But the language they use. I don't understand who they're trying to appeal to. Do they think they'll sell more tickets, just because they use dirty words?"

"I don't know," his father said. "You'll have to ask them."

She smiled bitterly. "The next time I see a producer, I'll mention it."

Albert was trying to watch cartoons. They were too young for him, but they were all that was on. Mutants with super powers battled the transforming heroes. What he really wanted was to be in his room, but his mother thought he should spend more time with the family.

"You have to learn the social skills. You don't want to grow up to be a hermit, do you?"

Actually, when he thought about it, the idea seemed rather nice. A little shack on an island out near the Keys, surrounded by water stretching to empty horizons. A small rowboat for fishing. Traps for crabs and lobster. The night filled with stars. One boy against it all, surviving by his wits.

He lay on the floor, the terrazzo cold against his stomach, and watched television. Under the legs of the sofa, out of sight of his parents, a spider moved complicatedly to the wall.

"I just don't understand these people."

His father blew smoke at the ceiling.

*   *   *

That Saturday he bolted his lunch and grabbed his bicycle.

"Where are you going?" his mother asked.

"For a ride," he shouted back, already gone, disappearing down the street. He imagined himself becoming smaller and smaller until he vanished from her sight.

He followed the road out, putting all the identical houses on their uninterrupted white sand behind him, heading into the plastic center of the state. He hit the coral rock ruts with a feeling of freedom. At last. And then stopped. Sawhorses and cones blocked the road and heavy earth-moving equipment waited nearby.

There were other roads. He went around the construction, traveling south, until he found another canal, and then followed it, watching it widen, overspilling one bank and forming inlets and shadowed nooks. Fish drew circles on the still water. The sky was distant and pale. An old refrigerator, pocked with bullet holes and partially covered with vines, sat at the side of the road and beside it lay the body of a water moccasin, the head neatly lopped. Albert stopped and stared. His breath quickened. There was danger.

He continued and discovered that this road was washed out in spots. As he carried his bicycle down the embankment and across the water and back up the other side, his excitement increased. No car could follow him now. He was on his own.

The road narrowed. The scrub closed in from each side and there were times when Albert could no longer see the water. All that remained were green leaves and tangled stems and small insects hovering in swarms. He pictured himself lost in the swamps, forced to live like a pioneer. He imagined pushing through a cluster of trees and finding the last of the Seminoles. They would adopt him and raise him as one of their own.

The canal reappeared, become nearly a lake. Albert found a clear spot, a crumble of rock weakly overgrown by vines and moss and shaded by a tree. He sat and watched the water. A snake swam by, drawing sinuous lines on the surface. A white heron landed thirty feet away and walked through the shallows, intently looking near its feet.

It was all like this before, Albert thought, and wished away the developments and the cars and the people. A hundred years ago it was the same. A land of water and birds and fish. Albert imagined how it might have been.

★   ★   ★

The weather changed. The temperature dropped. A single storm passed, trailing from a light gray cloud. The sky became dry and more distant. Albert stood in the front yard and watched it approach. The sun still shone, but the rain was a curtain drawing closer. He waited. The rain approached the houses across the street, darkening their colors. Each drop made craters in the white sand. It was coming. It was coming. And then there were no more drops, but sheets of struck silver. Albert waited and the rain intensified, beating against the street and bouncing up. A breeze started, cold and damp. It was so close. He felt he could almost touch it. He waited for the deluge, the sudden shocking change from dry to soaked, but then the rain retreated, drawing back and moving away. He stood, expectant, and watched it disappear.

*   *   *

Mona, the next-door neighbor, was painting her toes again. She sat on a chaise lounge with a drink beside her. She wore a t-shirt without sleeves and a pair of shorts ripped out at the sides. Albert liked to talk to her, he wasn't sure why. Their conversations were filled with pauses and silence.

"How's it going?"

She looked up from her toes. There seemed to be so much of her, more than he remembered. She smiled. "Okay."

He watched her work. The brush held so delicately. The toes waggling, the leg bent and reaching up and up, until he saw the white edges of her panties showing from the bottom of her shorts. The sun beat on his back. The heat dropped down. The white sand spread everywhere.

"Albert!" his mother called. He didn't want to leave.

"I think I have to go."

Mona waved with her free hand. "Anytime."

He thought about that. She seemed to like him.

"What were you doing?" His mother's face was twisted.

"I wasn't doing anything."

"What were you doing? What were you doing?"

They talked about it that night at dinner.

"I don't think you should go over there anymore." His mother appeared closed off, somehow. She looked away as she spoke.

His father stared at his plate and ate.

"Why not?" Albert wanted to see her again.

"I don't think she's a good influence. I don't think she's a person we should associate with."

Albert thought she was nice.

"You never know what's going on over there. It could be anything." He tried to imagine what that might be. "Mom." He knew he was whining. He couldn't help himself.

His father looked up from his plate. "You heard your mother. That's all there is to it." But his glance seemed to say something else, something Albert didn't understand.

*　　*　　*

Osceola had been the King of the Seminoles. Albert was reading about him. He lay on his bed and imagined General Dade and the troops marching down the state, looking for war, but finding only swamp. The Indians snuck out at night and killed the soldiers. They laid traps. They fired their arrows and ran. Dade had followed them into the Everglades and simply disappeared. Five thousand men swallowed up into death.

Albert heard that the Indians had stripped their captives and tied them to the trunk of a tree in a mosquito bog and left them overnight. In the morning, the prisoners would be dead, all of their blood drained out, nothing remaining but white shrunken bodies. Albert imagined dying that way, the clouds of mosquitoes settling like a blanket on the helpless, struggling skin.

*　　*　　*

Relatives were visiting, arriving in three sets of cars. The space in front of the house grew crowded. An aunt, an uncle, two grown cousins.

"You have to be nice," his mother said. "You have to live with others in this world, you know."

All he'd wanted was to stay in his room. Mona was outside again. He could see her from his bedroom window. "They won't mind," he said. And knew they probably wouldn't. "Tell them I'm studying."

But his mother insisted. "They want to see you."

His uncle worked in auto parts and complained about the Cubans. His cousins didn't work at all. His aunt never seemed pleased.

The adults talked. There was nothing for him to do. He was upset and angry. He lay on the floor with his chin in his hands, staring at the TV, as if it were on. He'd watch it anyway, he thought. In the darkened screen, he saw their reflections. His father laughing with his uncle. His mother chatting with his aunt. It seemed so strange, seeing them all like that, on TV.

*   *   *

They were going to the mall. "You have to get out of the house, sometime," his mother had said.

He didn't want to go. He felt stupid, following his parents from store to store. He looked out the window as they drove. They were traveling south. They passed the canal and the rock road, and he noticed that this one, too, was now blocked off. In the neighboring fields, there were tiny red plastic pennants marking off the lots. A billboard with a picture of a house stood at the corner. He looked past it all to the empty sky.

*   *   *

His parents were talking. Welfare mothers were destroying the country. Everyone was getting something for free. The Cubans were running things as they wished.

"We let them into the country," his mother said. "We took them in. We supported them for years and what the hell do they do? They take over, as if they owned the place."

"They do." His father was browsing through a magazine. There were boats on the cover and girls in swimsuits.

"They do what?"

"They own the place. They bought it. That's the American way."

His mother stood, climbing up from the couch in her anger. "With our money. With money we earned and saved and then just gave to them."

His father looked up and smiled. As if it all were somehow funny.

*   *   *

Albert built a trap in the back yard, digging a hole in the earth. He
placed sharp sticks at the bottom, pointing up, and then covered it
with a thin sheet of paper. He sprinkled white sand over the paper and
looked at the spot. He adjusted the length of the sticks until the paper
rested at the same level as the rest of the yard, indistinguishable. He
imagined his parents walking out back, his mother hanging laundry
on the clothesline, his father catching the sun. Albert tested it himself, putting his weight down until the stakes began poking through to
the sole of his shoe. He left it like that for two full days, and only then
filled it in.

Louis Phillips IN THE HOUSE OF
SIMPLE SENTENCES

Sentence number one: *We, in spite of
nightmares, still fall asleep.* Variations on
that sentence include:

1. In spite of nightmares we fall asleep
   still.
2. We fall asleep still in spite of nightmares.
3. Still we fall asleep in spite of nightmares.
4. In spite of nightmares, still we fall
   asleep.

And so forth. I had not fallen asleep, but
I could have sworn that the old man sitting across from me had said, "I am God."
Yes, he had said it all right. Out loud. Everybody heard him, and that included
four or five women, two men, myself, and
Cappy, who owned and worked behind

the counter of Cap's Café. The man who had said it was seventy or eighty years old, had a beard, a mane of white hair, a black coat that hung to his ankles, and a ragged pair of pants, capped with a flowered sport shirt. Cappy insisted that the old man was a bum. I, all of eleven at the time, was not so certain.

Two women sipping coffee at the lunch counter didn't look up. They went on drinking, smoking their cigarettes, and talking as if nothing had happened. I sat across from the old man at one of the tables. Every day, after school, I came into Cap's place to sweep up and run errands. Cappy didn't pay much, but it was work. Besides, Cappy was a good guy. Everybody liked him. He had a humped back and he wasn't any taller than I was. He liked to play games, and I was good at checkers and chess. When business was slack, Cappy and I played games, and he tried to tell me about women. I was very interested in women. Even when I was sitting across from the man who said he was God, I tried to listen to what the women were saying.

★   ★   ★

Sentence number two: *The ocean behind me had turned dark brown, almost black.* The ocean smelled like the coat of Zeus, for Zeus was the old man's name. He repeated it three times and spelled it out, letter by letter, as if there were any other way to spell it, while I wrote it on a napkin. ZEUS.

But what ocean was it? Was it a real ocean? Or was it an ocean that existed only in the mind's geography? I woke up thinking that the ocean was making a terrible pounding sound. I thought how awful for the ocean to turn such an unnatural color. It cannot be a good omen.

Outside the café the Florida sky had also turned black. The sky matched the ocean of my dreams. The old man, clinging to his cup of free coffee, said, "I am the thrower of lightning bolts."

I thought I should ask Zeus: How can you throw the lightning bolts when you are sitting in Cap's Café?

But I did not ask him the question. Instead I told him my dreams. It was a mistake.

The woman at the counter, the one smoking cigarettes with her friend, was named Hilda. She worked at a shop called The Corset Box. She told her friend, "You know there are Jews who actually put flowers on Hitler's grave?"

"I don't believe it," her friend said.

"It's true." The woman blew out smoke rings, and the circles fell into one another.

"I think I had better get back to the shop before it rains," the second woman said.

"I know somebody who actually did it," Hilda insisted. She opened her red pocketbook and searched for some change to leave on the counter.

"Why?"

"They wanted to show how magnanimous they are. I think they're sick. They ought to be shot."

"The whole world is sick," Hilda's friend said. She stood up and pulled at her skirt. Her slip had been showing.

I thought: someday I am going to know more about the world. To dream of a dark and choppy ocean, Zeus said, means that the dreamer needs supreme courage for events that lie ahead.

Yes, I thought, I need courage for the events that lie ahead. Cappy sat in front of the counter and sipped coffee. He was wearing his apron. Otherwise he would have been mistaken for one of the customers. He sat with his back toward Zeus. Cappy had no use for gods. It was God who had given him the hump on his back. Maybe the women loved him all the same, I thought.

The women went outside where it was starting to rain.

"Who's the woman in the red dress?" Zeus asked.

"Hilda," I told him.

"What's her last name?"

"Aronoff."

"I'd like to lay her," Zeus said. He grinned at me. His teeth were very crooked, very yellow. But what did teeth have to do with gods? He didn't look like a god. He looked like a drawing in my first-grade primer. "I didn't mean to shock you," he said.

"You didn't," I lied. I was eleven, but I was a very stupid eleven, even though I was my school's spelling champ. In a few days I was scheduled to go to the county spelling bee. If you won the county and then won the state, you got a free trip to Washington.

*  *  *

Combining sentences we get: *Because I had no courage, the sea behind me had turned dark brown, almost black.*

My father is walking along the beach. He tells me about a woman he knows in a pink trailer. The pink trailer is at the end of the beach. The woman in the pink trailer owns a horse, a black horse. The black horse has slammed my father's right hand against the trailer door and has broken it. It, the hand. My father says, "The horse has broken my hand." He speaks to me as if I were a small child. But this is many years later when I am an old man myself.

Question. Not a sentence. *Who lives in that trailer if it is not my mother?*

When Cap's Café closes at six o'clock, my mother will pick me up to take me home. I want Zeus to leave before then. I do not want Zeus to meet my mother.

Suppose the ocean is life, as it often is. Often it is. Often I could walk down a narrow street between a tight row of white houses. At the end of the street is the ocean. It is dark green. Not brown. Not black. But the ocean smells like the rags of Zeus. Because I have no courage, the ocean is not green. Because I have no courage, the ocean smells foul.

"My wife, Hera, died a long time ago," Zeus says. He pours spoonful after spoonful of sugar in his mug. I do not understand how he can drink anything that sweet.

"If your wife is a goddess how can she die?" Cappy asks, but Cappy does not turn around to ask his question. He sits with his back to the god.

"Gods die," Zeus insists. "Gods die all the time. I died a couple of times myself, when people forgot all about me. But I've got staying power. I live on another planet and only every once in a while I return to Earth. I like walking the earth, going to and fro upon it. Everything about the earth—its oceans, its mountains, its animals—reminds me who I am. You, son, are fortunate. You can grow and change. Gods cannot grow, gods cannot change. I always am whatever I was. But you can become something else. And you will."

"Pop, drink your coffee and go," Cappy says, still not looking at the man. Cappy is in his late forties, about as old as my father, and he has seen a lot of characters come and go. Cappy himself is a character, but I never once heard him claim that he was a god.

"How do I know you're a god?" I ask the man, staring into his clear-blue eyes. Everything about Zeus is old, except his eyes.

"You don't want me to prove that, son," Zeus says.

"Why not?"

"Because it means somebody has to die."

"If you are a god," I ask him, watching the storm through the plate-glass window, "can you go anywhere you wish to go?"

Zeus shakes his head.

"Why not?"

"Because I have my own destiny to contend with. I can control anything, but I cannot control the Fates."

I don't know what the old man is talking about, but I don't ask him. I want him to go away.

"Jesus," Cappy says. "Why don't you get out of here before I call the cops." I know what's bothering Cappy. People like Zeus drive away customers. But nobody's going to come out in the rain.

"It's pouring out," Zeus says. He thrusts his cup and saucer in my direction and winks. He wants a refill. I go get him a refill. Cappy looks at me with hatred.

"It's raining," I tell him.

"Everybody's got an excuse," Cappy says. "Especially God. He's got the most excuses of all."

When I bring Zeus the cup of coffee, he says: "Beware of scorpions. Florida's filled with scorpions, isn't it."

"Some parts of it are, I guess."

"That woman Hilda is as beautiful as a swan," Zeus says. "I think I'll go look her up."

"Why don't you do that," Cappy says. "See if she gives you the time of day."

I know something that Zeus doesn't. Cappy's got a crush on Hilda himself, but he doesn't have the nerve to do anything about it. Hilda's pretty down-to-earth and she always has a snappy answer.

I think: if he's a god, why doesn't he fly? Why doesn't he float in the air, surrounded by flames? If he is Zeus, as he claims, why does he sit at a small table in Cap's Café, hunched over a white mug of coffee like an old man waiting to die? Finally he stands up and leaves. He walks out into the rain as if it is nothing at all. Good riddance to bad rubbish, Cappy says. He doesn't really mean it, but he says it anyway. It makes him feel good.

★   ★   ★

I live in the house of simple sentences. Nobody at home talks much, so I don't tell them about Zeus. My parents wouldn't know what to make of it. I feel that religion should change with the times. My father feels that religion should never change. If it is the Truth, how can it change? We have terrible shouting arguments about it. It is the Greek style. We have a lot of feelings, but we do not know what to do with them.

★   ★   ★

Every Saturday morning at Cap's Café, the cops—at least the three who ride the horses through the main street of town—drop in for free breakfast. I finally understand why I get paid so little for my work. Cap gives everything away. Actually, I am underage. Cap has to pretend that I really am not working for him. Everybody else, however, knows the truth. Even the cops.

One is a lieutenant. The other two men don't have any stripes. They are young, and the youngest of the three is a blond-haired man named Honninger. When the three patrolmen sit down, their gun holsters hang over the sides of the tiny red stools. Their guns, their handcuffs, the bullets in the wide belts, their brown leather jackets—it all speaks of authority.

"Who is that old guy who goes around claiming he's God?" Honninger asks. I don't get to answer, because Cappy, clapping platters down on the yellow formica counter, tells him: "Arrest the old geezer the next time you see him. It's for his own good. He's as looney as they come. He's not playing with a full deck. He ought to be up in Chattahoochee with the rest of the clowns. It's for his own good." I figured that out myself, he tells me. "The reason God came to Florida is not because he needs a vacation, but because he wants to be close to Chattahoochee."

Chattahoochee is where they send the insane. My parents and I had passed the place a couple of times during our drives across the state. The people inside the asylum wear straitjackets and talk in sentences nobody understands. It's a standing joke in all the families in Florida.

Honninger's left hand is thickly bandaged. He cut himself disarming a robber. "Funny thing about that old geezer," he says. "I saw his picture in the paper a few weeks back. I could swear he's the same guy in that three-car pileup on U.S. 1. When they rushed him to the hospital he was DOA."

"What's DOA?" I ask.

"Dead on Arrival. Like these eggs," the lieutenant says. He laughs at his own joke.

"Well, he's not dead now," Cappy says, sliding the ketchup bottles down to me. I stack them up by twos, mouth to mouth, so that the blood from one can run into the other. "He comes in here every night like clockwork, freeloads a meal, fills the kid's head with wild stories. He ought to be run out of town. It's for his own good."

"He doesn't come in here every night," I tell Cappy. "It's only every once in a while."

"Well, you're not the one buying him coffee, are you?" Cappy says. He smears the grill with cooking oil. Some days I wonder if I smell like onions myself. "Anyway he's costing me customers."

"You don't have customers," the lieutenant says, laughing. "All you have is people that come in here and eat. Only places that have table-cloths can claim customers."

"Maybe the old guy had a twin brother," Honninger adds. "Maybe it was his twin brother that was killed in the crash and maybe that's what drove him wacko."

"Maybe you ought to take up psychology," the third cop says. His name is Bill. I know all the cops in town. There aren't that many. I also have learned that the gods have brothers. Are brothers. Hades lives under the earth. Poseidon is god of the sea. But is it a real sea, or only a sea of the imagination? A tiny sea found at the end of a narrow lane.

"It's got to be his twin brother," Honninger insists. "Or else he died and came back to life."

"And maybe there are little green men on Mars," Bill says.

"The paper says another UFO has been sighted," Cappy says.

"Always a UFO sighting," the lieutenant sighs. "That's all the calls we get these days. I tell you the whole state is going off the deep end."

On Saturdays I put in a full eight-hour day. When I get off work, I see Zeus walking down the street with Hilda on his arm. It's weird, I think. But I won't tell Cappy. Cappy's feelings would be hurt.

Maybe it's a way of proving to me that he's a god.

\*　\*　\*

More sentences. The blood of one runs into the other. The wind is blowing the branches aside so that the moonlight can reach us. He would be hurt. He claims to be the captain of a ship. Hence, Cappy.

\*　\*　\*

Sentenced. A person is brought before the gods and is sentenced to live. But who sentenced the gods to live? That is the unaskable question. Many years later I dream that I am walking along the ocean at night. Out on the ocean is a series of screens. Motion picture screens. War movies are being shown. And science fiction films. Images are landing from another planet and the tide is washing them in and out.

Unidentified Flying Objects. And the waves are white. The sea beyond is black. Scorpion-black. A light shone on the darkness.

*   *   *

It is the week before Christmas. In Florida, Christmas does not stand out the way it does in the North where there is the possibility of snow. In the Catholic church, my mother and my sisters are listening to the priest read from the Gospel of John:

> In the beginning was the Word, and the Word was with God, and the Word was God. The same was in the beginning with God. All things were made by him; and without him was not any thing made that was made. In him was life; and the life was the light of men. And the light shineth in darkness; and the darkness comprehended it not.

I have stayed home with my father, for we are cleaning out the garage. When he leans over to pick up a rake from under a wheelbarrow, a scorpion scurries forth and stings my father on the thumb. My father, taken by surprise, straightens up, gives a cry of pain or surprise, a gift to the unknown, and leaps back. I watch the scorpion run down the rake handle, then onto the dirt floor. My father picks up a shovel and goes after it, pounding the insect into the ground. I tell my father to call the doctor, but I know what my father is thinking. Doctors cost money. He continues to clean out the garage as if nothing has happened. I watch his thumb swell.

When we go inside the house, my father takes a razor blade, cuts an X on his thumb, and sucks out the poison. But he's not feeling well. So he lies down to sleep.

I must find Zeus before it is too late.

1. I must find Zeus.
2. You must find Zeus.
3. We must find Zeus.
4. See Zeus change into a swan.
5. See Zeus carry away innocent victims.

6. Run, Jodie, run.
7. In the beginning was the Word and the Word was God.
8. See God.
9. See God die.

At the Catholic church, the Church of the Little Flower (was there anywhere in the world the Church of the Big Flower? the Huge Flower?), there is only the choir rehearsing for its program of Christmas music. I love the smell of a church. The smell of candle wax. The smell of the Holy Water. The stained-glass windows that comprehend the light. The choir singing:

O Magnum mysterium et admirabile sacramentum, ut animalia viderent Dominum natum, jacentem in presepio. O beata Virgo, cujus viscera meruerunt portare Dominum, Jesum Christum. Alleluia.

If God speaks to us, He speaks to us in dead tongues. I run into the church and I run out. I am looking for the wrong god in the wrong place. Even I know that, but I have the presence of mind to call Hilda. Hilda Aronoff. When she answers the phone, I tell her who I am and I ask if she can tell me where Zeus is.

"Try the park," she says. "That's where he usually sleeps it off."

And off I go to the tiny park with its bandshell and sundial. The sunlight falls across the flowers in such a way that it becomes Time. Is Time. The park is deserted. I am running through a world in which no one lives except when memory brings them alive. Even the policemen on horseback are nowhere to be found. Nothing is to be found but the light falling across the hibiscus. And at home, if my father is dreaming, what is he dreaming? *O Magnum mysterium.*

In front of the tiny bandshell, where soon people will be gathering to sing Christmas carols,

O come, all ye faithful,
Joyful and triumphant,
O come ye, O come ye to Bethlehem.
Come and behold Him,

Born the King of Angels:
O come, let us adore Him,
O come, let us adore Him,
O come, let us adore Him,
Christ, the Lord

are row after row of green wooden benches, and there in the very back lies the old man asleep, his grizzled face toward heaven. Come and behold Him. And the stench about him. And the flies crawling down his coat. I shake him. I shake him hard. "Mr. Zeus, wake up." But he will not wake. I pound on his chest with my fists. But nothing will open those eyes. There is a dried river of blood at the corner of his mouth. And in his hands is nothing.

"The scorpions. You warned me about the scorpions!" I cry. "You must do something."

I look at his hands. How swollen they are. How swollen his entire life has been.

And from the church, the bells are ringing their old familiar carols. What can any of us do, when the gods need as much help as we do?

Running back through town, I finally locate my friend Honninger. Honninger is flirting with a teenaged girl in front of the movie theater, and so he is not pleased to see me.

"Zeus is dead," I tell him. "He's in the park, near the bandshell, and he's dead."

"No, Jodie, he's not dead. He's just drunk."

"I tried to wake him up."

"Dead drunk."

"No," I tell him. "I know the difference. He wasn't breathing. There was blood coming out of the side of his mouth."

"For Christ's sake," Honninger says, holding his hands up to the sky. "That bum is more trouble than he's worth." The teenaged girl looks on with admiration, confusion, and fear. I want to fall in love. I want to tell her, Hey, I'm the spelling champ.

"All right, Kid," Honninger tells me. "I'll take care of it. It's nothing for you to worry about."

"I'll go with you," I tell him.

"No, you go home. It's nothing for you to get involved with." He mounts his horse. The sound of the heavy hooves on the road fills my heart with wonder.

At home, the house is filled with tragedy. Everyone is seated around the kitchen table and my mother's eyes are all teary. My grandmother has died. My father's mother. In the morning, my father must fly to Boston.

*   *   *

My father insists on going through a ninth-grade spelling book, and so we sit outside the house, sit in the front yard, where he calls out the words to me. There is very little light. I wonder how he sees. What is going through his mind with his mother dead? All those words waiting to be placed into sentences:

Extract
Carrion
Bereaved
Dynamo
Verbatim
Intrigue
Fossil

Letter by letter they are spelled. Word by word, sentence by sentence, we form our lives and speak our tenderness. Dreams we have, but they are not large enough. Perhaps they are large, but we are not large enough.

Is it possible to use all the above words in a single sentence?

*From the dynamo, I, bereaved, say verbatim I shall stoop to intrigue in order to extract fossil carrion.* Impossible? Perhaps. No doubt nonsense.

My father looks up from the spelling book and sees a strange light orbiting far off. It is not a star. It is not a planet. It is not a plane. My father points it out to me and we sit and study it for nearly twenty minutes. Long enough for me to get goose bumps.

"There's something funny about that light," my father suggests. My heart is in my throat and I begin to tremble. Perhaps I am just exhausted.

My life is an Unidentified Flying Object. I am looking at something in the sky, something very strange, something beyond our planet. It is my father's mental state objectified. He suggests that we go inside to call the police. I am terrified. My six-year-old sister is in the living room. She is howling with terror. She is hysterical. The thought of visitors from another planet is overwhelming. I cannot bring myself to go outside to look at the sky, with its strange whirrings.

When my father gets off the phone, he says: "I'm not the first to report it. They said that they got fifteen or twenty calls already. The air force is going to send up a plane to investigate." He pauses, and takes my sister into his arms.

"By the way," he says. "Honninger said for me to tell you not to send him on any more wild-goose chases."

"What goose chase?"

"I don't know. He just said it wasn't funny. You sent him to look for somebody who wasn't there."

"Wasn't there?"

"I'm just telling you what he said."

I do not understand and take my misunderstanding into another room, as I take them now into another life, where we, in spite of nightmares, still fall asleep.

"Summer is a dead season," the motel
owner says.

What tropic rampage of life around his
pastel pillboxes: scarlet hibiscus and
purple bougainvillea entwine with pale
clematis, innocent honeysuckle and Virginia creeper mingle with poisonous pink
oleander.

My mother's neighbor is waiting outside
in his sapphire Lincoln Continental. I
watch him from inside, here by the regis-
tration desk. He does not seem to notice
me. Perhaps he feels it indiscreet to be
observed leaving a motel with me. He was
kind enough to come here for me. He is
vain enough to comb his waxy silver hair
for me.

My brother took over my mother's
Volkswagen when he flew in this morning.

He is also not afraid to sleep in her bed tonight. This afternoon he is meeting with her lawyers.

The motel owner flips the Yellow Pages for the closest coffin store. His first time to look up this item. Also mine.

Finally, among Fruits & Vegetables (Wholesale), and Fuel Injection Systems, Fund-Raising Counselors, and Furs, we find numerous Funeral Directors. I write down six addresses, thank him, walk out to the car.

After the motel gloom, the sun is terribly bright, and I am warm in the black silk dress borrowed from my mother, or rather, her closet. Strangely, it fits.

My mother's neighbor gets out, shakes my hand solemnly, opens the other door for me. He squeezes my arm, as if to offer condolences, or something else.

We have talked long on my previous visits. Fortunately now he is saying he does not know what to say. I show him my list of addresses.

"Those are scattered all over the suburbs," he points out, "or in the seedier sections of town."

I think of certain foreign cities where one whole street, fragrant with pine shavings and incense, devotes itself to the craft, and funeral revelers gong full blast all across town so everyone knows and in some way shares in the celebration.

She would have shunned such exotic show, as well as funeral parlors.

Cold in the car, I roll down the window, welcome the heat which billows inside, licks the white leather seats with its stream.

"That doesn't help the air conditioning," he murmurs, leaning toward me. He keeps squeezing my hand.

"That doesn't help your driving," I murmur back.

He continues to career through the streets as if late for a wedding.

The first showroom stands among beauty parlors and package stores, used-car dealers and billiard halls, in a neighborhood my mother would not have frequented. Nor would my mother's neighbor. He is busy unfastening my seat belt with more than condolent warmth.

Terribly cold in the showroom. The salesman, large in a dark shiny suit with a faded carnation in the lapel, extols the value of velvet linings.

"But my mother hates velvet. Besides, velvet's too hot for this climate."

"Then rayon? Or satin? Or best of all silk, see how nicely striped—"

Like Grandmama's love seat, I think.

"Feel here," he says, "how soft this padding is—And see here, these handles are hinged for ease of pallbearing—"

I think how my brother and my mother's neighbor and her lawyer and maybe her dentist will all together give a jolly Heave ho, even a *Yo, heave ho*—

"And let's consider oak versus walnut—"

Or whatever wood lasts almost forever, and with age might improve.

"My mother insists on cremation. No point in sarcophagi at $4,995."

The salesman inhales. "For a dignified burial service—"

Distaste on his florid face. He doesn't want his coffins in the fire. He shows me the line in the catalogue that guarantees imperviousness to ground water.

No, as far as he knows, twenty years in the business, there are no reusable coffins.

My brother and I divided the chores: should I have left this one to him?

The salesman steers us from coffin to coffin. Each appears more substantial, more plush than the last. Some have handles of brass.

I remember the Mother's Day card of padded satin trimmed with pink lace I sent her once, in part as a joke, but also . . . It reached her in the midst of her myriad causes. She scribbled back on a plain pre-stamped post office card: *Why waste your money on kitsch?* I never sent her another.

In her sensible striped beige dress she is still lying cold back home until they come for her. My brother left the air-conditioning on HIGH. That will also keep the flowers from wilting.

She would be annoyed at the stiff bouquets. "Sympathy gifts," she often said, "should go for worthier purposes. And lilies are so depressing, gladioli rigid."

On the way home, we will surely pass a field or empty lot. I will gather her favorite daisies, as if for a bridal bouquet. I won't let them burn.

"Black is becoming to your fair skin." My mother's neighbor's whispers caress my hair. "But you're pale today beneath all those freckles. As soon as we've finished this business, I'll take you to lunch, feed you a juicy steak, or better, calves liver, washed down with good burgundy. You need extra protein and iron to carry you through this ordeal."

How my mother's neighbor sounds like my mother, except that she seldom served meat. It is she who lies terribly pale, back there, beneath her freckles of age.

"They'll fix her up nicely," the salesman is saying, "and a pink velvet lining will be most becoming. When the coffin rests open and you approach to kiss her, you'll note the fine workmanship under the lid."

Years since I've kissed my mother. When she was drinking, I couldn't even approach. Despite all her goodness . . .

I insist that $4,999 is too much. So is $3,999. Even $2,999.

"This coffin is only $2,955." The salesman plumps up the plush, "The Basic Package with Options."

The $2,955 Package lies at the back of the showroom. Brass handles like door knockers. Let me in, let me in, in the dead of the night.

"I know it's a difficult choice," murmurs my mother's neighbor. His fingertips trickle over my forearm. "Shall I help you, honey, make up your mind? And after the funeral is over, and your brother leaves, I'll find an excuse to take you for a few days to the beach . . ."

The salesman is distracted. His secretary, her coiffure glistening blond, helmet-stiff above her magenta blouse and black patterned slacks, needs him to sign several death certificates. He excuses himself, it'll just take a moment in his office.

Another door leads to a smaller showroom.

"Look over here," I tell my mother's neighbor, who is running his fingers over a gleaming Cadillac of a coffin near the front window. "Absolutely crammed with coffins back here."

Plain pine in the corner, and what feels like plywood pasted over with wallpaper, or self-sticking shelf paper, to simulate walnut bordered with teak. A smaller coffin, gold foil embossed with dancing lilies, sized for a child.

"Prices are much better here," I tell him. "And it's warmer, away from that air conditioner."

My mother's neighbor is wiping sweat from his neck with a large white handkerchief.

I finger the dacron paddings. Orange blossoms and pink roses, forget-me-nots, and here's one printed with blue anchors. I think of the long-ago pajamas, patterned with little green trains, my mother found at a church bazaar and gave to my brother for Christmas. He swore they were too large, then, before he had grown into them, he passed them on to me unworn.

The salesman hurries in. He looks embarrassed. His long arms try to shepherd us back toward the main salesroom. At the threshold he positions himself, arms folded, between the boxes and us.

"These coffins are for Latinos." His voice is low surf.

"But my mother was Latin." He looks with surprise at my blue eyes, death-white skin, tell-tale red hair. My mother's neighbor also looks astonished. Both perspire in the moist air that follows us from the back room.

"She was likewise Oriental and Black."

I point past them.

"I'll take—that one over there in the corner, daisies printed on oilcloth. My mother will be happy in that, and yes, I know it's plywood."

Think how well it will burn, I muse, and write him his check. Some question as to whether he will accept it.

Back in the icy Lincoln Continental, my mother's neighbor sits very tall, and does not take my hand.

**Enid Shomer** | TAKING NAMES

I'd never served on a jury before. In fact,
I hadn't been downtown for years—ever
since they built the Falling Waters Mall.
Stan assured me I'd have no trouble spotting the new courthouse. "It'll be the only
building with portholes over the en-
trance, he said, "like a big ship in dry
dock." He drove me to the kiss-and-ride,
and from there I took a bus.

The woman in the information booth
pointed me to an elevator before I got
close enough for her to hear my question.
Everyone got off at four and streamed
into the jury pool room.

I sat down and picked up an old copy
of *Life*. "Nine o'clock. Let's get going,"
a man at the microphone announced.
"Anybody here who can't serve this
week?" I leaned forward, thinking of Stan

alone at the farm with all the grafted trees that needed repotting. About fifty people stood up, waving their jury duty notices and talking. "Form a line," he ordered over the hubbub. I read about John Hinckley wanting to go home for Christmas until I heard the man's voice again. "Listen for your name," he said. A long scroll of computer printout spilled from his podium. "It's a punishable offense to be absent, so make sure I get you." As he went down the list, one by one people slumped back in their chairs, as if released from a magnet.

"Now you wait. When we need you, we'll call you. No leaving the room. You've got two TVs, books, cards, magazines, checkerboards, puzzles, restrooms, and a coffeepot."

The woman next to me had brought knitting—blue yarn with a silver fleck running through it that matched her tinted hair. Across from us, a group was forming to work a thousand-piece puzzle. "I'm good at finding the borders," I said, diving into the confetti-like mess. The box lid pictured an iceberg drifting at sundown, the colors of sky and sea nearly indistinguishable. Hard on the eyes but a good test of concentration.

A bell rang. "Williams, DeBaro, Feldman, Sanchez—that's Rosario—Gold, Eaugalle, Chesterton, Whelan, Eisenblatt, Samuels, Lattore, Jabotinsky, Wood, and Helms." He read the list rapidly, as if they were all one name. We congregated near the double doors. Then he led us like schoolkids across the marble hall.

The courtroom was beautiful, with dark walnut paneling and molding. I half-expected carved faces where the walls joined the high ceiling. The light was dim, and voices were muffled by thickly upholstered blue chairs.

The judge explained the procedures with great patience. He sounded like Johnny Cash and had a long, sallow face. "The victim was a young child, and some of the evidence is graphic." He looked at his hands forming a steeple on the bench in front of him. "It won't be pleasant," he cautioned, "but it's your duty." Two women behind me spoke up at the same instant. "I'm a grandmother," they said. "I couldn't stand it."

"We need grandmothers," he said. "Are you sure?"

They were both sure.

After we gave our addresses and occupations, two lawyers fired questions at us. Had we read about the case in the papers? Had we been abused as children? Did we know an abused child or abusive parent? More people were excused. Then we were removed to the jury room while they haggled over us.

"Helms," the bailiff read, then five more names and two alternates. So that was it. I had a case, a duty to perform, then home to Stan and the nursery where five hundred citrus trees were waiting to be repotted. Valencias and Parson Browns. Mineola tangelos and Satsumas. The grafts had taken well and were ready for two-gallon containers and new homes. It always pleased me to think of my trees taking root all over the country in climate zone 10.

Elvis Thornberry, the defendant, entered the room, accompanied by a guard and a washed-out-looking pregnant woman who sat behind him. The D.A. aligned his pad and pencil.

Elvis didn't look like the famous Elvis. He had sandy hair thin as seedlings and stooped shoulders. His chest caved in under a limp white shirt and brown polyester jacket. He was a man you'd never notice unless he held a gun to your head or saved your life.

The D.A. promised to present circumstantial evidence convincing enough to take us beyond a reasonable doubt. The public defender assured us that a crime without a witness was difficult to prove.

At lunch, I asked the knitter what was happening in the jury pool room. "Same as when you left," she told me. "The young ones are plugged into Walkmen. They might as well be on the moon." I turned to dump my sandwich wrapper. "Oh, a big bunch was called for a cocaine case, but most of them got excused. They're afraid to serve," she whispered. "I hear you can get a person's legs broke for under a hundred dollars these days." "Hmm," I said. I was glad that Elvis Thornberry didn't look like he had those kinds of connections.

"And," she went on, "I played solitaire for nearly an hour without a five of hearts." She spun the counting spool on her knitting needle and stuffed the yarn into her bag.

\*　　\*　　\*

Elvis, his wife, and their toddler, Elvis, Jr., lived in a truck on the beach for two months before they found a cheap rental in the Palm Breeze Trailer Court. Elvis told the authorities that the refrigerator had fallen on his little boy. But when the police checked, they found no dents in the floor where he said it landed. We studied pictures of the floor. The refrigerator was banked so deeply in the gummy linoleum that I was pretty sure Elvis had lied.

Next were the photos of Elvis, Jr., not as terrible as I had dreaded because he didn't look dead and there were no outward signs of violence. This, the coroner explained, was because he had been killed with a single blow, a blow named the knee-slam by child abuse experts. The killer had lifted three-year-old Elvis over his head like kindling and smashed the child's abdomen across his upraised knee. All the damage done in one stroke, irrevocable and irreparable. I remembered the citrus counties ravaged by the '84 freeze: 160,000 acres destroyed in Marion, Lake, Orange, Polk, Hillsborough, Osceola, Sumter, Pasco, and Hernando. Only the coastal groves like ours spared.

The prosecution rested. Then, without rising from his chair, the defense rested. Not one witness. During his closing argument, Elvis's lawyer leaned over the jury box banister, pleading that no man should be put behind bars for a lifetime on the basis of his kitchen floor. We retired to reach a verdict.

The first ballot was five guilty, one abstention from a young TV cameraman who didn't understand the difference between Murder Two and Manslaughter. The foreman read the definitions from a sheet the judge had provided.

The next vote was four guilty, two abstentions. The cameraman still didn't get it, he said, and now the woman next to him was confused by the legal jargon, too. We didn't know each other's names so the conversation was blunt. Comments were offered around the table without apology or explanation, like chips in a poker game. "Murder is more brutal, then?" the cameraman asked. "Yes," we said.

The next vote was unanimous for Murder Two. The foreman rang the buzzer, and we returned to the beautiful room. No one was in the gallery, now a place of doom for Elvis Thornberry. The silence was cold and penetrating, like the nights in the nursery before we light the smudge pots when a freeze threatens. Soon there would be fire and the falling and rising of voices and heartbeats.

The judge read the verdict and polled each of us individually, tying our names to the word "guilty" forever. We passed into the grandeur of public record.

Back in the jury pool room, smoke rings hung in the stale air like complicated nooses. The boss man crossed our names off his list and said we'd get our checks in ten days. "What about the sentencing?" I asked. "The judge takes care of that. You're finished," he said.

At home, I told Stan about the case. He said I should get it off my mind. "The trees," he said. "Think about the trees."

But I kept thinking of Elvis Thornberry and Elvis, Jr. Two weeks later I phoned the judge's chambers. "He got life," his secretary told me. "He was a convicted felon in Kentucky and Tennessee, but they couldn't tell you that."

"So he'll be there for as long as he lives?" I felt relieved.

"Oh no," she said, after putting me on hold. "Legally, he's eligible for parole in seven years, but His Honor recommended no hearings for at least fifteen."

Good, I thought. Maybe by then I'll have forgotten his name and his face. I turned to the latest citrus grower's bulletin, which reviews the major threats to citrus: hard freeze, Medfly, canker, Phytophthora foot and root rot, orange dog, and histeza, the only incurable virus. It attacks the bud union, the graft, the scion.

William Snyder, Jr. | THE FERDINAND MAGELLAN

One Saturday morning there was a ship
in my lake. I saw it through the mist. You
could hear the engines thumping and the
fush-fush of the screw. A ship. The bow
waves broke on the beach something
crazy. It must have missed my sign: "No
Wake." Just a joke for the neighbors.
There's never been as much as a five-
horse here. Lake's too small. The waves
from that ship were no joke. A Sunfish
was capsized and Smoltze's punt was
washed up. Dock three houses down was
splintered.

And the waves tore hell out of the
beach. Everybody's. Including mine.
Worst was, I'd paid a man to sand and
grade my strip not a month before. Lucky
the stern wake was rolling south. No
houses there.

166

Made some Folgers, poured my Honey Grahams, then sat on the patio and watched the sun come up. And watched the ship. The old anhinga that the wife and me named Rush stood in the yard. Watching, too. Went out front and got the *Sentinel*. No ship stories.

Called the sheriff. "Sure," they said, but said they'd send somebody. Went back out back. After a bit the wife called out about the Grahams were open.

The mist began to rise. The ship was big. Gray hull riding deep. Just an inch or two of the Plimsoll showed. Couldn't see a flag. Name on the bow said, *Ferdinand Magellan*.

Wife called, "Get the front. What's a sheriff doing here?"

Led him around back. "Son of a bitch," he said. "Where's he going?" He meant the ship.

"Don't know," I said.

The wife called out: "What's that doing here?"

"Don't know," I yelled in. "That's what I called the sheriff about. Any ideas?" I asked him.

"Nope," he said.

Johnson next door came over. Toting a shotgun.

"Can't do much with that," the deputy said. "It's gonna need the all of Fort Bragg or the Seventh."

"Or a miracle," Johnson said.

The lake's all retired. They were all out pretty soon, standing in backyards or on their docks. The ones still standing. Rush flew around to the south.

"What we got here is a ship," Edwards said. "Name of Ferdinand Magellan." Said the "g" like "maggot."

"Magellan," I said. "G, like jam."

"Mashellan, makshellan," he said. "What we got here is a ship in our lake. What are you going to do, chief?" He meant the deputy.

"I'll call the sheriff," the deputy said.

It did make a man wonder, how a ship could be steaming in the lake, making wake, goin' nowhere. Seemed like it would go aground on the north side at the Nashevits' and I could just see the hull come bulling up the beach, cleaving up their five-room. But it didn't.

I kept smoothing down my grass where people scuffed it up traipsing around. And kept watching my beach getting ruined. "Grandaddy shit," I said and slipped inside, then out the front. Walked around to the Nashevits,' untied his Sears and rowed. Nobody noticed. They kept pointing at the ship and traipsing.

Bow waves rolled up high. The Sears surfed 'em. Kept the oars out to steer. The ship looked like Orlando downtown. Sailors by the rail. Threw a rope. Caught it. Sailor pulled me into the boarding stairs. I grabbed the platform and crawled up and sailors helped.

One had blankets. One wore white and had a black bag. They un-hitched the Sears and set it loose. Dammit. It pipped and jogged away in the swells.

Up on deck the sailors cheered. That was funny. I waved and did a bow but they eased me down on a stretcher and covered me up with blankets. All I did was row out from the Nashevits'. All's I wanted was to get that ship the hell off the lake.

The man in white said, "We take you down for check."

"Check what?" I asked, but they carried me down and put me on a cot. "You may have exposure or shocks," he said. The only "shocks" I had was the ship and my beach. "Name?" he asked.

"Shingle, Wilfred Shingle."

"How long in boat?"

"Ten minutes." He looked in my mouth and ears, checked my pulse and what not. "Do you know where you are?" I asked.

"Twenty east, eighty-one west. Two days from Valparaiso."

"You're in Blue Lake, Florida, USA," I said.

"You must beg pardon," he said. "Not expecting guest."

"I wasn't planning on it either," I said.

"Will call soon for lunch," he said.

"Just had breakfast," I said. "Going to Shoney's for lunch. I'd like to see the captain." He led me up to the bridge. Through the port-side window I saw the wife, fifty, sixty yards away, milling with the people, pointing at the ship. Sheriff vans and a cruiser there, too.

The captain had gray hair. "Welcome to the Ferdinand Magellan," he said. "You are fortunate. There are no vessels within a hundred and thirty-one kilometers."

"I guess to hell not," I said.

"Sir?" he asked.

"Look," I said. "That's the wife. White shorts." He looked at me. "Well, look," I said. Then I yelled, waved, smacked the window, jumped and waved but the wife kept pointing and talking. "Where are you going?" I asked the captain.

"Through Panama and on to Hamburg."

"Grandaddy!"

The bow wake broke on the swells and whitecaps and the stern wake, a long, stirred-up white ribbon, stretched away aft. Then the wife fell away in the distance.

Abraham Verghese | TENSION

It is three in the morning. The coach is
awake and cold and shivering. He has
heard a sharp sound, like the report of a
rifle.

He knows what it is: one of the thirty
Donnay rackets he carries for his player
and that are stacked in the clothes closet
has imploded, collapsed in on itself from
the tremendous tension of the strings. It
is a familiar sound, but still, each time it
startles him, makes his heart race, more
so when it wakes him from sleep. He
looks around the room, as if the sound
still echoes in the corners.

He had asked other coaches whether
this ever happened to them and they had
looked at him strangely. It is only his
boy—he still thinks of him as a boy—

who wants his rackets strung at such an extraordinary tension, twice that of McEnroe. Ninety pounds means they are dancing on the edge of the tolerance of the wooden frame. It is difficult to find a stringer willing to work with such tension, to risk having it explode, sending projectiles of wood splinters and gut in his face. There is only one man in Sweden whom they trust.

Ninety pounds of tension makes the racket feel as stiff as a skillet, but it is what the boy wants. It suits his big, looping ground strokes, gives him a control and precision that no one in the world can match.

On several occasions, the rifle-crack sound has shattered the calm of a first-class cabin at thirty thousand feet, causing flight attendants to scream, drinks to be spilled, looks of panic to come over the faces of passengers. The boy never flinches or blinks when this happens. He sits, observing quietly, while the coach explains, pacifies, pulls out the frame from the bag and cuts out the strings before they warp the frame. If the frame is warped, they give it away as a souvenir.

Once the implosion happened in the customs lounge in Milan and instantly the machine-gun-bearing carabinieri surrounded them, muzzles raised. And the previous year in Britain, just before they stepped out of the locker room for a quarterfinal, the coach was double-checking the tension, holding the racket in one hand and slapping the heel of his other hand against the strings. The racket shattered and gut and wood wrapped around his wrist like a handcuff. "It must have been more than ninety pounds," the boy said, walking away, even as the coach tried to free himself.

*   *   *

He lies still, knowing he must get up, open the bag, and cut out the strings. The rackets are stacked on top of each other, like a fine china service in green chamois. He idly wonders if it is possible for one racket to snap and set off a chain reaction with the others inside the giant duffel bag. He tries to imagine that sound.

He searches the suite for the thermostat and, finding it, turns off the air conditioner.

He listens at the door that separates his room from the boy's; he thinks he hears something. The door opens softly and she stands there. He is embarrassed to be seen there in nothing but boxer shorts, as if he were eavesdropping. She too was awakened by the sound, has come to the door, and now looks at him as if he has some answer for her. He shrugs. She smiles, sadness in her smile. They both turn to look at the boy: He sleeps, facedown, his arms spanning the width of the bed, his head buried in the pillow, his blond hair tangled and covering his shoulder blades, his spine rising and falling slowly. Surely in sleep his heart beats even more slowly than its usual sixty or so a minute. Once in the press it was reported that his heart pulsed at thirty-six beats a minute. It has become perpetuated as a truism, quoted so much that no one would believe him if he disputed it. Thirty-six is an aberration. Perhaps it gets that slow in sleep. "Do you think he hears the sound in his dreams?" he whispers.

She thinks about this. She leans to his ear. "When he dreams, he concentrates on what he is dreaming about and ignores everything else."

It is the seriousness of her reply that makes him laugh, reach out and touch her on the shoulder, gently. Their communication is usually wordless, and their topic is almost always the boy. His touch tells her to go back to bed, to try to sleep. His communication with the boy is like that too. After years of traveling together they speak only when one of them is moved to. The girl has been with the boy for a few years—they are married now—and she has slipped into an orbit much like that of the coach. They are two satellites around the boy, the star. She and the coach have been sucked up, consumed by his needs. She has let her own career lapse, stopped competing on the women's tour. She had given up her ambitions in order to further his. It is perfectly reasonable, she is a talented player, but compared to him . . .

She closes the door and he thinks he hears the creak of the bed as she climbs back in with the boy.

*    *    *

He finds the racket and cuts out the strings. He checks the exact order of the rackets. The previous night he and the boy had held their "harpsichord recital"—her name for the ritual that goes like this: They lay out fifty rackets on the floor of the coach's room. The boy, a racket in each hand, taps the strings of one racket with the frame of the other. They both lean forward and listen intently. If necessary, he pings it again. Based on the pitch, he places the racket on one of two piles. When they are done, they go through the rackets that have made the cut, the ones whose sound resonates with some inner standard both coach and boy have memorized. They now rank the rackets: The first six will be used in that order and the order is never changed. If, during a match, a string breaks, the boy will walk to his bag and pick up the next one without a second thought. The racket whose string just snapped is the fourth racket. Tomorrow they will have to go through the remaining twenty-four rackets and pick a sixth.

He replaces the rackets and contemplates going back to bed, but he knows he will just toss and turn there. As he grows older, he sleeps less and less. It is, the doctor told him, tension. How many pounds? he wanted to ask. He declined pills because, for the most part, he wasn't tired from lack of sleep. But he misses the escape into sleep, he envies the way the boy rises from a chair, says good night, and falls on his face on the bed into deep sleep for ten hours. More and more he thinks of the boy as a perfectly balanced creature, put on earth for only one reason, to play tennis. Everything they do, from the vigorous massage the coach administers, to the meticulous watching of the boy's weight, is designed not to interfere with the symmetry of the body that allows it to play tennis the way it does. A few ounces too many or too few might change the balance, alter the delicate levers around the joints that allow him to hit the ball just so.

*    *    *

He slides open the door to the balcony and steps out of the icy room and leans against the railing. He almost chokes as the Florida air clogs his nose and throat, like a hot, wet rag. He can feel sea spray in the wind. His sweat glands are jarred awake. When he looks at his forearm, he can see a fine sheen of sweat forming underneath the hairs.

He sits without moving for three hours. The sea on this half-moon night is full of sound, like a creature that is awake and playfully trying to rouse the world. Nights like this, awake, he plays in his head with his invention, what has now become his obsession. He is consumed with an idea for a racket. He has a name for it already: the Protagon. The racket is strung in such a way that the main strings descend to a focal point within the shaft. Within the handle is a camshaft that allows the player to adjust the tension by turning a knob in the base of the handle. Once he mentioned this idea to the boy, who listened with detachment and mild curiosity, as though to say, Why do you even think of such things? Surely your life with me as my coach is a full life, yes?

Yes. His life as the boy's coach is a full life. Or, rather, he has no life of his own. He took up this life willingly In the process, he has become part of one of the greatest records in tennis history: five Wimbledon titles, six French Open titles. But he knows that the life is winding down. The boy's game isn't erratic or fading, but the boy, who can be out there all day and night, getting the ball back one more time till he wins, is bored. And then there is McEnroe. Thus far the boy has imposed his baseline game on others, like Connors, and even on McEnroe when he first appeared on the scene. The coach has ideas, ways to counter an ascendant McEnroe. The boy probably knows already what he needs to do. The coach can tell the boy is trying to decide simply if he *wants* to change his game, not if he can.

The coach isn't reluctant to give up the travel and the luxurious but stupefyingly monotonous hotels. It is a sybaritic existence that can fascinate only people who have just enough money to experience it occasionally. To live in such places year-round is to long for an uncarpeted floor, for a kitchen, for an overstuffed, worn armchair, for the familiar creak of a shed door. He will willingly unload the burden of making travel arrangements, scheduling practice time, lining up partners, timing meals before matches, enduring press conferences, meeting with sponsors, planning the calendar a year or two ahead. But, for the first time in their partnership, he has greater ambition for the boy than the boy has for himself. The U.S. Open title eludes them, as does the Australian Open. He does not want the boy to finish his career without winning all four Grand Slams at least once. But, he can sense that the boy is winding down. The other life—whatever is out there after tennis—is beckoning him. And when that moment comes, the coach will be silent, help him make his exit, stifle the arguments against retirement that even now he rehearses in his mind.

But the Protagon will be the coach's own legacy. It will be a record of his own, some tangible way in which his name will survive independently of that of his ward, be spoken separately from the boy's. A coach, in the sense of someone telling the boy how to play, had always been superfluous. There was nothing to tinker with in his game. His powers of concentration were awesome, and of his own creation. In an interview once the boy had said, "I try to reduce the game to its simplest level: I try to get the ball back over the net one more time than my opponent."

The adjustments the boy made for the grass of Wimbledon—a surface on which no one thought he could be dominant—he had made himself: He had worked on his serve; he had developed the backhand slice approach specifically to hit to Connors's forehand; he had worked on the drop volley, a shot that still looked so awkward when he executed it, but one that caused the ball to drop over the net and die, unanswerable. The coach was in reality a gofer, a valet, a masseur, a connoisseur of the boy's body.

The Protagon will not be a racket for a touring pro. Instead, he pictures someone out there, a club player, a man with some other profession—a doctor or a lawyer—who will benefit from this racket. He pictures this man going out to hit, and finding that nothing is going quite right. That his baseline tactics are not working. At this point the player can simply twist the grip on the racket, drop the tension five or ten pounds, and have the ball come off the racket like a trampoline, use it to serve and volley, use it to block service returns, dispense with much backswing on the ground strokes. The player could, in other words, emulate McEnroe.

Or, on a hot, muggy day, if the ground strokes seem to be working well, the owner of the racket can crank up the tension, convert it into a stiffer wand, use it to camp behind the baseline and take huge swings at the ball, give it topspin and loft, control, and, like the boy, pin his opponent behind the baseline—

He hears someone open the door between the two rooms. He hears the sound of a toilet flushing.

He gets up, stiff from sitting outside for so long.

He must look for the room-service menu.

It is time to order breakfast. And to pick another racket.

**Steve Watkins** | CRITTERWORLD

First the rumors.

No, Henry's Meats didn't come around with their knives to carve steaks from the body. Mutt & Jeff's Grill didn't serve elephant-burgers.

Nobody sawed off the feet for umbrella stands. Nobody caught any weird African diseases, no elephantiasis. The little girl from Michigan, the one who got trapped in the car, she might have seen a psychiatrist for awhile, but if she did it was back up North so I don't see how anybody could have known for sure about that story, true or not.

And the elephant's name wasn't Stash, like "trash." It was Stash, like in "lost."

But people will say anything, I know that now, especially in a little town like ours, and I guess the best thing is not to even listen, though I don't see how that's possible unless you go deaf. You could still do everything you wanted if you were deaf. You could even make great music, like Beethoven; you just wouldn't be able to hear it is all.

I told my mother that after what happened to Stash. My mother was the only one I talked to for a long time, maybe about a month. But she just hugged me and said, "Oh Charlie, do you know what? That Beethoven story is so sad it always makes me cry."

We were there when it happened, of course—me and Jun Morse and George Mabry—out by 301 a mile south of town, sitting in the ditch across the road, pretty well hidden behind the tall weeds and under the billboard that said "Critterworld, Florida's First Zoo" which I always thought was kind of a lie because it made you think *first ever* when it was really just the first you got to when you crossed the state line. Jun and George were doing their Advanced Geometry homework. We were all three in the accelerated class. In fact, we *were* the accelerated class. They drove us over to high school from eighth grade so we could sit in a room full of eleventh graders who tried to cheat off our tests. I liked it more than Jun and George, though, because I shared my book with this one girl named Sharla, who was a cheerleader but still pretty nice, and she would scoot her desk right next to mine and sometimes when we were both hunched over the book my elbow touched her boob but she didn't move and either didn't know or didn't mind, and I kept it there as long as I could until I lost all the feeling in my arm.

Anyway, the other guys were doing geometry and I was watching Stash when it happened. One minute he was standing there, this hundred-year-old elephant, not moving except for the ends of his flappy ears, and it might have been a breeze doing that. The next minute he seemed to sort of wobble. He lifted his chained leg, looked at it as if he'd just realized what they'd done to him, even though he'd been chained to that iron ring in front of Critterworld for as long as anybody could remember. He raised his trunk. He swung his head from side to side, made a noise that sounded like all the air rushing from his body, then fell sideways on top of the Volkswagen.

I stood straight up and stepped on George's homework. All I could think about at first was why did they park their car so close to Stash? The explanation later, the one the father of the little girl gave to the Jacksonville paper, was they didn't think Stash was alive. Stash was so still, and so dusty from standing there all those years by the highway, that they thought he was a statue of an elephant, like over in Weekee Wachi they have that brontosaurus that's really a gas station, or like out West my mother told me about a World's Biggest Prairie Dog.

Since there's nothing once you get south of town except scrub brush, slash pine, and Critterworld, and since the little girl's parents were inside the Critterworld snack shop, I was the first to hear her screaming inside the car. And initially I didn't believe it was somebody screaming, because Stash flattened the car so badly and I couldn't see how there could be anybody inside. George was yelling at me to get off his geometry homework, too, so that made it hard to hear anything else. George is just anal about his homework anyway—writes everything out on graph paper in this tiny block print that looks like a computer wrote it, which you might say is sort of the case, because when they did the eighth grade aptitude test it was old George Mabry that not only scored in the 99th percentile, but actually answered all the questions and didn't miss one. They announced it at an assembly. Jun and I and two girls were in the 90th percentile, but Jun—whose real name used to be John until he decided he needed to change it— told me all the tests really measured was your ability to take tests. Somehow to him that meant that being in the 90th or even the 99th percentile was, to use his favorite phrase, a meaningless abstraction, but I didn't see how it was meaningless since my whole life seemed to be about taking tests, so it was comforting to know I was good at it. When you make all As, you just figure they're grading on the curve and most of the kids in class aren't too smart, so your A is a relative thing, to use another one of Jun's favorite phrases. But when they rank you with the whole state of Florida, you have to figure there are some pretty smart people out there that you're up against.

Not that I ever felt as smart as Jun or George. Even though everybody lumped us together as the eggheads of junior high and all because of our grades and because we hung out together and because we played chess in home room, I always thought I was pulling something over on the teachers, working really, really hard to seem like I was as smart as them, when the truth was that I'm not actually all that intelligent. I said that to my mother after the time I got accused of cheating on a science test. A kid had told the teacher I looked on George's answer sheet, when all I was really doing was seeing how far along George was on the test, which of course was a lot further along than me. Nothing happened, though, because Mrs. Crow said she knew I would never cheat, and besides, what was that kid doing looking around during a test anyway? Still, I was pretty upset, and I told my mother I thought I was getting an ulcer from trying to pretend I was as smart as George and Jun.

What she said was, "Of course you're smart, Charlie. Just maybe not in the same way as your friends. You have an intuitive intelligence."

The funny thing was that nobody really cared if I was smart, or if Jun was, or if George was. I mean, teachers cared, and our parents cared, and George and Jun certainly cared about themselves. George already had a correspondence going with the registrar at M.I.T., and I'm not making that up. But other kids didn't care, and I only cared in a weird way because being smart, or pretending to be smart, was about the only thing I was good at. It was all I had. I couldn't play basketball, even though I worked at it all the time. I wasn't big enough or fast enough or strong enough. I didn't know how to talk to girls, except for smart girls about school subjects, and except for that cheerleader, Sharla, who talked to me sometimes about things, like the difference between dancing and dance. Dancing was what she loved to do; dance was what she wanted to study when she got to college. But she had a football-player boyfriend, and whenever she was with him I pretty much ceased to exist.

But there I was, anyway—to get back to the story—standing on George Mabry's graph paper, staring across the road, shaking my head to figure out if that really was somebody screaming. It was Jun who made the first move. He stood beside me and said, "Stash! Wow!" and then he said, "Squashed bug!" He grabbed my arm and we both ran across the highway to the car. George was too busy collecting his papers and books to come right away.

We could just see the little girl's face through what was left of the passenger door window; Stash had pretty much flattened the driver's side. The girl was flat on the floor of the car, screaming in a way that sounded more like squealing—like: "Hreeeee-hreeeee-hreeeee"— and I think it was as much to get her to stop as anything else that I started pushing like crazy against Stash to get him off the car. That's how stupid I was.

Jun ran inside Critterworld to get help. He told me later that when he came back out with the parents I was hitting Stash's head with my fists and yelling at him to get up, but that's not how I remember it. I just remember pushing and pushing, and dust rising off Stash in little puffs right in my face, and not really figuring out he was dead until the girl's father shoved me out of the way and I stepped back and looked into one of those big elephant eyes that was wide open but already dusted over, too. A dozen cars stopped, some of them right there in the highway, before the sheriffs finally showed up. The little girl had quit squealing by then—partly because she'd figured out she wasn't going to die, and partly because Jun got her a bottle of Coke from Critterworld and stuck about ten straws together into one long one to reach her mouth. The father yelled at Jun when he first brought it out, but the mother said, "Let the boy help, Clyde," and the father got a little nicer after that and they threaded the straw through a crack in what was left of the window and down to the girl trapped on the floor.

After that, Jun moved off a short ways from the crowd. He couldn't stand crowds. He told me once that he was an ascetic, and that there were two kinds: the ones that choose it, as a means to something, and the ones that are born to it, the ones like him. That was supposed to explain his aversion to crowds. At the time I didn't even know what he meant by *ascetic,* and when I looked it up I had the wrong spelling so I went around for a long time with the wrong definition in my head. I did the same thing with *cavalry* and *Calvary,* too, but that was in second grade.

I didn't want to leave Stash when Jun moved away. Everybody was so mad at him for dying and crushing the VW and trapping the little Michigan girl, I guess I felt like Stash needed somebody on his side, an advocate or something, even though he was dead. Not that I said anything to anybody. I laid my hand on the bottom of his foot, which was crusty because it was so old, but still not hard like you might expect, and I tried to remember everything I had read about elephants. The only line that came to me, though, was this one: "The powerful feet can trample an attacker into the ground, but are so softly cushioned that a whole herd of elephants can troop through a forest without making a sound."

George Mabry, meanwhile, wasn't having any problems remembering. He was over in front of the monkey cage where they kept the psycho-monkey that everybody flicked cigarette butts at, and he was lecturing some kids about elephant penises. For such a math-and-science nut, it's amazing how much George Mabry went in for the dirty stuff. He told those kids that an elephant's penis weighs sixty pounds, and it gets four feet long when the elephant gets aroused, and sometimes, if the elephant is chasing a cow, he might even step on it. And he told them about how the penis is shaped sort of like an S, and the muscles at the end work on their own to poke around under the cow's belly to find the hole, which is way up underneath, not right there between the hind legs.

For some reason it really bothered me that George was telling them all that. I knew it, too, of course—Jun had given both of us the same book to read—but George was just showing off how much he knew, and what a dirty mind he had. Those kids, though, they didn't deserve to know that stuff. They hadn't earned the right like we had. It didn't seem appropriate, or fair, or something, that they should get it so cheaply, and for a minute I hated George Mabry, standing there in his high-water pants and nerd glasses with that hair he never washed, trying to be cool with those elementary school kids, trying to be cool like I knew none of us would ever be cool, not him or me or even Jun who always knew what to say and never had to show it off like George the M.I.T. nerd.

I saw all of us in that second as these three very brainy but mostly very pathetic guys who didn't have any friends but one another, and even those friendships as a sort of last resort because nobody else would have us. I looked at Stash's old yellow tusks, or what was left of them since they'd been sawed off short before I ever knew him, and I looked down between his legs and saw just this shriveled worm of a penis, and I felt like crying and I felt like everything that had happened was my fault, as dumb as that may sound, but it was how I felt and in some ways how I still feel, no matter what my mother said later to cheer me up and no matter what sometimes I can think of to tell myself.

The girl was still trapped in the car, and the sheriffs, as it turned out, didn't have a clue for getting her free, and that's the way things stood for awhile, except for one thing I haven't mentioned yet, which is why Jun and George and I happened to be there in the first place, hiding out in the ditch across the highway from Critterworld. It was because we were studying old Stash and looking for a way to kill him ourselves.

⋆   ⋆   ⋆

Critterworld is the saddest place in Florida, maybe even in America. I only went inside once, and that was on a field trip in elementary school. Stash out front was so familiar to us that we hardly noticed him—all except Jun, who made a point of saying how much Stash disgusted him—and the psycho-monkey in the cage was already mean way back then from picking up lit cigarettes. When people came near he attacked the bars and tried to throw things, but for some reason he couldn't stop himself from picking up cigarette butts and burning his hands. All us kids crowded around the cage and teased him with monkey noises that day of the field trip, which frustrated him and made him crash wildly around, hurling himself at the bars as if he wanted to kill us, or kill himself trying.

Pay a dollar and you could go inside where they had the two-headed turtle collection, and the Siamese piglets disintegrating in a giant jar of formaldehyde. The whole place smelled of formaldehyde, as a matter of fact—that and the vomity smell of very old, very wet straw. There were the snakes, of course, and all the girls cried when they saw the white rat shivering in a corner of the aquarium where they kept the boa constrictor. And there was the bald eagle with the broken wing that hadn't healed right so it couldn't fly. And the albino squirrels, and the furry chinchillas, and the Shetland pony. In the petting area they kept a lamb and a goat and a calf and a live piglet and a goose, but Jun told me Critterworld sold them all for slaughter except the goose once they grew past the cute-baby stage. Nobody liked the goose because he bit kids.

Our first plan—or rather Jun's first plan—was to get rid of all of Critterworld, maybe burn it down, but we quickly dropped that because it was too ambitious. "And besides," Jun told us, "the point is not to draw attention to ourselves or to the deed."

"Then what is the point?" I asked him—this was in home room a couple of weeks before everything happened, and Jun and George were playing chess while we debated our course of action.

George put Jun in check just then and Jun glared at me as if it was my fault, but also as if to say, "We can't keep going over and over this for you, Charlie." He was mad at me for bringing it up again, but I was still having a hard time figuring out why it meant so much to Jun to kill something. I mean, I understood the reasons he said, but Jun seemed so obsessive. That was the word my mother used for it later, anyway, and she said she thought it had something to do with Jun's father, who used to be head of maintenance at the hospital but lost a lot of jobs because of drinking and now ran a service station north of town out by the interstate. That made a lot of sense in a Sigmund Freud kind of way, I guess, but somehow when you're in the middle of things it all seems a lot more complicated, and with Jun, who could talk me into just about anything if he talked long enough, I'm still not sure.

The point, as he had explained a hundred times, was to kill a thing that had compromised itself so much that it no longer had a self. Something that wasn't true to its nature. Jun started talking about "essence" like it was something you could put in your book bag or hide in your locker, and he said Stash represented all those things that had lost their essence, and that's why we had to do away with him. George, who liked the idea from the start—but from a purely scientific perspective, as he kept reminding us—suggested killing the psycho-monkey instead, but Jun got really mad about that and said didn't we understand anything, and said the monkey was the only animal at Critterworld worth living.

Jun had gotten the idea from a story we read in another advanced class on World Literature. It was that Japanese book, *The Sailor Who Fell From Grace With the Sea,* which I personally hated but which Jun read about ten times and carried with him everywhere like a bible. It was about a bunch of kids who dissected their cat because he didn't catch mice anymore, and later they dissected a sailor, I think because he was dating their mom. That was when Jun decided he was an ascetic, which he said made plenty of sense because his family was Catholic and the Catholics had an ascetic tradition of sitting in the desert and fasting and wearing hairshirts, and Jun said he saw a connection between that and the Japanese ascetics, which was what he said those kids were in the book, and he went on his own fast for purification which lasted a couple of days until he went to bed one night and slept through all of the next day and the next night, too, and his parents took him to the emergency room thinking it had something to do with his hemophilia. Jun said he had a visionary dream about knocking off Stash during his two-day sleep, and he convinced George and me to learn everything we could about elephants. He said we had to understand what Stash was supposed to be to experience the tragedy of what he was instead.

At first I went along because Jun was so persuasive, and because he said all we had to do was kill Stash, not dissect him. Plus it was usually easier to do what Jun wanted than to talk him out of it, and besides, he often lost interest in projects before we saw them through to the end. So we read the elephant book. We discussed elephant lore. We figured out that Stash was an African elephant rather than an Asian elephant—bigger ears—which I was happy about once I learned how they trained elephants to work in India which was to make a hole in the back of their skulls and poke inside the hole with an iron bar.

Studying Stash himself was my idea. We were having a hard time coming up with a way to kill him—George, in an uncharacteristically stupid moment, recommended dynamite; Jun said poison—and I suggested gathering first-hand data on the subject while we tried to figure it out. Jun agreed because, as he put it, we needed to become more elephant than the elephant. And of course the idea appealed to the scientist in George, who must have been the most empirical guy in the state.

So that's what we were doing when Stash died—or what I was doing. Jun just shrugged about it later and said it was coincidence; he said Stash saved us a lot of trouble by dying when he did, but something in his voice sounded false, and I wondered if maybe he wasn't more upset than he was letting on. His mother let him paint a St. George and the Dragon mural on his bedroom wall, which seemed to take his mind off ritual slaughter for awhile, and then we took up the Russians in that World Literature class and Jun decided to become a humanitarian. My mother believes in God, which means she has a stock answer for things that can't be explained, and I go to church with her every week thinking one day it will rub off on me, too. She said God was watching out for us by taking Stash, but I still have my doubts.

⋆　⋆　⋆

After two hours trapped in the VW under Stash the little girl started squealing again—"Hreeee, hreeee, hreeee"—and nothing her mother or her father said could get her to stop. The sheriffs were useless, talking on their radios, calling more and more sheriffs to come out. They tried pulling Stash off with a wrecker truck, but that didn't work, and they were afraid he might shift and crush the car worse if they jerked at him hard. Finally, though, Mr. Funderburke, the guy who owned Critterworld, got Steve's Sod Farm to send over three tractors and together they were able to drag Stash off the car. The welder burned the girl's arm with his blowtorch cutting through the metal, but just a little, just a spark, and the sheriffs took the whole family to a motel in town, compliments of Critterworld. Now the problem was what to do with the body. It became like a big joke there in the Critterworld parking lot: people saying, "How do you get rid of a dead elephant?" then cracking up, as if it was the funniest thing in the world. Stash must have weighed a couple of tons.

Woody Riser, the tree-service man, finally showed up with the biggest chain saw I've ever seen. He consulted with the sheriffs and with

Funderburke, then he lugged his chain saw over next to Stash. The sheriffs herded everybody back a ways—there must have been a hundred people by then, and more coming all the time—and they formed a line around the body. Woody Riser mixed gas and oil for his tank, slipped on his safety goggles, then pulled the cord. On the third pull it coughed around and caught, and the noise was so loud that the little kids covered their ears. He went for a leg first, aiming carefully just above the knee where the skin was taut, but I guess he should have checked how tough the flesh was because the chain saw kicked back on him and took a bite out of Woody Riser's own leg.

Things got a little crazy after that.

A couple of sheriffs put Woody Riser in their car and left for the hospital, and the rest of the sheriffs gave up on crowd control while they huddled with Funderburke to figure out what to try next. Right away people started pushing close to Stash. They all wanted to touch him, but some pulled out knives and poked at him with their blades. I saw a guy sawing at Stash's tail, and a couple of kids tugging on a tusk. Somebody else went for a piece of the ear.

George and Jun stood next to the psycho-monkey cage—the monkey had gotten hold of a cigar and they were watching him try to smoke it—but I didn't want to have anything to do with them for awhile. I wanted to leave, but I also wanted to stay, and it was about then that I saw Sharla, that cheerleader from my Advanced Geometry class, standing by herself at the edge of the crowd.

I went over to her and stood there for a couple of minutes before she noticed me. "Oh, hi, Charlie," she said. Her eyes were red from wanting to cry, but she hadn't cried yet. I tried to think of something to say back to her—something sensitive or clever—but nothing came except, "How's your geometry?" She didn't have a chance to answer, though, or to laugh in my face and tell me how stupid I was, because a couple of pickup trucks pulled into the crowd and a bunch of football players from the high school got out with axes. "Elephant Patrol!" they shouted. Everybody laughed except for me and Sharla, and the crowd pulled back to give the guys room to operate. Even the sheriffs seemed to think it was pretty funny, and they ignored Funderburke, who started yelling at them to stay away from Stash. "He can be stuffed," Funderburke kept saying. "He can be stuffed." Nobody listened.

"Isn't that your boyfriend?" I asked Sharla. I thought I recognized one of the football players.

"Oh, David wouldn't do that," Sharla said, obviously worried that David would. "He's just with them. He wouldn't—" One of the football players climbed onto the hood of his truck and shouted: "County High one time!" The crowd roared, and an axe ripped into Stash's side. "County High two times!" Another axe sliced the trunk. "County High three times!" Two football players—one of them Sharla's boyfriend—hacked at Stash's legs. "County High all the damn time!" They attacked.

It must have gone on for a long time, guys passing off the axes when they got tired, always somebody new to step in for a few whacks at Stash. A couple of people left, offended, but more came, and the Critterworld parking lot turned black with blood. I didn't see too much, though, because I followed Sharla across the highway where she sat and cried in the ditch where George and Jun and I had been.

I'd never seen a girl that upset before, and I didn't exactly know what to do, so I just patted her on the back like my mother used to do to me when I was little. I wanted to tell her that her sorry boyfriend didn't deserve her anyway, but that didn't seem quite appropriate even though it was true. She cried harder and harder, but nothing could block out the thwack of axes or the pep rally cheers as they worked over Stash in front of Critterworld. I heard the psycho-monkey screaming, too, and figured he'd gotten to the ash-end of his cigar, and then, after a long time, just about when I started thinking I should leave Sharla alone because I was probably just bugging her, sitting there patting on her like I was, she turned her face to my shoulder and she cried onto my t-shirt and I put both of my arms around her as far as they would reach, and we stayed like that for a while longer until it was all over and nearly dark and a couple of her girlfriends came looking for Sharla to give her a ride home.

She wiped her eyes and climbed into the car, and she said something to me through the back window, but they were already pulling away so I didn't catch it. Maybe it was just "Goodbye" or "See you in class," or maybe she just said my name. Pretty soon I was the only one left, sitting there in the ditch, except for Mr. Funderburke, who just stood in the parking lot like the broken man he was. The crowd was gone, the sheriffs, the football players with their axes, even George and Jun. I got up slowly and walked back across the road to get a last look at what was what. But now here's the really funny part: For all their chopping and their pep rally and everything, Stash was still there. Sure, he was cut to hell and bleeding everywhere, and his trunk and his tail were gone, and the ears were tattered and all like that, but he was still there. They could have swung their axes for another whole day and Stash would still have been there. Even dead he was too much elephant for them, and I wished Jun was there for me to show him, and to tell him that, and to make him understand.

They got those sod farm tractors back the next day and dragged Stash into a field behind Critterworld. They got a bulldozer and dug a big hole and dropped him in on a bed of wood soaked in gasoline. The fire lasted all night, and I got my mother to drive me out to see it. There were cars all up and down the road.

Some people say that Stash haunts that field now, that somebody stole his trunk and he looks for it on full moons, that passing motorists have seen him standing at 3 A.M. on his old spot in front of Critterworld. All that standard ghost story stuff. They even say that nothing will grow on the spot where Stash was cremated, but I guess you can write that off as rumor, too, because I've been out there a couple of times since and the grass is as green there as anywhere.

Joy Williams | THE BLUE MEN

Bomber Boyd, age thirteen, told his new
acquaintances that summer that his father had been executed by the state of
Florida for the murder of a sheriff's
deputy and his drug-sniffing German
shepherd.

"It's a bummer he killed the dog," a girl
said.

"Guns, chair, or lethal injection?" a boy
asked.

"Chair," Bomber said. He was sorry he
had mentioned the dog in the same
breath. The dog had definitely not been
necessary.

"Lethal injection is fascist, man; who
does lethal injection?" a small, fierce-look-
ing boy said.

"Florida, Florida, Florida," the girl murmured. "We went to Key West once. We

did sunset. We did Sloppy's. We bought conch-shell lamps with tiny plastic flamingos and palm trees inside lit up by tiny lights." The girl's hair was cut in a high Mohawk that rose at least half a foot in the air. She was pale, her skin flawless except for one pimple artfully flourishing above her full upper lip.

"Key West isn't Florida," a boy said.

There were six of them standing around, four boys and two girls. Bomber stood there with them, waiting.

\* \* \*

May was in her garden looking through a stack of a hundred photographs that her son and daughter-in-law had taken years before when they had visited Morocco. Bomber had been four at the time and May had taken care of him all that spring. There were pictures of camels, walled towns, tiled staircases, and large vats of colored dyes on rooftops. May turned the pictures methodically. There were men washing their heads in a marble ablutions basin. On a dusty road there was the largest pile of carrots May had ever seen. May had been through the photographs many many times. She slowly approached the one that never ceased to trouble her, a picture of her child in the city of Fez. He wore khaki pants and a polo shirt and was squatting beside a blanket upon which teeth were arranged. It had been explained to May that there were many self-styled dentists in Morocco who pulled teeth and then arranged them on plates and sold them. In the photograph, her son looked healthy, muscular, and curious, but there was something unfamiliar about his face. It had begun there, May thought, somehow. She put the photographs down and picked up a collection of postcards from that time, most of them addressed to Bomber. May held one close to her eyes. Men in blue burnouses lounged against their camels, the desert wilderness behind them. On the back was written, *The blue men! We wanted so much to see them but we never did.*

\* \* \*

May and Bomber were trying out their life together in a new town. They had only each other, for Bomber's mother was resting in California, where she would probably be resting for quite some time, and

May's husband Harold was dead. In the new town, which was on an island, May had bought a house and planted a pretty little flower garden. She had two big rooms upstairs that she rented out by the week to tourists. One was in yellow and one was in gray. May liked to listen to the voices in the rooms, but as a rule her tourists didn't say much. Actually, she strained to hear at times. She was not listening for sounds of love, of course. The sounds of love were not what mattered, after all.

Once, as she was standing in the upstairs hallway, polishing a small table there, her husband's last words had returned to her. Whether they had been spoken again by someone in the room, either in the gray room or the yellow room, she did not quite know, but there they were. *That doctor is so stuck on himself* . . . the same words as Harold's very last ones.

The tourists would gather seashells and then leave them behind when they left. They left them on the bureaus and on the windowsills and May would pick them up and take them back to the beach. At night when she could not sleep she would walk downtown to a bar where the young people danced called the Lucky Kittens and have a glass of beer. The Lucky Kittens was a loud and careless place where there was dancing all night long. May sat alone at a table near the door, an old lady, dignified and out of place.

*   *   *

Bomber was down at the dock, watching tourists arrive on the ferry. The tourists were grinning, and ready for anything, they thought. Two boys were playing catch with a tennis ball on the pier, a young boy and an older one in a college sweatshirt. The younger one sidled back and forth close to the pier's edge, catching in both hands the high, lobbed throws the other boy threw. The water was high and dark and flecked with oil and they were both laughing like lunatics. Bomber believed they were brothers and he enjoyed watching them.

A girl moved languidly across the dock toward him. She was the pale girl with the perfect pimple and she touched it delicately as she walked. Her shaved temples had a slight sheen of baby powder on them. Her name was Edith.

"I've been thinking," Edith said, "and I think that what they should do, like, a gesture is enough. Like for murderers they could make them wear black all the time. They could walk around but they'd have to be always in black and they'd have to wear a mask of some sort."

Sometimes Bomber thought of what had happened to his father as an operation. It was an operation they had performed. "A mask," he said. "Hey." He crossed his arms tight across his chest. He thought Edith's long, pale face beautiful.

She nodded. "A mask," she said. "Something really amazing."

"But that wouldn't be enough, would it?" Bomber asked.

"They wouldn't be able to take it off," Edith said. "There'd be no way." There was a pale vein on her temple, curving like a piece of string. "We didn't believe what you told us, you know," she said. "There was this kid, his name was Alex, and he had a boat. And he said he took this girl water-skiing he didn't like, and they were water-skiing in this little cove where swans were and he steered her right in the middle of the swans and she just creamed them, but he wasn't telling the truth. He's such a loser."

"Which one's Alex?" Bomber asked.

"Oh, he's around," Edith said.

They were silent as the passengers from the ferry eddied around them. They watched the two boys playing catch, the younger one darting from side to side, never looking backward to calculate the space, his eyes only on the softly slowly falling ball released from his brother's hand.

"That's nice, isn't it?" Edith said. "That little kid is so trusting it's kind of holy, but if his trust were misplaced it would really be holy."

Bomber wanted to touch the vein, the pimple, the shock of dark, waxed hair, but he stood motionless, slouched in his clothes. "Yeah," he said.

"Like, you know, if he fell in," Edith said.

★   ★   ★

One Sunday, May went to church. It was a denomination that, as she gratefully knew, would bury anyone. She sat in a pew behind three young women and studied their pretty blond hair, their necks and their collars and their zippers. One of the girls scratched her neck. A few minutes later, she scratched it again. May bent forward and saw a small tick crawling on the girl. She carefully picked it off with her fingers. She did it with such stealth that the girl did not even know that May had touched her. May pinched the tick vigorously between her fingernails for some time, then dropped it to the floor where it vanished from her sight.

After the service, there was a coffee hour. May joined a group around a table that was dotted with plates of muffins, bright cookies, and glazed cakes. When the conversation lagged, she said, "I've just returned from Morocco."

"How exotic!" a woman exclaimed, "Did you see the Casbah?" The group turned toward May and looked at her attentively.

"There are many Casbahs," May said. "I had tea under a tent on the edge of the Sahara. The children in Morocco all want aspirin. 'Boom-boom la tête,' they say, 'boom-boom la tête.' Their little hands are dry as paper. It's the lack of humidity, I suppose."

"You didn't go there by yourself, did you?" a fat woman asked. She was very fat and panted as she spoke.

"I went alone, yes," May said.

The group hummed appreciatively. May was holding a tiny blueberry muffin in her hand. She couldn't remember picking it up. It sat cupped in the palm of her hand, the paper around it looking like the muffin itself. May had been fooled by such muffins in public places in the past. She returned it to the table.

"I saw the blue men," May said.

The group looked at her, smiling. They were taller than she and their heads were tilted toward her.

"Most tourists don't see them," May said. "They roam the deserts. Their camels are pale beige, almost white, and the men riding them are blue. They wear deep blue floating robes and blue turbans. Their skin is even stained blue where the dye has rubbed off."

"Are they wanderers?" someone asked. "What's their purpose?"

May was startled. She felt as though the person were regarding her with suspicion.

"They're part of the mystery," she said. "To see them is to see part of the mystery."

"It must have been a sight," someone offered.

"Oh yes," May said, "it was."

After some moments, the group dispersed and May left the church and walked home through the town. May liked the town, which was cut off from other places. People came here only if they wanted to. You couldn't find this place by accident. The town seemed to be a place to visit and most people didn't stay on. There were some, of course, who had stayed on. May liked the clear light of the town and the trees rounded by the wind. She liked the trucks and the Jeeps with the dogs riding in them. When the trucks were parked, the dogs would stare solemnly down at the pavement as though there were something astounding there.

May felt elated, almost feverish. She had taken up lying rather late in life and she had taken it up with enthusiasm. Bomber didn't seem to notice, even though he had, in May's opinion, a hurtful obsession with the truth. When May got back to her house, she made herself a cup of tea and changed from her good dress into her gardening dress. She looked at herself in the mirror. I'm in charge of this person, she thought. "You'd better watch out," she said to the person in the mirror.

★   ★   ★

Bomber's friends don't drink or smoke or eat meat. They are bony and wild. In the winter, a psychiatrist comes into their classrooms and says, *You think that suicide is an escape and not a permanent departure, but the truth is it is a permanent departure.* They know that! Their eyes water with boredom. Their mothers used to lie to them when they were little about dead things, but they know better now. It's stupid to wait for the dead to do anything new. But one of their classmates had killed himself, so the psychiatrist would come back every winter.

"They planted a tree," Edith said, "you know, in this kid's memory at school and what this kid had done was hung himself from a tree." Edith rolled her eyes. "I mean this school. You're not going to believe this school."

Edith and Bomber sat on opposite sides of May's parlor, which was filling with twilight. Edith wore a pair of men's boxer shorts, lace-up boots, and a lurid Hawaiian shirt. "This is a nice house," Edith said. "It smells nice. I see your granny coming out of the Kittens sometimes. She's cute."

"A thing I used to remember about my dad," Bomber said, "was that he gave me a tepee once when I was little and he pitched it in the middle of the living room. I slept in it every night for weeks right in the middle of the living room. It was great. But it actually wasn't my dad who had done that at all, it was my gramma."

"Your granny is so cute," Edith said. "I know I'd like her. Do you know Bobby?"

"Which one's Bobby?" Bomber asked.

"He's the skinny one with the tooth that overlaps a little. He's the sort of person I used to like. What he does is he fishes. There's not a fish he can't catch."

"I can't do that," Bomber said.

"Oh, you don't have to do anything like that now," Edith said.

*   *   *

The last things May had brought her son were a dark suit and a white shirt. They told her she could if she wished, and she had. She had brought him many things in the two years before he died—candy and cigarettes and batteries, books on all subjects—and lastly she had brought these things. She had bought the shirt new and then washed it at home several times so it was soft and then she had driven over to that place. It was a cool, misty morning and the air smelled of chemicals from the mills miles away. Dew glittered on the wires and on the tips of grasses and the fronds of palms. She sat opposite him in the tall, narrow, familiar room, its high windows webby with steel, and he had opened the box with the shirt in it. Together they had looked at it. Together, mutely, they had bent their heads over it and stared. Their eyes had fallen into it as though it were a hole. They watched the shirt and it seemed to shift and shrink as though to accommodate itself to some ghastly and impossible interstice of time and purpose.

"What a shirt," her child said.

"Give it back," May whispered. She was terribly frightened. She had obliged some lunatic sense of decorum, and dread—the dread that lay beyond the fear of death—seized her.

"This is the one, I'm going out in this one," her child said. He was thin, his hair was gray.

"I wasn't thinking," May said. "Please give it back, I can't think about any of this."

"I was born to wear this shirt," her child said.

*   *   *

In the Lucky Kittens, over the bar, was a large painting of kittens crawling out of a sack. The sack was huge, out of proportion to the sea and the sky behind it. When May looked at it for a time, the sack appeared to tremble. One night, as she was walking home, someone brushed against her, almost knocking her down, and ran off with her purse. Her purse had fifteen dollars in it and in it too were the postcards and pictures of Morocco. May continued to walk home, her left arm still feeling the weight of the purse. It seemed heavier now that it wasn't there. She pushed herself down the street, looking, out of habit, into the lighted rooms of the handsome homes along the way. The rooms were artfully lit as though on specific display for the passerby. No one was ever seen in them. At home, she looked at herself in the mirror for bruises. There were none, although her face was deeply flushed.

"You've been robbed," she said to the face.

She went into her parlor. On the floor above, in either the gray room or the yellow room, someone shifted about. Her arm ached. She turned off the light and sat in the dark, rubbing her arm.

"The temperature of the desert can reach 175 degrees," she said aloud. "At night, it can fall below freezing. Many a time I awoke in the morning to find a sheet of ice over the water in the glass beside my bed." It was something that had been written on one of the cards. She could see it all, the writing, the words, plain as day.

Some time later, she heard Bomber's voice. "Gramma," he said, "why are you sitting in the dark!" The light was on again.

"Hi!" May said.

"Sometimes," Bomber said, "she lies out in the garden and the fog rolls in, and she stays right out there."

"The fog will be swirling around me," May said, "and Bomber will say, 'Gramma, the fog's rolled in and there you are!'" She was speaking to a figure beside Bomber with a flamboyant crest of hair. The figure was dressed in silk lounging pajamas and a pair of black work boots with steel toes.

"Gramma," Bomber said, "this is Edith."

"Hi!" Edith said.

"What a pretty name," May said. "There's a hybrid lily called Edith that I like very much. I'm going to plant an Edith bulb when fall comes."

"Will it come up every year?" Edith asked.

"Yes," May said.

"That is so cool," Edith said.

\*     \*     \*

A few days after she had been robbed, May's purse was returned to her. It was placed in the garden, just inside the gate. Everything was there, but the bills were different. May had had a ten and a five and the new ones were singles. The cards were there. May touched one and looked at the familiar writing on the back. *It never grows dark in the desert,* the writing said. *The night sky is a deep and intense blue as though the sun were shut up behind it.* Her child had been a thoughtful tourist once, sending messages home, trying to explain things she would never see. He had never written from the prison. The thirst for explanation had left him. May thought of death. It was as though someone were bending over her, trying to blow something into her mouth. She shook her head and looked at her purse, turning it this way and that. "Where have you been!" she said to the purse. The pictures of Morocco were there. She looked through them. All there. But she didn't want them anymore. Things were never the same when they came back. She closed the purse up and dropped it in one of her large green trash cans, throwing some clipped, brown flowers over it so that it was concealed. It was less than a week later that everything was returned to her again, once more placed inside the gate. People went through the dump, she imagined, people went through the dump all the time to see what they could find. In town, the young people began calling her by name. "May," they'd say, "Good morning!" They'd say, "How's it going, Gramma!" She was the condemned man's mother, and Bomber was the condemned man's son, and it didn't seem to matter what they did or didn't do, it was he who had been accepted by these people, and he who was allowing them to get by.

\*   \*   \*

Edith was spending more and more time at May and Bomber's house. She ate dinner there several times a week. She had dyed her hair a peculiar brown color and wore scarves knotted around her neck.

"I like this look," Edith said. "It looks like I'm concealing a tracheotomy, doesn't it?"

"Your hair's good," Bomber said.

"You know what the psychiatrist at school says?" Edith said. "He says you think you want death when all you want is change."

"What is it with this guy?" Bomber asked. "Is there really a problem at that place or what?"

"Oh there is, absolutely," Edith said. "You look a little like your granny. Did your dad look like her?"

"A little, I guess," Bomber said.

"You're such a bad boy," Edith said. "Such a sweet, sweet bad boy. I really love you."

The summer was over. The light had changed, and the leaves on the trees hung very still. At the Lucky Kittens, the dancing went on, but not so many people danced. When May went there, they wouldn't take her money and May submitted to this. She couldn't help herself, it seemed.

Edith helped around the house. She washed the windows with vinegar and made chocolate desserts. One evening, she said, "Do you still, like, pay income tax?"

May looked at the girl and decided to firmly lie. "No," she said.

"Well, that's good," Edith said. "It would be pretty preposterous to pay taxes after what they did."

"Of course," May said.

"But you're paying in other ways," Edith said.

"Please, dear," May said, "it was just a mistake. It doesn't mean anything in the long run," she said, dismayed at her words.

"I'll help you pay," Edith said.

*   *   *

With the cool weather, the tourists stopped coming. When school began, Edith asked if she could move into the yellow room. She didn't get along with her parents, she had been moving about, staying here and there with friends, but she had no real place to live, could she live in the yellow room?

May was fascinated by Edith. She did not want her in the house, above her, living in the yellow room. She felt that she and Bomber should move on, that they should try their new life together somewhere else, but she knew that this was their new life. This was the place where it appeared they had gone.

"Of course, dear," May said.

She was frightened and this surprised her, for she could scarcely believe she could know fright again after what happened to them, but there it was, some thing beyond the worst thing—some disconnection, some demand. She remembered telling Edith that she was going to plant bulbs in the garden when fall came, but she wasn't going to do it, certainly not. "No," May said to her garden, "don't even think about it." Edith moved into the yellow room. It was silent there, but May didn't listen either.

Something happened later that got around. May was driving, it was night, and the car veered off the road. Edith and Bomber were with her. The car flipped over twice, miraculously righted itself, and skidded back onto the road, the roof and fenders crushed. This was observed by a policeman who followed them for over a mile in disbelief before he pulled the car over. None of them were injured and at first they denied that anything unusual had happened at all. May said, "I thought it was just a dream, so I kept on going."

The three seemed more visible than ever after that, for they drove the car in that damaged way until winter came.

# CONTRIBUTORS

Frederick Barthelme's books include *Bob the Gambler, Chroma, The Brothers,* and *Painted Desert.* He edits the *Mississippi Review* and teaches at the University of Southern Mississippi.

Tom Chiarella chairs the English Department at Depauw University. His fiction has appeared in *The New Yorker, Esquire, Story* and other magazines, and he is author of a nonfiction manual, *Writing Dialogue.*

Philip Cioffari teaches creative writing and acting at the William Paterson University of New Jersey. His fiction is widely published and his plays have been produced at American Theater of Actors in New York City.

Steve Cushman is a graduate of the creative writing program at the University of Central Florida. He lives in Orlando.

John Henry Fleming is the author of *The Legend of the Barefoot Mailman* (Faber & Faber, 1996), a novel about Florida. He grew up in Lake Worth, and he teaches at Saint Mary's College of California.

Aracelis Gonzalez Asendorf was born in Cuba and emigrated to the United States with her parents as a child. She lives in Tampa with her husband and two children.

Jeffrey Greene moved to Bartow, Florida, when he was two. He now lives in Maryland, but much of his fiction, including his first novel, *Lilianna,* is set in Central Florida.

William R. Kanouse is a poet and playwright living in New Jersey. He teaches creative writing and theatre arts at Ocean County College.

Karen Loeb lived in St. Petersburg for eleven years, where she wrote about alligators only occasionally. She teaches at the University of Wisconsin–Eau Claire.

Alison Lurie is the author of *The War Between the Tates, Foreign Affairs* (winner of a Pulitzer Prize), and most recently *The Last Resort.* She divides her time among Ithaca, New York, Key West, and London.

Wendell Mayo has published stories in more than sixty magazines, and his 1996 collection, *In Lithuanian Wood,* won the Premio Aztlán. He directs the Creative Writing Program at Bowling Green State University.

Jill McCorkle has published five novels, including *The Cheer Leader* and *Carolina Moon,* and two collections of short stories. She lives near Boston, Massachusetts.

Peter Meinke's collection of stories, *The Piano Tuner,* won the 1986 Flannery O'Connor Award. His most recent book is *Scars,* in the Pitt Poetry Series. He lives in St. Petersburg.

Patrick J. Murphy is a native of Hialeah who moved for a while to California, then returned to live and write in Tallahassee. His story collection, *Way Below E,* was published by White Pine Press in 1995.

Louis Phillips was born in Massachusetts but grew up in Hollywood, Florida. He has published more than thirty books and teaches at the School of Visual Arts in New York City.

Elisavietta Ritchie lives in Washington, D.C., but has lived in Malaysia, Cyprus, France, and, most recently, Canada and Australia. Her books include *Elegy for the Other Woman* and *Re-inventing the Archives.*

Enid Shomer's collection *Imaginary Men* won the Iowa Short Fiction Award in 1993. She teaches writing at the University of Arkansas, Fayetteville.

William Snyder, Jr., has made his living as a janitor, short-order cook, seawall builder, street performer, and guitar teacher—among other occupations. He now teaches writing and literature at Concordia College in Moorhead, Minnesota.

Abraham Verghese is a professor of medicine at Texas Tech University and lectures on medical humanities. His first book, *My Own Country,* was a national best-seller.

Steve Watkins teaches writing at Mary Washington College in Fredericksburg, Virginia. He is the author of *The Black O: Racism and Redemption in an American Corporate Empire.*

Joy Williams has written three novels and two collections of short stories as well as a history and guide to the Florida Keys. She is a recipient of the Strauss Living Award from the American Academy of Arts and Letters.


Susan Hubbard has published two collections of short stories, *Blue Money* (1999) and *Walking on Ice* (1990). Her stories have appeared in *TriQuarterly, Mississippi Review, America West,* and *Ploughshares.* She teaches creative writing at the University of Central Florida.

Robley Wilson is the author of four story collections, a novel, and three books of poems, most recently *Everything Paid For* (University Press of Florida). He is professor of English at the University of Northern Iowa and edits *The North American Review.*